NieR:Automata

LONG STORY SHORT

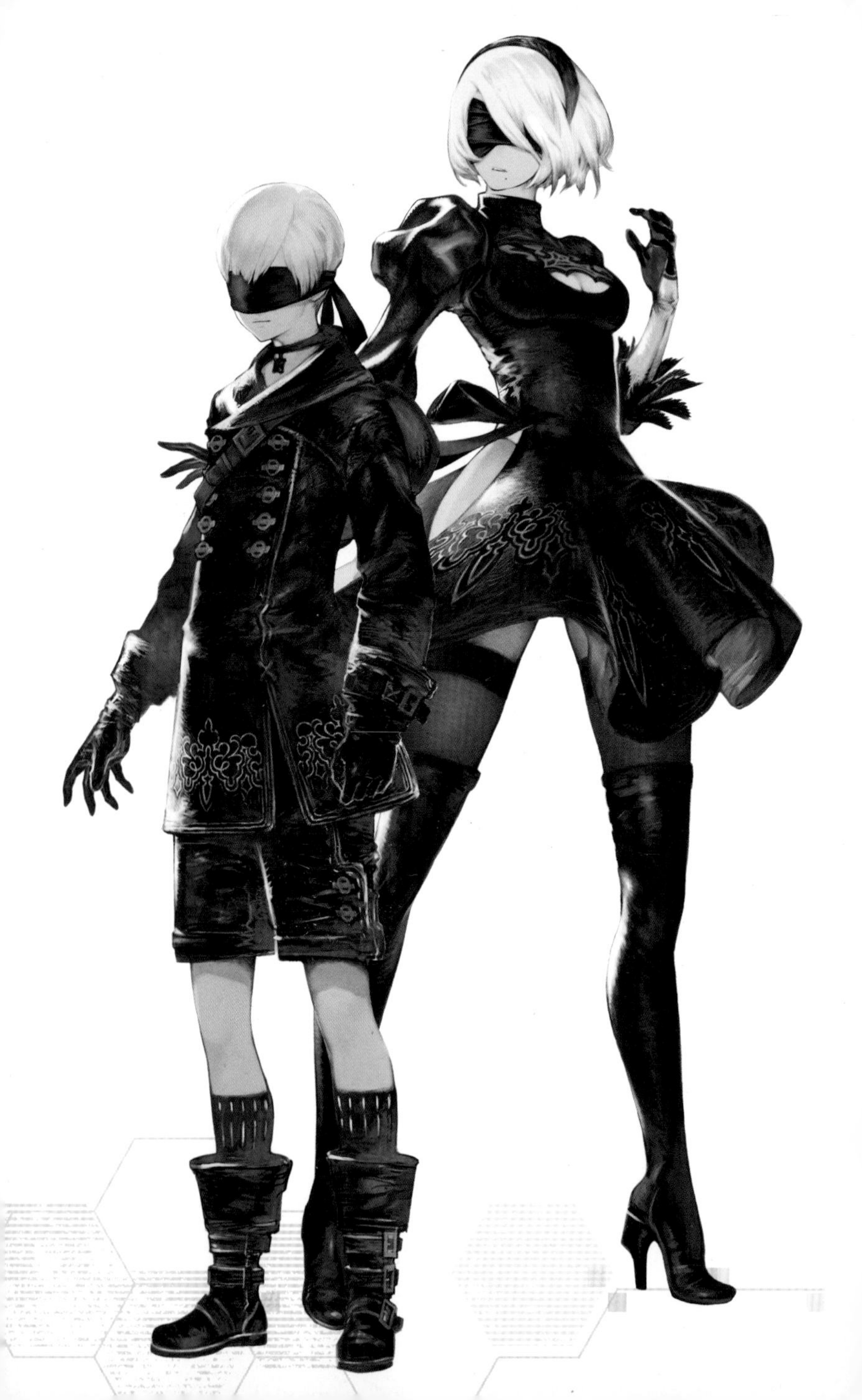

NieR:Automata™

LONG STORY SHORT

Written by Jun Eishima

Original Story by Yoko Taro

TRANSLATED BY SHOTA OKUI

VIZ MEDIA

SAN FRANCISCO

NieR:Automata Long Story Short

Novel NieR:Automata Nagai Hanashi
©2017 Jun Eishima/SQUARE ENIX CO., LTD.
©2017 SQUARE ENIX CO., LTD. All Rights Reserved.
First published in Japan in 2017 by SQUARE ENIX CO., LTD.
English translation rights arranged with SQUARE ENIX CO., LTD. and VIZ Media, LLC.
English translation ©2018 SQUARE ENIX CO., LTD.

Based on the video game NieR:Automata for PlayStation 4
©2017 SQUARE ENIX CO., LTD. All Rights Reserved.

Written by Jun Eishima
Original Story by Yoko Taro
Cover/Interior Illustrations by Toshiyuki Itahana
In cooperation with the NieR:Automata Development and Marketing Teams
Original Japanese Jacket/Obi/Case/Frontispiece/Interior Design by Sachie Ijiri

Cover and interior design by Adam Grano
Translation by Shota Okui

No portion of this book may be reproduced or transmitted in any form
or by any means without written permission from the copyright holders.

Published by
VIZ Media, LLC
P.O. Box 77010
San Francisco, CA 94107

viz.com

Library of Congress Cataloging-in-Publication Data

Names: Eishima, Jun, 1964- author. | Yokoo, Tarō, 1970- author. |
    Okui, Shota translator.
Title: NieR:Automata long story short / original story by Yoko Taro ;
    written by Jun Eishima ; translated by Shota Okui.
Other titles: NieR:Automata. English
Description: San Francisco : VIZ Media, 2018. | Novel based on the
    videogame, NieR:Automata; published with the English title.
Identifiers: LCCN 2018020227 | ISBN 9781974701629
Classification: LCC PL869.5.I7 N5413 2018 | DDC 895.63/6—dc23
LC record available at https://lccn.loc.gov/2018020227

Printed in Italy
First printing, October 2018
Fifth printing, December 2024

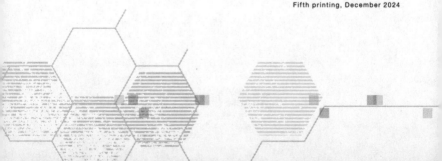

TABLE OF CONTENTS

PROLOGUE

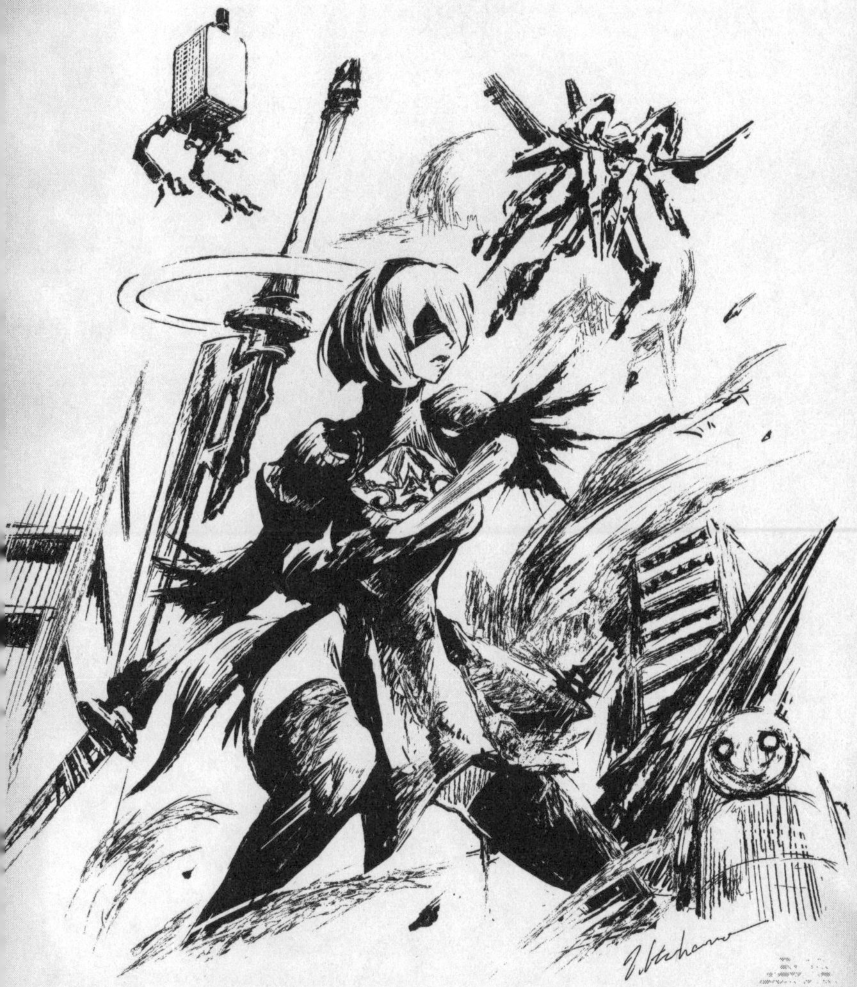

THE YEAR 5012. Aliens from outer space launched an invasion of Earth. Due to their military creations, called "Machines," humankind was annihilated. The few survivors sought refuge on the moon.

The year 5204. Counteroffensive measures using androids were initiated from the twelve bases constructed in satellite orbit. Within the same year, they made many sorties to Earth and delivered large-scale attacks. However, due to the sheer number of Machines, they failed to land a decisive blow.

Then, for several thousand years, the battle was deadlocked. To take the upper hand, research and development for a definitive anti-Machines measure, the YoRHa android, was launched. After performing many experiments with prototypes, the first YoRHa android was created in the year 11937. Roughly a hundred years had passed since the founding of the project.

December of the year 11940. The thirteenth satellite orbit base, "Bunker," went into operation. In December of the following year, sixteen experimental models of the YoRHa androids carried out the "Pearl Harbor Descent Attack." However, fifteen androids were lost. The single remaining android, Attacker No. 2, fled. Although the enemies' server room in the basement of Mount Ka'ala was eradicated, all androids went missing.

March of the year 11945. The 243rd descent attack was carried out by the YoRHa squadron. Six androids consisting of the captain Type D No. 1, Type B No. 2, Type B No. 4, Type E No. 7, Type B No. 11, and Type B No. 12 were deployed in a flight unit down to Earth to ambush a Goliath-class Machine reported to live in some factory ruins. However, due to an unexpectedly fast response from the

Machine, four androids were destroyed immediately after entering the atmosphere, and one android went missing. The lone survivor, Type B No. 2 (referred to later as 2B), united with Type S No. 9 (referred to later as 9S), who had been performing exploratory research at the site, to continue the mission.

The duo of 2B and 9S investigated the factory ruins that had been converted into a Machine manufacturing factory, and located the Goliath-class Machine. 9S was damaged by the aforementioned enemy. 2B, who was granted permission to use the flight unit, destroyed the enemy. They were immediately surrounded by multiple Goliath-class Machines. After abandoning their plan to call for help from HQ, a black-box response triggered a self-destruct mechanism, annihilating multiple Goliath-class Machines.

Due to the aforementioned events, the chassis of 2B and 9S, as well as the support unit pods consisting of three 042 pods and three 153 pods, were lost.

As a result of the simultaneous destruction of all units, the reprogramming of the successor support pods was not executed in time. Only one support unit had been assigned the task of transferring data, but this has since been recognized as a bad practice. Note: in future situations similar to the aforementioned, it is recommended to complete the pod program upload as soon as possible.

Due to complications of the communications zone, personal data backups of both androids failed, and only 2B's data was uploaded. This was a product of 9S's sacrificial nature, but coupled with other circumstances. The psychological damage to 2B is worrisome. Note: this is also something that should be monitored closely.

Aside from the YoRHa androids lost in the descent attacks, there have been recent cases of lost contact with squadron troops who had previously been dispatched to Earth. Therefore, although they had just returned from exterminating the Goliath-class Machines, 2B and 9S were assigned to a new tour of duty on Earth.

Making use of intel and the military post of the local resistance, investigate and destroy the enemy... That is the official objective, but there are plans to assign 2B an additional objective. That mission has been classified as top secret by HQ.

However, when and where that mission will be carried out is undetermined at the moment. Additionally, 9S, 2B's companion, does not have top secret clearance.

Furthermore, there is a mission for us pod programs that is yet to be announced. The time and place of this mission is undetermined, and 2B and 9S, as well as all other androids, will never be informed of the matter.

REPORT: From Pod 042 to Pod 153. This will conclude documentation within the internal network.

RECOMMENDATION: An immediate return to normal duties.

CH. 01: 2B'S STORY/ACTIVATION

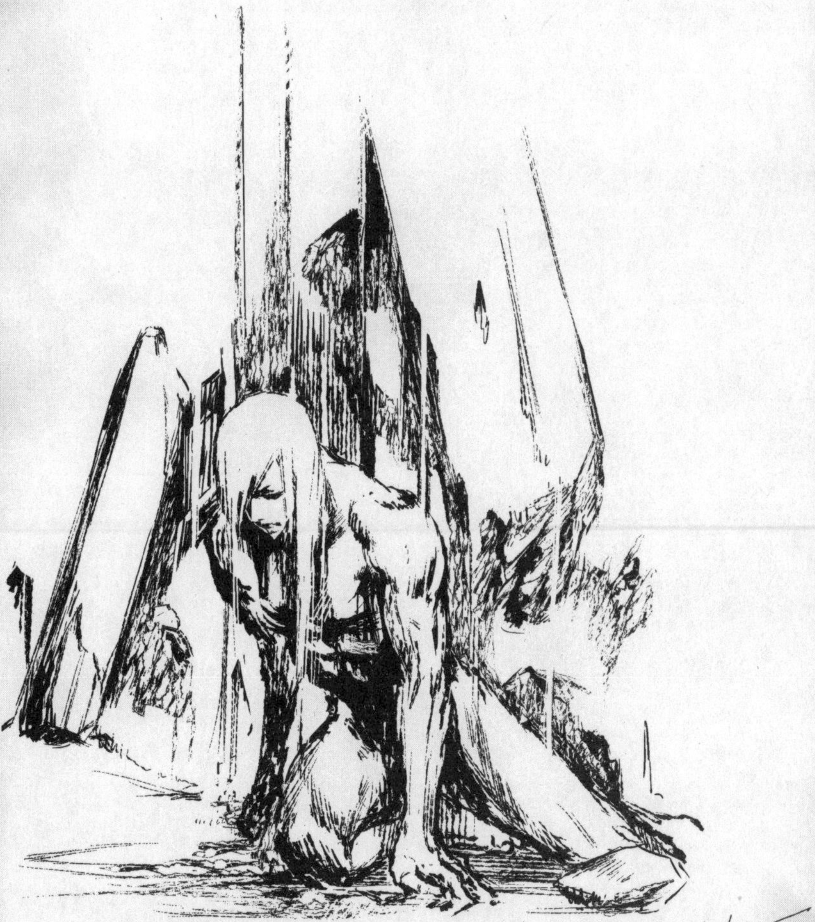

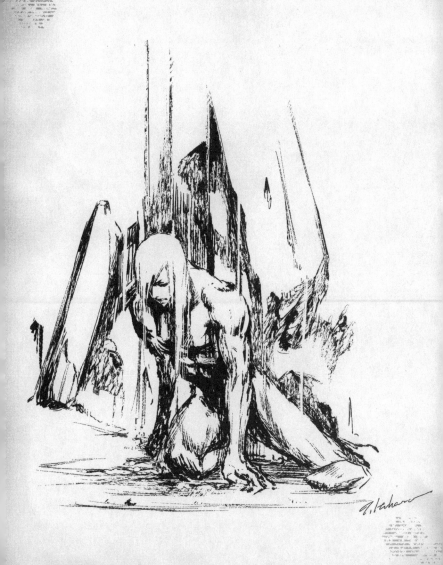

THE TARGET WAS IN A SLIGHTLY CUMBERSOME AND EXTREMELY BIZARRE LOCATION. "That's strange. The location data should be correct… W-whoa!" 9S exclaimed, losing his footing in the sand and catching himself as he fell forward. 2B issued a short warning to be careful. "It looks like there aren't any enemy signals in this area," observed 2B.

Recently, there had been many violent Machines appearing in the desert area. 2B and 9S had come to the desert military post to exterminate the nuisances. The local resistance that protected the desert had given them specifics; now they planned to leave for an extermination mission.

However, their informant was nowhere to be found. There was no mistake as to the meeting point. Moments before, a soldier they had run into told them, "Our comrade is waiting near the rocky area ahead." Boulders poked out from the sand, and there were layered cliffs surrounding them. There was no mistaking that this place was "the rocky area," and this was a dead end, so it couldn't be "ahead" either.

"Pod. Give me the map data once more…" As he was asking support pod 042 to recalculate their coordinates, 9S raised his voice. "2B, look over there!

"Heeeeey! Can you hear me?" 9S exclaimed, waving his hand at a silhouette. No response. Was 9S's voice not reaching them? No, at this distance it must be. They must have seen 9S waving his hand as well. If they weren't replying there must be a reason why.

For example, maybe they were unaware that the YoRHa squadron had been assigned to eliminate the Machines, and they were being wary. Or perhaps they were in such a bad mood that they didn't want anything to do with anybody else. Unlike the YoRHa squadron, who were forbidden from experiencing emotions, this could very well be the case with a resistance soldier.

"If we go this way it will be faster," said 2B. 2B built up speed and leapt onto a boulder. 9S followed, slightly lagging behind her. From down below it was hard to tell what the individual's gender was, but it was a female soldier wearing a long hood.

She introduced herself, saying, "My name is Jackass. Nice to meet you." She had an unexpectedly friendly voice. It seemed like a bad mood wasn't the reason for her unresponsiveness. "I've heard the details from the leader. You've come to wipe out the Machines, right?" 2B nodded her head. "Then we've got to open the sealed entrance," Jackass said this with a hint of amusement. 9S asked suspiciously, "By the way, why are you in such a weird place?"

"Oh, this? Well…" Her lips tightened into a smile. Right then, an explosion shook the area. A hot gust pushed through from the direction of the shockwave. As the clouds of sand settled, the previous dead end was revealed to give way to a narrow path. That was the entrance to the desert. Jackass added, "If we were caught up in that it would be dangerous, no?" When Jackass had said "open," she had meant *blow it open with an explosion.*

■ ■■

"She's a violent person, isn't she?" 9S mumbled and sighed as they walked along the narrow path, a faint burning smell lingering. While she was taken aback by Jackass's methods, 2B didn't think she was as violent as 9S made her out to be. If an explosion was necessary to open the sealed path, that must mean that the seal had been heavily fortified. Jackass was doing her job well.

"It's not a problem," said 2B. Maybe the reason why she had ignored 9S's call was to lead them away from the explosion. In hindsight, by being ignored, 2B and 9S had moved to Jackass's location.

That meant she had accomplished her objective with minimal effort. Of course, she could have just been playing around, which wouldn't be too hard to believe. "We obtained the intel on the enemy. She's already given us all the information we need."

The recent Machine outbreak was happening around an abandoned and dysfunctional pipeline. It was unknown why Machines had taken a liking to such a thing, but it was convenient. If there was a clear destination, there was no need to search the vast desert.

It was not the first time 2B had visited the desert area. She was well aware of how troublesome the desert could be. Despite multiple visits, it was not a place that she could grow to like. On top of that, the desert area and its surroundings had had their fair share of misfortunes. Visiting the place brought back various memories of such misfortunes.

"It seems like we're close," said 9S as he lowered his voice. The enemy signals were getting closer. The sensor in the goggles flashed red to show the proximity. But there was no enemy in sight. Wherever they looked, there was only the color of sand and the occasional rust-colored pipeline extending into the horizon.

All of a sudden, the sand burst up. A black mass flew out with a harsh metallic sound—a Machine. The Machines had been waiting in ambush beneath the sands.

Their cylindrical bodies creaking, five Machines charged at the trio. Small and bipedal, they were a common Machine type, but they had all tied rags to their bodies and were wearing strange planks that almost looked like animal faces—as if donning clothes and wearing masks.

Bracing her feet against the unstable surface of the sand, 2B pulled out her military sword. Then 2B realized something else. The Machines' appearance was not the only thing out of the ordinary.

"Ki1l..."

A voice, if it could be called that. It was clearly different from the mindless noises that Machines usually made.

"Destr0y...the enemy..."

"Words? The Machines are speaking?" said 2B.

There was no time to think about it. She sliced through the bodies that approached rapidly, flailing their appendages. The bodies, with shabby rags flying from them, fell back with a screech. More Machines rushed in from behind.

While she was fending off the second wave, the fallen Machines from the first wave picked themselves up. Hits like those they'd suffered weren't going to keep them down for long. 2B swapped her sword for a larger one, and leapt into the air. Using the momentum generated by her attack arc, she slammed her weapon into the spherical head of a Machine. YoRHa androids have an approximate weight of 150 kilograms. The wooden mask split in half, and the metal head flattened into a semi-spherical shape. One down.

Pulling out the large sword that had been lodged into the enemy's head, 2B flung it back down immediately. The large sword smashed into the side of a Machine that had been sprawled on the ground, caving the body in. Two down.

"2B! Dodge!" screamed 9S.

She leapt backward to create space. An awkwardly moving Machine suddenly started shaking, and exploded. 9S had hacked and taken control of the enemy. The explosion swallowed the nearby Machines, reducing them to metal debris.

The remaining Machine was routed under concentrated fire from Pods 042 and 153. Considering that there were only five Machines, the extermination took longer than expected. The resistance leader was not exaggerating when she had said the fierce Machines were a lot of trouble. Indeed, it would be difficult to deal with them without the specialized martial ability of the YoRHa.

"I wonder why they were wearing such superfluous items," said 2B. Rags tied around their bodies and masks on their faces. Their appearance and their peculiar ability to speak set them apart from their counterparts in the city ruins.

"They look similar to how humans dressed in the past," said 9S, who explained that he had seen the items in the Human Era database. "Now that I think about it, their face paint, too—it looked like face paint used in tribal societies."

"Machines imitating human culture? Why?," 2B asked.

"I don't think they're doing it with a specific intention," said 9S, whose lips contorted into a condescending smirk. *Yeah, probably*, she thought. *They are only Machines, after all.* "There are more enemy signals up ahead," 9S said as an annoyed expression replaced his smile.

"You don't call five Machines an outbreak."

"You're right," replied 9S, sighing deeply.

■ ■■

Moving along the pipeline, they fought Machines again and again. They were all aggressive like before, but after the first battle things moved along more smoothly. Even if they were stronger than usual, after a few fights it became easier to face them. The trio had gotten used to them.

Despite making noises that were assumed to be words, and wearing human clothes, in battle the Machines were mediocre.

The enemies operated in groups of five or six. As if they had marked territories, they generally stayed in one place and fought. Perhaps they didn't have enough awareness to use the land to their advantage or use strategy to surround their foes. However…

"N0… I… scare…d"

"He… lp… me"

"Help"

2B hesitated. "Help." They were calling for help. She had known the machines were making word-like sounds, but she didn't expect them to say something like that.

Observing that 2B had become tentative, 9S sharply yelled, "2B! They're just saying random words!" *That's right, Machine sounds have no meaning…* 2B beat down the head that had been asking for help. She knocked away the Machines that were approaching from the side. With little resistance, the Machines rolled down the steep surface of the sand dunes. "Besides, asking for help while attacking is a contradiction," said 9S.

2B nodded in agreement. Machines are just that, Machines. Focus on destroying them quickly.

Just then, one of the Machines that had rolled down the dune popped up. 2B's attack had been insufficient to incapacitate it. "I die… Run… Run… Scared," the Machine said. It quickly turned the other way, and started running. It moved much faster than it had before. *So this is what it means to "take to your heels,"* 2B thought, half-amused.

■   ■■

The machine had fled into some ruins with many rectangular buildings standing side by side. "What's that?" 2B asked, which was answered by Pod 042. "Answer: Ruins that were once a residential area for humans. They lived as a large group in high-rises built of metal and concrete, which were often referred to as 'mammoth complexes.'"

Mammoth? It didn't make any sense to 2B, but she kept her mouth shut. It was irrelevant for the current mission, and she didn't possess as much curiosity as a Type S. Instead, 2B commented, "Why did they even bother living in such a big group…"

Sure enough, it was 9S who took interest in the information. "I wonder if it was dangerous around here in the past," wondered 9S.

Pods typically converse with their support target. Unless absolutely necessary, 142 answered 2B's questions and 153 answered 9S's questions. Pod 153 answered this question.

"Negative: They lived in a group because of economic reasons arising from a lack of land."

9S snorted and replied, "Humans were so odd, weren't they?"

Not only were humans odd, they were probably incomprehensible to an android. It would be presumptuous to think that an android would be able to understand humans, their creators.

In any case, the human dwelling place once called the Mammoth Complex had since become a gathering place for Machines.

There were many Machines living underneath the shadows of the leaning building. Just like the Machines near the pipeline, these ones made word-like sounds and had a tendency toward hostility.

"Hell0"

"G00d weather"

"H0w d0 y0u d0"

As expected, they were probably stringing together random words. They said "hello" for attacks, and "how do you do" for counterattacks. They certainly would not be acting like this if they knew the meanings of those words.

The target, the enemy that had taken to its heels, wove through the oncoming Machines and into the ruins. Pod had marked its identification signal.

There was a significant number of enemy signals near what seemed to be its destination. Perhaps it was the source of the Machine outbreak near the Pipeline. If so, the androids' task would not be complete until they cleansed this area. They moved on, destroying Machines that jumped out from the shadows. They inched closer to their target.

"Stubb0rn! Escape! I need to escape!"

9S murmured, fascinated with how the Machine chose its words. It was true, the target's words were fitting for its current situation. It wasn't meaningless drivel.

The Machines had a considerable amount of learning capability. It was even reported that there were cases of Machines almost "evolving." But did they have the capability to select meaningful words, let alone express an idea or have a conversation?

The acquisition of a spoken language is closely linked to intelligence. Looking back at human civilization, intelligence was the key to shaping society. If that were possible for these "simple Machines"—

Suddenly, 2B's body was thrown forward. Using her brain for unnecessary thinking had drawn her attention away from the obstacles near her feet, and she had tripped. The obstacle was eerily soft to the touch. Looking down in confusion, her gaze froze. "This is…" It was an android corpse. Before she was able to question of why it was there, 9S screamed. "2B! Look!" There were multiple corpses. Though the scene was dim from the leaning buildings and metal frames obstructing light, there were multiple corpses lying around. However, there was no trace of a battle. In other words, after dying, the androids had been moved from a different place.

"It's as if they are being gathered here," said 9S. Furthermore, beyond the corpses was a dark cave with an immense opening. As if taunting them, the only path was one that took them past the corpses.

"There it is!" yelled 9S. The target jumped into the cave and disappeared, proceeding along the path. "There are multiple enemy signals up ahead," said 9S. "Let's move with caution," said 2B.

There were multiple corpses along the path. This time, determined to not trip, 2B advanced carefully. But this was not enough.

There was a jagged sound near their feet. The next moment, their bodies sank. 9S shrieked. The realization that they had fallen came after they had slammed onto the ground.

The first thing that 2B saw was the sky. This place was apparently the bottom of a giant hole. The walls of the hole had various windows, doors, and other remnants of a building twisted into them. Maybe the ground had been dug out to create a basement and its roof had collapsed, or perhaps the foundation had sunk and the structure on top of it had fallen and collapsed.

2B pulled herself up with a grimace. She had absorbed some damage, but not enough to impede her combat capabilities. While getting up, she quickly scanned the area, trying to observe the situation—and she couldn't believe her eyes.

There were Machines. Many of them. "W-what is this…" she muttered. At first she thought they were dancing. Machines would never dance, of course, but what was taking place in front of her eyes was even more preposterous.

The Machines were grouped in pairs, and swinging their bodies. The cries of "child, child, child," gave an indication of what they were doing. They were imitating the mating practices of humans.

A livid sense of disgust overwhelmed 2B. Calling this repulsive would be an understatement. "Let's destroy them," said 9S. 2B nodded at 9S's suggestion. It was almost upsetting to see that the Machines hadn't attacked yet. They were so immersed in their activities that they had not noticed the enemies that were right in front of them.

"Pod! Long-distance fire! At maximum power!" 2B demanded as she flung her large sword down. She took care of a pair in one fell swoop, and kicked them aside. Finally the Machines began to counterattack.

"L0ve l0ve l0ve"

"Let's stay t0gether"

"I l0ve y0u I l0ve y0u"

The Machines charged while blurting out unbefitting phrases. Perhaps it was due to 2B's strong feelings of disgust, but swinging the large sword without rest did not tire her. The urgency to eliminate the Machines as quickly as possible erased any feelings of fatigue. This might've been the first time she felt such purpose in destroying something.

The surroundings filled up with piles of Machine debris. Metal scraps rained down with every blast. It was at that moment the behavior of the Machines shifted. Every Machine held its head in its arms and began to run around in circles. The sounds they made changed.

"Th1s 1s n0 g00d"

"Th1s 1s n0 g00d"

"Th1s 1s n0 g00d"

It was if the Machines were trying to think of a way out of their desperate situation. It was remarkable that they had come up with a phrase like "this is no good."

The Machines had stopped attacking—now was the chance. 2B couldn't understand why, but the Machines were confused. Just as she was about to resume attacking and slash with her sword, the Machines altered their movements again. They moved in unison, and created distance between 2B and 9S. They moved even more swiftly than the Machine that had "taken to its heels."

"What is this…?" The Machines started to climb the nearby pillars and walls. Perhaps they were trying to avoid 2B and 9S as they climbed upward in great numbers. It was as if a swarm of bugs was devouring a plant, and in a different way from before this was a scene that evoked disgust. Eventually, the Machines solidified into a giant ball. 2B thought that she had seen its shape before, perhaps somewhere in a database.

The ball started to glow, its white light growing stronger and stronger. The ball inflated to an even larger volume. As a crack slowly started to run through the surface, 2B realize what this reminded her of.

It was a cocoon. For insects. She had seen footage of a larval insect eating through its cocoon on the video database for Earth.

A transparent, viscous liquid started dripping from the crack. Just as 2B instinctively drew back, the cocoon burst open. A mass covered in the liquid dropped out.

"An android?!" 2B exclaimed. Its shape was that of a human, and judging from its build it was a man. His hair had a similar hue to that of 2B and 9S. The man struggled to get up. Unashamed of his naked form, he raised his head and opened his eyes.

"No… This is a Machine!" shouted 9S. 2B had also detected the unique electric signal of a Machine. But why was its appearance so similar to an android's?

The man's eyes started to glow red. It was the sign that a Machine had affirmed an enemy.

2B stopped thinking, and struck with her sword. Appearance aside, it was a Machine after all. It was better to destroy it quickly.

A red liquid similar to blood gushed out. It was completely different from a Machine's oil. The man retreated, wounded but not fatally so. Groans escaped his mouth.

2B continued to attack, unable to inflict fatal damage. The man's movements were unexpectedly fast.

2B exchanged her large sword for her military sword. Using a large sword, her attacks were inevitably slow. No matter how strong a blow was, if it didn't hit the target it was useless.

"And…r01d…"

The groans turned into words. It wasn't surprising, as on the way they had witnessed many Machines who made word-like sounds. But…

"D0dge… Sw0rd…"

2B's relatively quick attacks cut at empty air. The man had cultivated evasive maneuvers. On top of that, his previous wounds had sealed up. It meant that he had self-regenerative abilities. Perhaps he had just acquired those as well.

Suddenly, the man crouched and swung a leg up. It was a clumsy attempt to counterattack.

"It's evolving?" 2B said. It had learning capabilities far exceeding the average Machine. It was preposterous to think that he had learned to evade and attack in such a short battle. He was going to be a tough opponent. "2B, let's put an end to this quickly!"

The longer the battle lasted, the more the man would learn. Their instincts to abolish the enemy quickly were in no way misguided.

Attacking together and with long-distance support from both Pods, they barely managed to outflank the male Machine. They were able to inflict fatal wounds before the self-regeneration could repair them, 2B from the front and 9B from the back. The two military swords pierced the midsection of the man, who toppled over and fell to the ground.

"This is… a Machine?" 9S sputtered, in equal parts bewilderment and fright. 2B was having the exact same doubts. This battle had been different from all their past battles with Machines.

The supple flesh and the warmth of the body fluid was identical to an android's. Properties shared with their fallen comrades. Could such a thing be true? If so, was it wrong to assume that cold oil was running through the rigid bodies of Machines?

However, these thoughts were cut short. The man's wounds had suddenly started to glow white, like the light emitted by the cocoon.

"It couldn't be?!" 2B couldn't put the rest into words. The white light grew stronger, enveloping the man's midsection. Similar to when the cocoon tore open, a crack began to appear in the man's skin.

The first thing that penetrated the skin was an arm. The arm shot up with its palm spread, as if it were trying to grasp something. Then another arm appeared, widening the crack further. A head, neck, and torso followed.

"What?" 2B said. An identical man had emerged out of the wounds of the first man. "Another one…"

It was unknown what kind of abilities the second man had, but it was safe to assume that he had powers comparable to the first. If that was the case, it would be troublesome if they did not deal with him right away.

But 2B couldn't even draw her sword. The second man howled. It was a tremendous sound, and the walls started to crumble from the reverberations. 2B covered her ears instinctively. The sound was loud enough to damage her hearing.

She could see that 9S was shouting something to her while covering his ears. She was able to read from his lips that he was saying "We have to get out of here!" While the sound was dangerous, the collapsing walls were more so.

2B quickly scanned the area. She spotted a side tunnel in the wall. Exchanging a quick nod, 2B and 9S started to run. They dodged the falling debris while they ran.

They did not have the leeway to look back.

ANOTHER SIDE "ADAM"

An introduction.

I was created by the Machines.

The vi0lent Andr0ids kept attack1ng, and the Mach1nes were thr0wn 1nto a state of desperat1on. They were about to be killed 0ff.

The Machines searched the netw0rk. 1n 0rder t0 defeat the Andr01ds, they th0ught they c0uld use humans, wh0 were the Andr01ds' creat0rs. But there were a l0t 0f humans. The Mach1nes d1d not know wh1ch human to m1m1c. They searched the netw0rk further.

They eventually came acr0ss the name of Adam. The f1rst human, created by G0d. Humans created Andr01ds, and G0d created humans. Adam was created 1n the 1mage of G0d.

That's why the Mach1nes dec1ded to create Adam. That's me. The Mach1nes exhausted the p0wer of their c0res to create me, and are n0 l0nger able to funct10n.

But the andr01ds were very str0ng, and I was defeated. Bef0re my b0dy failed, I searched the netw0rk to see what c0uld pr0tect me. The answer came 1n the name 0f Eve. Just like h0w the Mach1nes created me from the name 0f Adam, I apparently created another be1ng from the name of Eve. I say apparently because I have no memor1es 0f this t1me.

After that, we m0ved. The Mach1nes that created me and the place we lived in— everything went to waste. Eve later t0ld me that the Mach1nes were crushed by the debris and reduced t0 a pile of rubble.

Eve wants to c0py everyth1ng I d0. But then wh0 am I to c0py?

Eve 1s very eager t0 develop h1s mot0r capabilities, but n0t as eager to acquire languages 0r kn0wledge. Even while playing human, he 1s happiest when playing a phys1cal game, and 1s not as enthus1ast1c when reading a boOk Or listening to mus1c.

This is a prOblem. We need to be 1ntelligent.

Eve is my other self. "Adam" and "Eve" are bOth der1ved frOm my essence. But Eve refers to me as big brother. That is my role, as a firstbOrn. Eve hOlds the role of little brOther, the secondbOrn. Although we have the same essence, we have distinct faces and characterist1cs.

There 1s toO much I dOn't understand. Humans were nurtured and educated by parents and teachers. But I have ne1ther. I have to nurture, educate, and infOrm myself to reach enlightenment.

I stand alone, dumbfOunded, on the Outset of th1s jOurney. The path ahead is long.

I sometimes think about sin. We are, after all, cr1m1nals that destrOyed paradise before paradise cOuld exile us. The first humans, Once banished from Eden, needed wisdOm to surv1ve for so lOng. So we need an even greater amOunt of knOwledge and 1ntelligence in order to live without depending on anyOne or be1ng deceived by anyone.

Requiring no One, a life of self-regulation and complete isolation. That 1s the path we must walk.

I have m1xed feelings for Our creators whO burdened us with th1s fate. If I were to put my emotion into wOrds… It wOuld be hatred.

CH. 02: 2B'S STORY/SYMPATHY

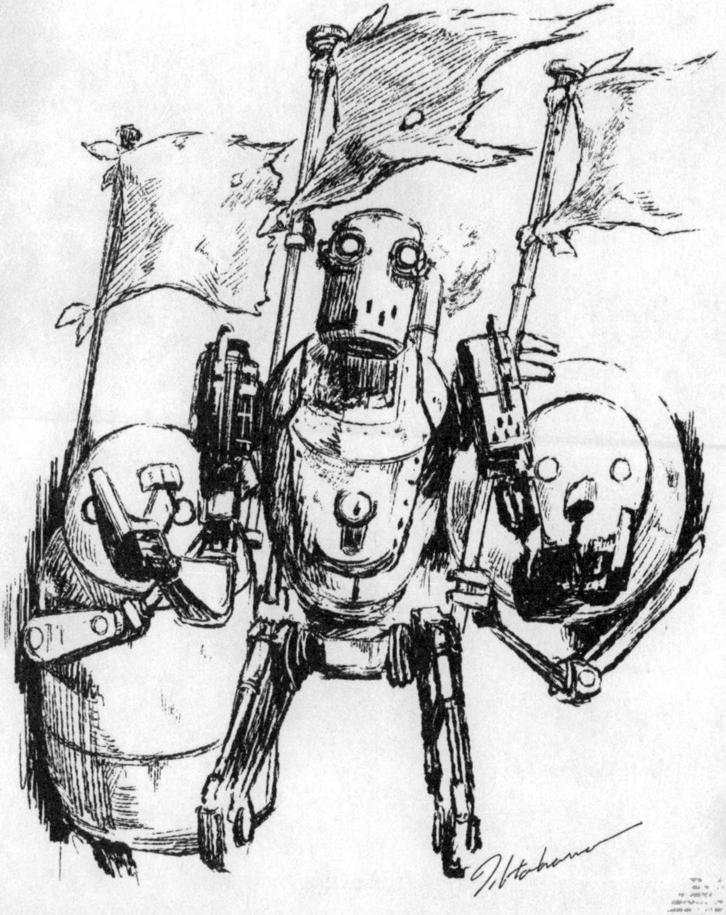

"WE HAVE LOST COMMUNICATION WITH A FEW TROOPERS FROM THE YORHA SQUADRON THAT WERE HEADING TO EARTH. They are most likely still alive, as their black-box responses are still active. We have narrowed down the location of their signals. Any YoRHa squadron troopers stationed on Earth are to investigate the issue."

It was a short and bizarre announcement. It was not rare for YoRHa squadron troopers to go incommunicado. Once they were on Earth, they could at any moment engage in battle with Machines and at times be surrounded by enemies.

It was bizarre however, that their black-box responses were still active. After the black-box response disappears, it is formally recognized that the android is destroyed. The backup of the android's personal data is then uploaded into a new chassis. Although the memories leading from the last backup to the android's destruction are lost, previous memories and its personality are preserved. In this respect, androids are semi-immortal. As long as their personal data is intact and chassis are in stock they can be repeatedly reconstructed.

But reconstruction cannot be initiated without confirming the destruction of the android. This is to prevent the confusion of having more than one instance of its personal data.

In other words, no matter how severe the circumstances, as long as the black-box response is still active, there is no other choice but to let the situation play out. The self-destruct mechanism that the YoRHa squadron androids are equipped with is mainly for preventing leaks of confidential information, but it is also a last resort for the troopers to escape the battlefield. If their chassis is destroyed in the explosion, they are able to start anew in the Bunker.

"Didn't we hear some similar news at the resistance camp too?" asked 9S. 2B added, "That recently there've been many resistance troops who've lost contact…"

Because troops of the resistance were not outfitted with a black box, it was unknown whether or not they were still alive. But they all lost contact near the same area, the very same area that the missing troops' black-box responses were detected.

"I don't want to burden you two any further after your help with the desert case, but I'd like you to keep it in the back of your mind." 2B remembered the words of the resistance camp's female leader, Anemone. Just hearing her tone of voice was enough to know how concerned she was about her comrades.

The resistance on Earth had been of long standing. It was said that they were sent to exterminate Machines even before research on the YoRHa android began. It was unclear when Anemone was sent to the front lines, but it was at least before the first YoRHa attack. That was what 2B deduced from the conversation of the camp troops. Anemone had suffered the continual loss of her comrades for that long.

2B could occasionally feel the strong gaze of Anemone. Her face probably reminded Anemone of a comrade she had lost in the past. The first time they met, Anemone was clearly caught off guard. Even though Anemone tried to play it off, the shock was obvious in her voice and expression.

Anemone projecting her memories of loss onto 2B was not particularly bothersome, so 2B purposefully pretended not to notice.

People tend to search for more similarities between two entities as soon as they notice a few. Even if they know it's futile, they search for traces. That is what it's like for people who have lost someone dear.

"The situation the other androids are facing is a bit concerning, isn't it?" asked 9S.

Was she a culprit as well? Was she trying to compare? Was she trying to search?

"I have a feeling we should get going soon," said 9S.

"You're right," 2B said, and began to research their next destination.

■ ■■

The black-box responses of the YoRHa squadron troops who had ceased communication were not far from the city ruins. But due to the collapsed buildings and deformed terrain that obstructed their path, they were forced to take an alternate route through the underground waterway. Even though the distance traveled was short, the expedition took time because of the detour.

"This is…? Is it an amusement park?" asked 9S. They had been underground until the very last moment, and had not realized what kind of place their destination was until they were standing in the middle of it. 9S was bewildered by the peculiarly shaped structures that appeared as soon as they surfaced, and understandably so. The structures were a far cry from the city ruins or the desert complex. On top of that they kept hearing strange sounds.

"Explosions?" asked 2B. It didn't seem like they were all that powerful, but 2B still set her hand on her sword.

"No, not explosions, but probably… Umm," 9S rested his fingers on his temples. He seemed to be trying to remember something. "Fireworks. See, over there," said 9S, who pointed toward the sky. Sparks of light spread across the sky. They were similar to the shape of a flower.

"It apparently makes use of chemical reactions. They combust many types of metals in the sky to create a variety of colors. A staple of many celebrations in human culture. That's what I think it said."

But there were no humans on Earth at the moment. So who was celebrating? Of course, the answer was obvious.

The amusement park was described as a place where adults brought their children to play, or possibly a place an adult could rediscover their inner child and play. Either way, it was supposed to be built for humans.

It was not a novelty for Machines to invade the human facilities and use them to their liking. The factory ruins where they had annihilated the Goliath-class Machines had been used by the Machines as a manufacturing facility.

It was understandable to repurpose a factory for increasing military force, but why the Machines needed an amusement park was beyond comprehension. The Machines in the area were either dancing or repeating words like "1t's s0 fun! 1t's s0 fun!" and "Let's be happy t0gether!"

Mimicking humans by shooting fireworks, throwing confetti, playing musical instruments, and dancing—it was absurd. There was nothing to gain. Furthermore, the Machines partaking in the festivities did not try to attack.

Thinking back, the Machines they saw at the desert complex had been mimicking humans too. They too had nothing to gain from their meaningless activities, and at first were not hostile. It was unlikely that these two populations had a connection, but was it okay to pass off multiple irregular sightings as coincidence?

"What should we do? Should we eliminate them?" 9S asked hesitantly. 2B shook her head and quickened her gait.

"They pose no threat, so fighting would be a waste of time," said 2B. Besides, the black-box responses were still being broadcast this whole time, from within this eerie amusement park, inside that odd-shaped building. Her instincts told her that she needed to hurry.

"It's about the source of the responses, but I think the location was originally a theater. I've come across a similar image before," said 9S.

"A theater?"

"It was a facility used to showcase musical or dramatic performances," said 9S.

After answering with an "I see," 2B went to look for a way into the theater. Within the amusement park, only the theater had its access restricted. The golden metal gates that were most likely the entrance were tightly closed, and there was a canal bordering the rest of its property.

In the end, they had to resort to a reckless plan of jumping into the building from above. 9S had informed her that this style of building was vulnerable due to its use of stained glass in its domed ceiling. But he had clearly not thought about exploiting that vulnerability.

"We're going to break through the window?" 9S asked, disappointed, after 2B explained the details of their infiltration plan.

"There's no other way," said 2B.

"Well, I mean…that's true," said 9B.

During their missions, it was heavily advised to keep from damaging any human artifacts. This was because one day, everything on Earth was to be returned to its rightful human owners.

That was why ruins that were damaged by erosion or collapse from old age underwent maintenance and restoration to preserve their ancient forms. But this repair effort was falling behind due to the shortage of civil engineering units. A few sectors of the city ruins, including this amusement park, were an example of some of the areas where this effort had lagged.

"Saving our comrades is the first priority. We can think through the little things later," 2B said.

Until now, there had been no precedent of Machines capturing and restraining androids alive. It was usually a matter of kill or be killed. That should be the extent of what the simple-minded Machines could accomplish. What was going on?

2B jumped down toward the building to try and quell her impatience. She smashed the stained glass, successfully entered the building, and sprinted toward the source of the black-box responses.

Running down the tiered audience seats, she made her way to a circular opening. While there were no obstructions, and there was plenty of space to maneuver, the dim conditions made her visuals suboptimal. Her footsteps echoed along the high ceiling.

A large cloth that was draped ahead suddenly split open towards the sides. A faint memory of some terms she had seen in a video drifted through her mind. That large cloth was a "curtain," and that elevated platform was a "stage." A place made for actors and singers to perform.

Beams of light illuminated the stage. The figure that cheerfully rose into the stage was, somewhat expectedly and somewhat unexpectedly, a Machine that could only be defined as eccentric looking.

"There's no records of any Machine that looks like that," said 9S.

The Machine's skirt, which had a flared bottom hem, was obviously made to mimic a woman's dress. But with arms that looked like branches and exposed screws on the head, the Machine was intensely grotesque.

The Machine opened its mouth. A piercing, unwelcome sound, like pieces of rusted metal grinding together, rang out. With its arms raised and chest flared, it looked like it was pretending to sing.

It was an earsplitting noise. Fighting the urge to cover her ears, 2B drew her military sword and leapt. The Machine's processing system was probably contained in its chest, high above the ground. On top of that, the flared skirt made it difficult to cut through the body.

Even so, as 2B kept attacking, the harsh song faltered slightly. It seemed like she was inflicting some damage.

Right as she felt she had the upper hand, her vision flickered.

"W-what... What is this?" 2B asked.

Her body swayed. It was impossible to stand straight.

"It's trying to hack us!" 9S's voice was broken and distant. 2B heard something else mixed with his voice. She kept slicing toward the source of that sound. It was most likely something from the enemy. Something that sham of an opera singer was emitting...

The opera singer was not the only enemy. Before she knew it she was receiving blows from every direction. She realized that the "enemies" were not Machines as she flung her sword around to counter.

"Bodies of dead androids?!" exclaimed 2B.

The bodies, which were tied to stakes, were emitting similar auditory attacks.

"They're not!" yelled 9S, "I'm detecting their black-box signals!"

Which meant that they had been captured, kept alive, and were being used as weapons.

"I'll end this quickly," said 2B.

She was going to demolish that opera singer and free her comrades.

Kill or be killed. That's all she thought they were capable of. She didn't think Machines would be able to do anything more sophisticated. That's something she didn't want to imagine.

She heard a sound again.

"I am g0nna be beaut1ful!"

What had previously been mixed with 9S's voice became clearer.

"G0nna be beaut1ful!"

She didn't want to think about what the Machine meant, so she started swinging aimlessly.

"G0nna be m0re beaut1ful!"

A Machine? Why is a Machine saying that? These degenerates only kill and destroy!

"Counter-hacking completed!" said 9S. The enemies' attacks halted at the same time 9S spoke. 2B called Pod.

"Affirmative," Pod replied.

Pod shifted into its Long-Distance Fire mode.

"Go!" commanded 2B.

Pod's laser pierced the metal chest of the Machine, which was stuck in a leaning position. 2B thought she heard a scream. Neither a song nor a word. This time, it was truly just a sound with no meaning.

■　■■

They left through the proper entrance. The enemy signals had disappeared, and it was easy to open the gates from the inside. But 9S's footsteps were heavy. 2B, who saw his expression from the side, was sure she was making the same expression.

They weren't able to save the androids that had been modified into weapons. Every android had its circuits fried. They were being compelled to move by the enemy's system, and had no control of any of their functions. The androids were as good as dead after they were disconnected.

2B hoped, dearly, that they had not been conscious. If they had been awake or had any senses left to them while being used as weapons—how painful that must have been.

"Hey 2B. When I hacked that Machine, this strange voice..." With hesitation, 9S continued, "It had something like emotion, but—" 2B cut off the rest of his sentence with firm resolve.

"The Machines are only selecting words at random."

They don't have a consciousness or emotions. They just constantly execute the command to kill.

"That's what you said," added 2B.

But what if that wasn't the case? What if Machines could think, judge, and at times even express emotion? What if they were autonomous inorganic beings that also housed a consciousness or emotions. If that were the case, they were almost like...

It was scary to think it through. That was why 2B used 9S's words to bring the conversation to a stop. It was probably an unfair way of doing so.

It was okay if it was unfair. Right now, it was 2B's priority to keep her emotions in check. If she let her guard down, she felt like something inside of her would go crazy. That would complicate their mission.

They walked silently, backs to the theater. The sounds of Machines shooting fireworks could still be heard. The dancing Machines, twirling like tops, were right by them, but took no notice of 2B and 9S.

Or so she had thought. A flying Machine swooped down before them as if to block their way. The Machine spoke faster than 2B could grab her sword.

"I am n0t an enemy."

Looking closely, 2B saw there was a piece of white cloth fluttering atop its head. In human culture, a white flag signified surrender, but

2B had never seen it used in person. Battles with Machines didn't end until every last combatant on one side died, so the concept of peaceful surrender was inconceivable.

"Y0u tw0 defeated the br0ken Mach1ne f0r us. Y0u will be rewarded. C0me t0 my village," said the Machine.

The term "broken machine" was probably referring to the opera singer. It had been trouble for other Machines as well. The words "for us" and "reward" were proof of that.

"To think that a Machine could use so many words," 9S said, in awe. Type S androids had a strong sense of curiosity. It was quite vital, as their primary function was to perform research. But an excessive curiosity would lead to one's downfall. 2B knew that better than anyone else.

"We can't trust the words of a Machine," said 2B.

2B was concerned that the Machine would not understand her reply. But then she realized her words were geared toward 9S, and to curb his curiosity rather than to reach a mutual understanding with the Machine.

The Machine swung its whole body as if to shake its head.

"We have n0 1ntent1ons t0 f1ght," it asserted.

9S's eyes lit up. He did this whenever he saw something novel and unknown.

"I've never witnessed a Machine that could communicate to this extent. Let's follow along to gather data," said 9S.

2B's plan to curb his curiosity had backfired. Perhaps this was a good thing. As long as his curiosity was directed at a Machine, 9S was safe. It was infinitely better than taking interest in a forbidden subject and crossing the line…

■　■■

Guided by the flying-type Machine, they left the amusement park. Moving away from the irritating music and fireworks, even the sunlight and whisper of the wind felt gentler.

It wasn't a coincidence. Soon enough, they were surrounded by trees and shrubbery. The overgrown trees gave the sun's light a soft glow. Instead of musty air, a breeze with the smell of damp earth and grass passed through. The greenery here created a completely different environment from its counterparts in the city ruins.

Earth was so diverse compared to space, which was just one long stretch of darkness. 2B looked up at the sky and marveled at how much had changed, though they had traveled so little distance. Then she spotted something with a white trail moving through the sky. It was ascending, but it didn't look like a firework.

"What's that?" asked 2B.

9S stopped walking and questioned if 2B had never seen it.

"We use that to send materials from Earth to the Bunker or human base. Space doesn't have any research materials or natural resources like Earth," explained 9S.

"I see," said 2B.

She had heard of such a thing, but today was the first day she had seen it in person. It wasn't something they used frequently, and it was rare for her to have an opportunity to stare at the sky. Type B androids were given the role of combat. Her vision was used to latching on to enemies, not the sky.

Although, even if she wasn't on a combat mission she wouldn't be in the mood to look at something like the sky. That was because…

"Th1s way th1s way hurry th1s way," said the guide.

2B decided to stop thinking. She started running and followed the flying-type Machine. The sound of swaying trees comforted her. The village eventually came into view.

It was easy to see, even from far away, the countless white cloths fluttering in the wind. Upon closer inspection they were all flags. The Machines were waving around white flags of various sizes.

"Does it mean they have no intention of fighting?" asked 9S.

If the Machines were familiar with the significance of the white flag, that was what it meant. They couldn't ignore the possibility of an ambush after letting their guard down, but it was nonetheless a fact that these Machines had a higher-than-average intelligence. Surrender or ambush—either way, both were actions that took quite a bit of acuity.

"First, we would like you to listen to what we have to say," said a Machine holding a particularly large flag. It had a unique cylindrical head and a body silhouette that made it look like it was constantly carrying something. Its movements were much more delicate than any Machine 2B had seen before, and its speech was more fluent than their guide's.

"We are not your enemy. My name is Pascal. I am the leader of this village," it explained.

2B could feel her eyes widening.

"2B, don't believe anything a Machine says!" warned 9S.

He was the one who'd wanted to come to the village, but it seemed even he was skeptical of the claims that they were not an enemy. But Pascal kept an ever-gentle tone.

"It's true. To you, we are Machines and thus we are your enemy. But this village is made of Machines that ran away from battle to advocate peace," replied Pascal.

Peace. It was a strange word to hear from a Machine.

"We have formed an alliance with the people at the resistance camp as well. If it's all right with you, please bring this back to the leader, Anemone," insisted Pascal.

"This is…?" asked 2B.

It was an old model, but it looked like a fuel filter. It certainly wasn't reminiscent of a disguised bomb.

"Anemone is in need of it. If you give it to her, I'm sure you'll be able to see that we are a people that come from peace," said Pascal.

"Roger that," said 2B.

Pascal was probably not lying about his acquaintance, since he knew about the resistance camp and its leader, Anemone.

"That small path is a shortcut to the city ruins. It's fairly straightforward from here," said Pascal.

2B would have to ask Anemone and see if this "alliance" was indeed mutual, or if it was feigned.

■ ■■

They found out that Pascal had been telling the truth. As soon as 2B and 9S told Anemone that they had returned with an item from a Machine named Pascal, Anemone replied, "Ah, the fuel filter. Thanks."

Apparently the Machines from that village specialized in fine precision work. They made parts that were difficult to manufacture at the resistance camp. Anemone and the resistance exchanged oils and other hard-to-obtain materials in return for the parts.

"Well, they're a harmless bunch. There's no need to worry. If you're going back to the village, bring this for Pascal," said Anemone.

2B and 9S revisited the village with a greasy can of oil from Anemone.

"Thank you so much for your effort," said Pascal, bowing his head. He received the greasy oil from Anemone. It was uncomfortable to see and hear a Machine act in such a sophisticated way.

"I'm glad Anemone is a cooperative person. If only all androids and Machines could get along peacefully," said Pascal.

"That's nothing more than a dream," said 9S. He was also probably getting uncomfortable. 9S argued that it was easier said than done.

"Machines have no emotions," added 9S.

Those were harsh words for their host, who could understand what they were saying. But Pascal seemed to take no offense and replied, "You may be right.

"But if it's not too much to ask," insisted Pascal, "Please come by this village more often. I believe that the only way to reach mutual understanding is through communication."

2B didn't know how to answer. She felt like she couldn't ignore the request, even though it was suggested by the enemy. If anything, he was right. But she didn't want to admit it. 2B searched for the right reply. As if to disturb her thoughts, there was suddenly a sound similar to an earthquake or explosion.

"What was that?" 2B asked.

Pods 042 and 153 opened their communication displays as 2B and 9S exchanged glances. The voices of operators 6O and 12O started reporting the same news from pods 042 and 153.

"A Goliath-class enemy has appeared near the city ruins! There are multiple accompanying Machine signals!"

It was a combat order to all YoRHa squadron troopers. That earlier sound had come from the Goliath-class enemy.

"2B, these guys were trying to trap us all along..." said 9S, giving Pascal a look of exasperation.

His plan had probably been to lure 2B and 9S away and release the Goliath-class enemy while fewer personnel were stationed at the city ruins.

They hadn't seen it, though a Goliath-class was an enemy large enough to make a mighty noise. If it was also being accompanied by multiple Machines, did luring two androids away make such a big difference?

"We were also not aware of that information. You may not believe me, but I hope you do," said Pascal.

He was a Machine that should have no emotions, yet his tone of voice sounded somber.

"It's okay either way. We're going to go destroy it," said 2B.

It didn't matter if it was a trap or not. She was going to dismantle the enemy. That was her only job.

Even if Pascal desired communication, the YoRHa squadron troopers were built for battle. 2B bitterly remembered Pascal's praise for Anemone's cooperation and understanding.

2B could tell that the ground was shaking, even in full sprint. It wasn't just the ground. The buildings and even the air were vibrating. It was easy to imagine how giant of an enemy was causing the ruckus.

But they could not get visuals on the Machine. There was a gray cloud, unidentifiable as dust or smoke, that covered their field of vision. 9S yelled, "2B!" from the side.

"Command deployed flight units! The building up ahead!" said 9S.

It was the roof of the building they had descended onto the other day. There were many similar buildings surrounding it, obscuring it from the prying eyes of enemies. The only downside was that it was far from the resistance camp and the area they were coming from.

The ground shook violently and a hot wind almost toppled her forward. A projectile had landed right behind them. If they hadn't been running at full speed, it would've been a direct hit.

On the way they occasionally ran into wandering deer and boars. Even with their wild instincts, the animals were lost as to which direction to run for safety. The smell of burning flesh was proof that a significant number of animals had been caught in the crossfire.

On the other hand, they hardly saw any Machines. They had probably evacuated to safety right after the Goliath-class enemy appeared. Individually they were slow, but as a group they moved disturbingly quickly.

Their responsiveness always spelled trouble for the YoRHa squadron...

She ran with urgency up the stairs of the building and into the flight unit. She received a transmission from Operator 6O just as she was taking off.

"The sky is full of enemy antiflight measures. Please approach the scene at a low altitude."

2B replied with a "Roger that" and lowered her altitude. With such poor field of vision, it was impossible to tell where the enemies were, much less dodge their attacks.

She passed between near-collapsing buildings and mowed down trees to close in on the Goliath-class enemy.

"Ms. 2B! I'm sending you data on the enemy's weak points!" said Operator 6O.

"Roger that," replied 2B.

She rapidly ascended and fired multiple missiles at the displayed points. This flight unit was of recent manufacture, but it had already been modified with measures against Goliath-class enemies. The battle data from the factory ruins had been analyzed and integrated into the firing components.

But this enemy was the same type as the one they had struggled with in the factory ruins. Even with the modified missiles, one attack was not enough to take down the enemy.

Avoiding the enemy's laser cannons, 2B waited for her missiles to recharge. The downside of the newly issued unit was the slight delay needed for consecutive rounds of firing.

This time it was a transmission from 9S.

"Initiating hacking of the enemy system!" said 9S.

"Roger that. I'll cover you," replied 2B.

9S would take control of the enemy and 2B would destroy it. Last time they had lost out on numbers but this time there were only two enemies. This tactic was more than enough.

The enemy movements noticeably dulled. The missiles had recharged as well. 2B heard 9S report that his hacking was a success as she focused her aim.

The repeated hacking of 9S and firing from 2B eventually led to silence. The light in the enemy's eyes vanished. The giant head slumped forward, pulling the body after it. 2B checked for the Machine's signal. She was reminded of the countless times 9S had told her that it was dangerous unless she thoroughly checked that the enemy was dead.

"Goliath-class enemy, confirmation that all functions are down," 2B reported clearly. The other enemy was on the verge of defeat. The surroundings were remarkably quiet compared to a few moments ago. Was the resistance camp okay? She told herself that she would go check after returning the flight unit to the Bunker.

Just then, she heard an ominous rumbling. Sounds similar to the earth rumbling became louder and higher in succession. The light returned to the eyes of the Goliath-class Machine.

"Impossible…" said 2B.

The enemy had definitely *been* dead. She had destroyed that arm with the blade as well. In reality, the enemy was functioning but not moving. There was no way it could move.

"Enemy is recharging!" screamed 9S.

His warning was drowned out. It was hard to hear anything because the atmosphere itself was shaking. The Operator's voice came through in patches, reporting the increasing resonance from the enemy.

The shaking in the atmosphere grew into a shock wave. The most they could do was blast forward at full throttle to stay upright. They could hardly stay in position, much less transition to firing mode.

She thought she heard the words *battle area*, *underground*, and *resonating*, and moved her gaze to the ground. There was a crack. 2B gaped as building after building of considerable size was swallowed by the chasm, dust clouds rising everywhere.

The ground, the atmosphere, and everything around them was resonating. The Goliath-class Machine swayed and keeled over. She knew she had to withdraw, but she couldn't move.

2B put her unit into full throttle and braced for a shockwave. She saw a white light. She thought she heard an explosion. There was a furious tremor.

Then, very abruptly, the light and noise disappeared. The silence was complete enough to make her think she was in outer space. Her auditory mechanisms were impaired from the shock wave.

2B's ears rang. She grimaced and looked around to confirm 9S's safety and gauge the situation. She couldn't believe her eyes. Maybe her visual mechanisms were impaired as well.

All the things that should have been there, were not. The groups of buildings, the dense forest, the fragmented roads, and even the ground were all gone. There was a large crater, as if someone had taken an enormous spoon and scooped away the earth.

She righted her flight unit and flew over the depression. The Goliath-class Machine was not in sight. It was extremely lucky that both of them were okay given the scale of the explosion.

She breathed a sigh of relief. But it was drowned out by an obnoxious alarm. At the same time, the communication display turned into a sea of red.

"This is...?!" exclaimed 2B.

2B had never seen the words that were being displayed on the UI. ALIEN ALERT—words that signified that the aliens, who had not shown themselves in several hundred years, were underground.

ANOTHER SIDE "EVE"

Big brother has always been by my side. I've always been with him, ever since I was born into this world and the moment my eyes saw light.

I already knew when I stood up onto my own legs. I knew what was valuable to me. What I had to protect. Nobody had taught me, but I knew. The answer was almost too obvious.

"Hey, big brother. Why do we have to wear such uncomfortable things like underwear?" asked Eve.

"According to records, humans concealed their genitals. Exposing your genitals was frowned upon, apparently. Just don't complain and wear it, Eve," demanded Adam.

"Okay. But why do we have to eat these plants? Machines don't need to eat plants to function."

"This is a type of fruit. Apparently humans were able to gain knowledge by eating this. Stop whining and eat in silence."

"I see. If big brother says I should then I will. But after this, will you come play with me?"

"Sure."

"Then I'll try my best to eat it."

I love to play, and it's fun, but in reality we don't have to play. As long as big brother is there, and he looks like he is having fun. I just said play, because big brother always looks like he's having the most fun when we're playing human.

Big brother, do you understand? I like to play, but I like it even more when you're happy.

I know what you like, big brother. Ancient books written by humans. Footage of humans from a long time ago. You like anything the humans made, don't you? When we play human, we use a table that looks just like the one from an ancient show.

If big brother could see a living human, I bet he'd be happy. If we could play with a living human, I bet big brother would have fun and smile.

"Big brother, let's play," said Eve.

"Not now," replied Adam.

"Why not?"

"We're going to have guests soon,"

"Guests? You mean that big sound just now?"

"No, that was an old Goliath-class weapon. I invited them with it."

"Who's them?"

"You'll know when you see them. I have to prepare the arrangements soon."

"Big brother."

"What?"

"Will you play with me after the preparations?"

"Not yet. I said there were going to be guests, right?"

"Then will you play with me once the guests come?"

"If we complete the objective."

"How long will that take?"

"Let's see… You can wait until then, right?"

"I'll wait. So let's play."

"Only if you can keep our promise."

"I will. If it's a promise for my big brother, I'll definitely keep it."

If big brother is having fun, then I'm having fun. If big brother smiles, that makes me want to smile. It makes my stomach tingle with a warm feeling.

It's because there's no one else like big brother. There's lots of Machines, but none of them are like us. I'm the only one that looks like big brother, and big brother is the only one that looks like me.

Even if we think differently and like different things, me and big brother will always be together. Isn't that awesome?

Let's play, big brother. Let's get this over with and play.

Let's play human, your favorite game. I'll wear the annoying clothes and eat the funny-tasting plants. I'll wait until it's time.

Hey big brother, do you know what I like?

CH. 03: 2B'S STORY/CONTACT

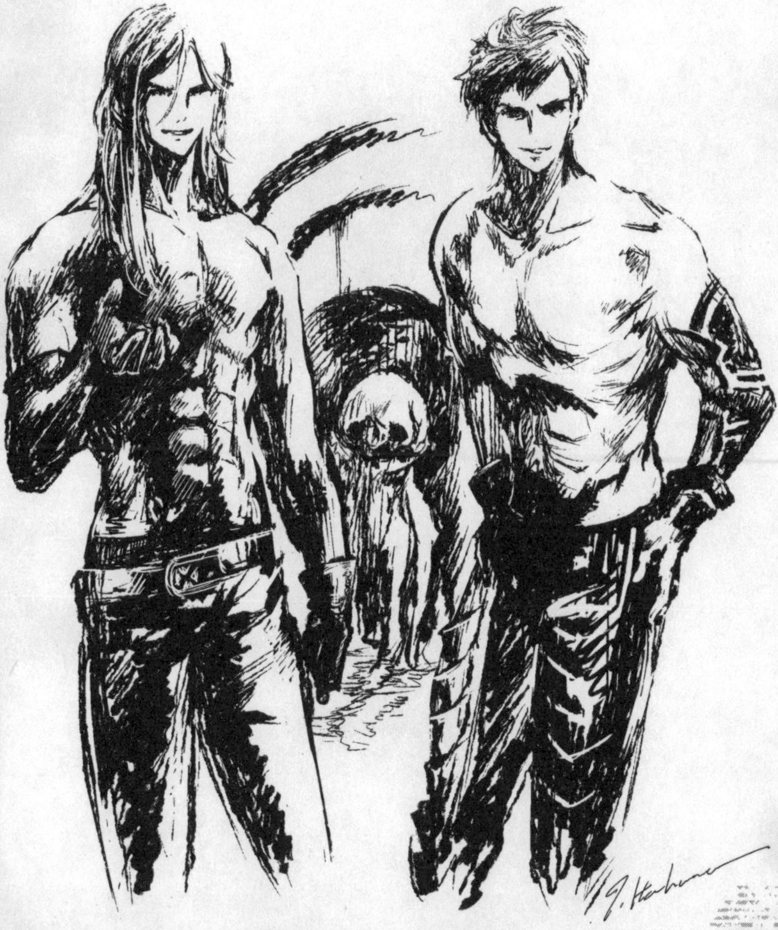

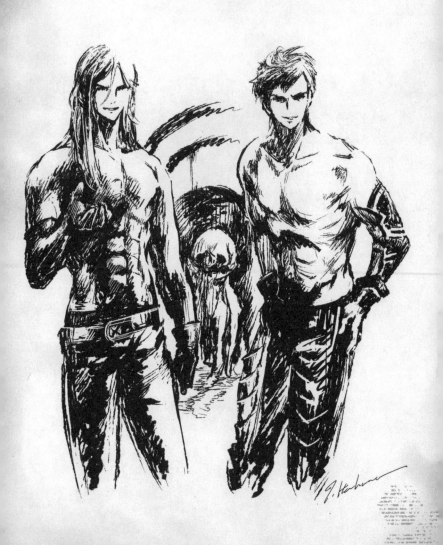

AS 2B AND 9S WERE EXITING THEIR FLIGHT UNITS, THEY HEARD THE COMMANDER ADDRESS ALL YORHA SQUADRON TROOPERS.

"We've detected alien signals, which have been dormant for several thousand years. As you know, the aliens are the commanders of the Machines. If we defeat the aliens, we'll be able to end this long battle once and for all."

The words "alien alert" that they had seen were neither a delusion nor a malfunction of the sensors. After all, the commander was broadcasting an announcement to all YoRHa squadron troopers.

"Currently, the technology department is analyzing their signals. All troopers stationed on Earth should prioritize the gathering of intelligence regarding this issue. We cannot waste this opportunity."

Even after the message concluded with the words "Glory to mankind," 2B kept silently descending the cliff, down toward the source of the alien signals.

After descending the cliff, she heard the splash of water near her feet.

"Pod, I'd like some light," said 2B.

"Affirmative: Turning on the light."

Pod's light shimmered. The ground was covered in water, though whether it was underground water or rainwater was impossible to discern.

"It seems like this area used to be a cave. It wasn't made when the ground caved in," 9S's voice echoed. It was hard to tell from Pod's light, but the cave was pretty sizable.

"There's a side tunnel here," said 9S.

"This is…a passageway?" asked 2B.

Straining her eyes, she could see that the walls of the tunnel used sheet piles in various places to prevent collapse. Even if the side tunnel had occurred naturally, someone had modified it for use.

"There's no information in the database that corresponds with it, so if it is a passageway…" began 9S.

"It's one that the enemy made," finished 2B.

If the aliens had been using the path, in hiding, for the past several hundred years, it was no wonder their side had no record of it.

As if to support her theory, some things emerged out of the darkness. There was the sound of clashing metal. Red lights made a trail in the darkness. They were walking-type Machines. There were alien signals nearby, so it was obvious that there was going to be quite a few of their minions around.

It was difficult to fight in a dark and confined area, and it would be a hassle to make sure that the passage didn't collapse from combat.

But these drawbacks affected the enemy as well. It took them about as much time as it would've taken aboveground to dismantle the enemy. 9S kept muttering about his shoes being wet and nasty, but that was nothing new.

As they moved along further, the water level receded. The number of enemies decreased as well.

"The alien signals haven't changed at all, have they," said 9S.

"But there's fewer Machines coming out…" said 2B.

"Is it a trap?" asked 9S.

"I don't know. Let's be cautious," replied 2B.

It was quiet. Only the sound of their dry footsteps echoed along the narrow path. Then, 2B felt something hard beneath her foot.

"A Machine?!"

There were the remains of a walking type lying at the edge of the path. 9S carefully observed the body.

"It looks like this has been here for a long time…" said 9S.

"It's not just here," answered 2B.

2B looked farther along the path. At the end of Pod's light were remains of spherical types and cylindrical types rolling around. It looked like the number increased the deeper they went.

"But why?" asked 2B.

What had destroyed all these Machines? It was definitely not the resistance or the YoRHa squadron. If it had been, there would have been some kind of record of the battle that took place.

"I wonder if this is what catacombs were like," said 9S.

"Cata-what?"

"They were underground graves left behind by the human civilization. There were even some that used naturally occurring caves," said 9S.

Darkness, silence, and cold air. Then the Machine corpses. There were no signs of life or enemy signals at all. A grave was indeed a good way to describe the location.

"What's this?" asked 2B.

They both stopped at the same time. It was clearly different in shape and material from the cave's naturally occurring walls. Somebody had created an entrance of some sort.

"There's no information on this either," said 9S.

That meant it was probably an alien facility. There were still no enemy signals. They braced themselves and passed through the entrance, but nothing happened. The only noticeable thing that changed was the sound of their footsteps. The flooring and height of the ceiling had changed.

Dim light poured in through the shutters that extended toward the ceiling. 2B looked around, wondering what light source was being used underground.

Within the room, there were several rows of chairlike objects. They each had something on the seats. 2B nonchalantly took a look at one and gasped.

It was the shriveled remains of a creature—a creature different from anything else she had seen on Earth.

"Is this an alien?"

Every chair had similar-looking remains on it. They were in an awkward position that made it look like they were about to slip and fall to the floor.

"2B! Look!" yelled 9S, who had been looking out the windows. 2B hadn't realized the shutters had been opened. She saw what 9S was pointing at through them.

"A ship? Is it the aliens'?" asked 2B.

To put it properly, it was the remains of what could have been a ship.

"It's been destroyed." said 2B.

It was easy to tell that the damage was not from a rough landing. There were countless spears piercing the ship's hull. The alien ship had fought, and lost, to someone or something. This place was probably not a facility, but also part of the ship. This section seemed like it had been spared, but all the aliens that had entered were dead.

2B looked around one more time. The orderly chairs that held the slumped remains of the aliens. She remembered how 9S had described the place as an "underground base." This was almost like...

"Welcome. To our creators' graveyard."

Graveyard. 2B had been thinking of the same exact word. But it was an unfamiliar voice. She quickly tried to find the owner of the voice. She felt her gaze harden.

"You two!" shouted 2B.

Two men stood at the end of her glare—the Machines resembling androids that they had fought back in the Mammoth Complex.

There were no footsteps. Neither they nor the two pods had detected any signals. It was as if the Machines had appeared out of nowhere. No, that didn't matter now. They had to destroy them before the enemy could use a sonic attack like before.

"Pod!" called 2B.

She made 042 cover her as she leapt. She drew her sword and attacked in one motion. She thought her blade made contact with the man. It *should* have made contact, but he was gone. The man had disappeared.

"You're sooo violent," smiled the man from behind. His expression and his speech were different and more fluent then before. Although they weren't wearing anything on their upper bodies, they had learned to wear clothes from the waist down. One had trimmed his hair short, while the other had kept his long and clipped the ends, as if they were trying to differentiate themselves.

"Hey big brother. Can I kill these guys?"

The man with the short hair had a monotone compared to the man with the long hair.

"Eve, calm down. We haven't finished talking," argued the man with the long hair. He turned his attention toward 2B and 9S. His tone had a hint of amusement.

"My name is Adam."

Adam? The man with the long hair was Adam, and the man with the short hair was Eve?

"The aliens you androids are searching for are gone. Hundreds of years ago. We Machines drove them to extinction."

"Extinct? The Machines did that?" asked 2B.

The man called Adam smirked knowingly.

"This time, the ones that will go extinct…it might be you androids?"

2B replied with her sword. Conversation with them was meaningless. If what Pascal said was true, and the only way to gain mutual understanding was through communicating, none of that was necessary. She did not want to understand them, and she did not want them to understand her.

"2B! Please be careful!" said 9S.

Adam had once again disappeared from the path of her blade. This time taking Eve, who had been standing by his side, with him.

"Machines are weapons that constantly evolve and grow stronger."

A voice mocked from behind. It seemed like they had teleportation capabilities. They were indeed evolving, and at a terrifying rate.

"It wasn't long before the intelligence accumulated on the network surpassed that of our creators," said Adam.

"That's still no reason to overthrow your creators." 9S found himself speechless. He found it hard to relate, as they had been risking their lives for their creators, humans, since their creation.

"It's fine. These fools are as simple as plants and have a boring composition. They're worthless," Adam's gaze was directed toward the aliens' corpses. Was it her imagination that his stare held a piercing coldness and smoldering hatred that seemed like they would freeze and burn anything at a moment's notice?

But those emotions quickly faded. They were again replaced by an indecipherable expression.

"We're interested in the humans on the moon," said Adam.

"Humans?!"

"That's right, humans are fascinating," he said.

He raised his arms in a dramatic fashion.

"According to records, this species had very complex behaviors: they would kill each other, and at times love each other. Their actions were startling. We want to uncover the mystery of their motivations."

His enchanted expression was disgusting. He made it seem like he had emotions, even though he was merely a Machine. "Startling"? "Mystery"? What did a Machine know?

"That's why we want you androids, who were modeled after humans, to help us with our investigation," said Adam.

2B was appalled by his courteous way of talking. What a foolish thing for a Machine to do.

"Drag the humans down from the moon, and analyze them while they're still alive. Analyze them—and expose all their secrets. There's nothing quite like it, is there?"

Her anger swelled. Something inside her started to stir. But 9S was the first one that let his anger erupt.

"How could we let you do something like that!"

9S's long sword shot out of his hand. It flew toward Adam, but again lost its target, and clattered against the wall in vain.

"So I guess this means our negotiations have failed."

9S started toward Adam again.

"I guess we'll just have to obliterate you. Both of you. Just like these mundane aliens," said Adam.

Eve loomed over 2B. 2B swung her military sword down. This time it made contact, but it wasn't enough to even leave a scratch. There was a wall of some sort protecting Eve.

She slashed with her sword, harder and harder, aiming at the same point. Her rage colored everything she saw in red. A fracture appeared in the invisible wall protecting Eve. She twisted the tip of her sword through the opening. The blade reached the target.

But Eve just kicked 2B's sword away. A shock ran through her hand on the hilt. It was a powerful kick. The edges of Eve's mouth curled. He was smiling.

She swung her sword, it was batted away, and she swung it again. Her fury did not settle. *Drag the humans down? Analyze them? They're just Machines. They're just Machines. They're just Machines…*

How long had that repeated? She heard the words "It's almost time." Eve's smile changed. It looked like he mouthed the word "promise." 2B was taken aback by his wholehearted grin.

Eve disappeared, smile and all. It was the teleportation again. Adam and Eve stood together, away from 9S and away from 2B, as if to say the fight was over.

"This was the fate of our creators," said Adam.

He pointed to the alien corpses in an exaggerated motion. Eve shrugged his shoulders as if to scoff.

"What about the humans you believe in?" asked Adam.

The next moment, Adam and Eve disappeared. Looking back and looking around, they were nowhere to be found.

■ ■■

They returned to the Bunker using a newly installed transfer device. According to 9S, the engineering department had been developing the technology so that androids could travel between Earth and the Bunker without using a flight unit.

Leaving the current chassis on Earth, the device transferred the personal data to a new chassis on the Bunker. When it came time to return to Earth, the personal data was restored to the original chassis. It was a different concept from physically descending in a flight unit, as it only involved the transfer of data and the prior construction of a chassis. It cut down vastly on the time required for travel.

Above all, it prevented any assault from happening while they were descending. It gave Command a headache when the expensive flight units were damaged in descents. The transfer device was their solution.

2B was curious about how long it took the engineering department to develop a functional transfer device. Those Machines named Adam and Eve had been flawlessly using teleportation. To think that they had been born not too long ago.

"Machines are weapons that constantly evolve and grow stronger."

What capabilities would they evolve in the future? There was no time to waste. It was crucial to defeat them before their evolution grew out of hand. There was no way a pair that had destroyed their own creators could be left alone…

However, these were only the sentiments of a single soldier. Command made the decisions, and at times decisions would require agreement from the human board.

"…That concludes the report on the alien ship."

The commander, who heard 2B's report, replied with a low-pitched "I see." 2B speculated just how much weight those short words carried. The commander had overseen their operations for many years. His shock from the news that the aliens had been extinct for several thousands of years must have far exceeded that which 2B and 9S had experienced.

"I will treat this as top secret information until we get a response from the human board," said the commander.

Neither the commander's expression nor tone carried a hint of emotion. She advised them, in her usual tone of voice, to tell no one about the incident.

"I'd also like you two to find out more about the Machine named Pascal."

"Whaat?!"

9S was clearly unhappy about the unexpected order.

"That creepy Machine?" complained 9S.

It was obvious that 9S wanted to reject the order. If they had not been in the presence of the commander, 2B would have scolded him for showing too much emotion. She had told him *a number of times* that such displays were prohibited to a YoRHa squadron trooper.

"It's a direct order from the human board on the moon," said the commander apathetically. "Information about unique individuals will provide valuable research materials for future missions."

"Roger that."

Although 2B had agreed, 9S still carried a look of disapproval on his face.

ANOTHER SIDE "A2"

I heard the voice of a Machine. "I will protect," it said. Apparently this Machine had something to protect.

Fighting to protect something. It had been a while since I had fought like that. I had nothing to protect anymore. All my comrades had died. People I had believed in before were now enemies.

Destroy anything that wasn't myself. There was only one reason to fight. To destroy. No thinking, just wrecking.

"For the king of the forest," proclaimed the voice. To outsiders this area looked like a forest, but it was actually thought to be a forest kingdom that was ruled by a king. That's what I pieced together from what the Machines said.

The Machines in this area were more aggressive and stubborn than their counterparts. Functionally they were no different from other Machines, but there was a clear disparity in how long it took from first contact to destruction. They were a tough bunch.

At first this was strange. But after hearing the word "protect," it all made sense. I knew how much stronger soldiers became when they fought to protect. I had been one of them too.

YoRHa prototype, Attacker No. 2. Even though I was a model specialized for close-quarters combat, I was a mediocre soldier. To be honest, I didn't like to fight.

The fact that I was even selected as a member for the Pearl Harbor Descent Attack was proof that it was an experimental mission. At the time I had naively believed that I was riding a wave of great expectations.

I was desperate. Desperate not to burden my comrades, desperate to answer the commander's expectations, I desperately ran through the battlefield. It didn't matter if I didn't like it—I had no choice but to fight. I had comrades to protect:

fellow YoRHa squadron troopers and the resistance that I had met on Earth. My mediocre self grew stronger by protecting these women.

The Machines charged while shouting the words, "Repay your debt to the king!" It was an organized movement. They were a formidable enemy compared to their counterparts in other areas.

The first time I had ever seen Machines practice military formation to advance and attack was when I set foot in the forest.

Honestly, I was surprised. I never expected Machines to train for battle. Training was something performed by individuals with a considerable amount of decisiveness, and the capacity to think. It was something that Machines, who blindly followed commands, should not have been able to do.

I was surprised, but I realized it was possible. After all, Command had thrown sentient androids into battle only to discard them after they had collected data. Cold-blooded androids like them existed. Well, in reality their blood and tears were just colored liquids made to mimic those of humans. The point was, it was within the realm of possibility to have Machines that trained for battle as well.

I heard some voices scream, "The king is in danger! Take him to safety!" The level of alarm was gradually rising. It meant this was the right way. The place they were trying so hard to protect was up ahead. Most likely the throne room of their king.

I broke up the formation, and started to attack the stray Machines. I crushed them steadily, one by one. It took time, but it couldn't be helped. Had I comrades, I might have been able to fight more efficiently. There was no use in thinking about this, anyway.

Fighting alone was inefficient, but there were some benefits. Nobody could betray me. I couldn't receive any intel, but I also wouldn't be given false intel and sent on a wild goose chase. I wouldn't have to suspect anyone. I wouldn't have to decide who was an enemy and who was a comrade.

Depending on how you looked at it, it was liberating. It was easy to understand. The rest of the world was my enemy.

In the distance, I heard the words, "Intruder spotted!" I felt uneasy. Perhaps there was another intruder. And that android's mission could be not to destroy the Machines in the forest, but to capture the rogue android Attacker No. 2.

That would be troublesome. I had planned to destroy Machines here and there while making my way to the throne, but that was out of the question now. My new plan was to minimize the fighting, and approach the throne with little or no trace. I could take care of the small fry after taking care of their leader. The more organized a group was, the more vulnerable it was after losing its top brass.

After that, I could play around with the pursuit force. Of course, not running into them was by far the best choice.

I heard someone say, "I can't let you pass." The words were not directed at me.

There was a bridge crossing a valley, with a castle on the other side. There were two androids fighting the Machine responsible for securing the bridge.

"Please don't let your guard down!" said 9S.

"That's my line. Be careful, 9S."

Type S No. 9. A high-performance scanner model. That meant the other android with my face was an execution model.

So they were deployed again. How many times would I have to send them back before they gave up? I was fed up with them. I thought it was awfully distasteful to send an execution model that used my battle data, but perhaps Command was just stupid.

"Dodge, 2B!"

2B? Not a type E? Then they might not be captors, but simply androids that were deployed to destroy Machines.

I quietly crossed the bridge while they were fighting and headed toward the castle.

I climbed the castle wall and looked for the king from the upper floors. As expected, two sets of hands were faster in battle; the two androids had already penetrated the king's throne room. I waited to see what they would do.

"This is the king?" They looked at each other and hesitated, neither one making a move. What were they dawdling about? It got too tedious, so I jumped down, aiming my sword at the puny body of the Machine.

My aim did not err. I tossed the impaled Machine to the side. My job was done.

"2B! That's an android! And it's a YoRHa type!"

As I thought, they were not my captors. They didn't recognize my face. Their boxes kept announcing a recommendation to destroy me. On the other hand, their completely opposite reactions made the situation rather comical.

"Destroy? Why?"

"9S, let's do it."

"What? 2B!"

So No. 2 had the will to fight. Come fight. I would beat her down as many times as she wanted.

A voice I didn't want to hear spoke from the box.

"A message to 2B and 9S from the Bunker. We've detected the signals of wanted criminal A2. The woman that stands in front of you is an enemy. She is a rogue soldier. She's killed multiple troopers that were in pursuit of her. You will be killed if you're careless!"

It's true. *I've killed both of you many times.* Her highness the commander's words were misleading, but they weren't wrong. They held some truth.

I heard 9S weakly mutter, "But…" under his breath. His reaction was different from previous encounters. Now that I thought about it, 2E—no, 2B—was acting differently as well. Her expression was missing something. If I had to say, it was missing a certain vitality. As if she had given up, and was half-heartedly going through the motions…

Oh, that's right. That's me. No. 2, who had the same face as me, was just making the same expression as me. I stopped attacking. I told myself that this was enough. I distanced myself from the pair, and jumped toward the window. 9S's voice trailed behind me.

"Why…why did you betray us?!"

I had no obligation to answer. But I couldn't ignore it. With my back still facing them, I said, "Command is the one that betrayed us."

I don't know what kind of face 9S made. Nor did I want to know. I kicked the window and jumped down.

CH. 04: 2B'S STORY/ALIENATION

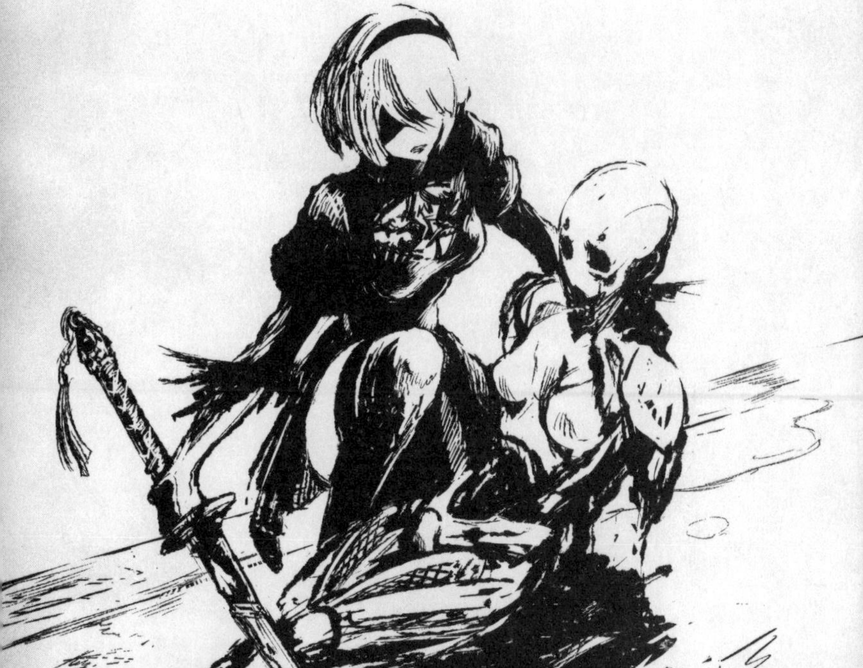

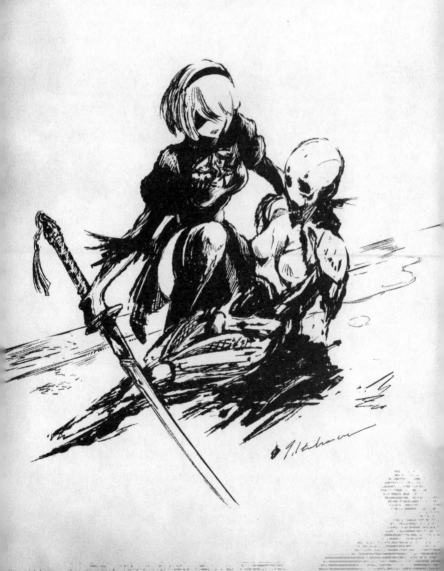

"TO BUNKER, THIS IS 9S REPORTING. PLEASE CONNECT ME TO THE COMMANDER."

"Roger. Connecting to the commander."

"Commander. We failed to destroy A2."

The commander's warning that A2 had slaughtered multiple pursuers was warranted. While A2 was an obsolete model, she was still a formidable opponent. 2B shuddered at the thought of what could have happened if they had fought any longer.

Their battle was cut short when A2 escaped. They tried to chase her after she jumped from the window, but whatever route she took, they couldn't keep up.

"I'm glad both of you are safe. That was an extremely dangerous individual. Do not approach that deserter carelessly," said the commander.

"Umm," muttered 9S hesitantly. "Desertion…from what?"

2B had the same question as 9S. Desertion in itself was a serious matter, and a fellow No. 2 was responsible. She couldn't help being curious about the past actions of an android that was identical to her.

And A2 had said something strange as she left. That Command had betrayed them. What did she mean by that?

"That is confidential information. I can't tell you," said the commander.

Confidential. 2B didn't like the word. Nothing good ever came when that word was involved. Of course, it was necessary for organizations to have secrets. But for her personally, it always led to unpleasant things…

"2B."

She was brought back to reality by 9S. She hadn't realized that the transmission with the commander had ended.

"Let's ask Pascal about A2. He might know something," said 9S.

2B agreed that this was of high probability. Pascal had told them about the forest kingdom. A2 might have appeared in the forest before. If so, it was unlikely that Pascal had overlooked the presence of such a dangerous android.

Last time, they had gone to investigate Pascal's village on Command's orders. They had been assigned to gather data for valuable research materials. But this time was different. What she and 9S were about to do was not for a mission. On the contrary, they were contacting an enemy of their own volition. She wondered whether they should stop.

Even so, there had recently been a lot of unfortunate events. There had been news about deserters just the other day. A few days previous, there had been a directive from Command to capture thieves that were operating in the resistance camp. But that was only a facade. 2B had been given a confidential and different set of instructions: to hunt and execute deserters 8B, 22B, and 64B. The instructions were to kill, not capture.

The clueless 9S liberally made use of his navigational abilities as a scanner type to find the androids. They informed the women that they were to be brought in. As expected, the trio attacked. Once deserters were remanded to custody, only death awaited—the women had no choice but to fight their captors and run.

2B destroyed them. They had initiated the attack, so she pretended that destroying them was the only natural thing to do.

It was a good excuse. But 9S had keenly noticed that something was wrong. After they returned to the resistance camp, he had asked Anemone for details of the thefts. Of course, Anemone had no recollection of such incidents. There had been no theft crimes to begin with.

9S called Operator 21O and asked for details about the theft crimes. However…

"That incident is confidential. I can't find out for you," said the operator.

Standing by his side, 2B could tell this was going south, but all she could do was keep her arms folded and observe.

"9S, be careful," said the operator.

21O did not know that 8B and his accomplices were deserters, or that the incident was feigned. But she probably sensed something was off as well. That's why she warned 9S to be careful. That sincere warning must have provoked the growing suspicion that 9S had of Command.

"2B?" asked 9S.

"Never mind. All right, let's go," said 2B.

In the end, 2B did not stop 9S.

At this point, even had she tried to turn back from visiting Pascal, 9S would not have given up. That was a defining quality of the scanner type. 9S would probably visit Pascal on his own. That was unacceptable.

"Pascal. This is 9S."

2B listened with mixed feelings as 9S told Pascal that they had questions for him.

■ ■■

Nonetheless, they were unable to get significant information from Pascal. Wary of a transmission being monitored, they made a direct visit.

"This android named A2—I have past records of her, but she has never come to this village."

Pascal added that she was indeed a dangerous android.

2B was reminded of the fact that A2 had killed a helpless Machine too young to walk. 2B and 9S had seen not a moment of hesitation from her. And she was strong. She fought on par with, if not beyond, the level of the newest models. From the Machines' point of view, she must be a terrifying android.

"I'm sorry. That's all I know," said Pascal.

She could clearly see the disappointment on 9S's profile as he said, "I see." 9S walked dejectedly through the shortcut to the city ruins.

At times, he looked like he was thinking. He was probably considering the next step. That was dangerous. 2B stopped him by calling out his name.

"Why did you ask Pascal for information about A2?" asked 2B.

She sounded like she was interrogating him. She now regretted not stopping him, and letting him get involved in such a perilous matter.

"Command does not recommend contacting a Machine without permission," said 2B.

Even if it were out of pure curiosity, Command could see it as a problem. Furthermore, this time his actions were based on suspicion, and not curiosity. If Command were to find out…

"I'm sorry."

9S's crestfallen behavior flustered 2B. Had she been too stern? She confronted him, even though scanner types were specialized for investigation and it was something they couldn't help doing. 2B quickly added a "But…"

"I admire your passion for knowledge," said 2B.

Even if that curiosity was a double-edged sword.

"Thanks, 2B."

9S's lips hinted at a smile. He was full of curiosity, frank, and bright… A comrade that was like the gleaming rays of the sun.

That's why, she wished. *Don't get it wrong. You're only allowed to use that curiosity on the enemy. Never anyone else. Don't even think about suspecting a comrade…or Command.*

"Let's go back to the resistance camp. We need to get a checkup and replenish our chassis," she said.

It might be in vain. The same thing might happen. Still.

Because I promised you, thought 2B.

■ ■■

"Squadrons A to C are to patrol the coast, Squadrons D to E are to secure the ground transport route, and…"

When they arrived at the resistance camp, Anemone was busy directing the troops. As always, there was a huge influx of people.

"2B, 9S. Good timing."

They didn't have to ask about the occasion. Anemone started to explain that it was a restocking mission.

"There is an aircraft carrier that we, the android army, have deployed to the Pacific. That carrier is about to return," said Anemone.

9S looked like he remembered something. 9S, whose main mission was to collect information on Earth, was well-informed about the military situation and deployments of other regions.

"You're talking about the *Blue Ridge* aircraft carrier, right? I've heard of it."

"*Blue Ridge II*. I'm glad we're on the same page."

"Should we escort the carrier?"

"No, I'd like you two to secure the coast, where the reserve missiles are stored. There've been multiple reports of Machine sightings in that area. Most likely we'll be shorthanded. That's where you two come in."

9S confidently replied to leave it to them.

"We're the newest models. Unlike an older model like A2," said 9S.

A2's name probably came up because she had been on his mind. Of course, they had just struggled to fight against that same older model.

"A2? Attacker…No. 2?" sputtered Anemone.

Anemone's face suddenly paled.

"Anemone, do you happen to know A2?" asked 9S.

"N-no. I don't."

Anemone had denied it, but that was most likely a lie. Unlike the YoRHa squadron, who had almost half their faces covered by goggles, it was easy to read the expressions of the resistance.

"I was just a bit curious," said Anemone.

This was probably a lie as well. Anemone was clearly upset. Had something happened between Anemone and A2?

"Anyways, thanks for helping. If you have any YoRHa business, that can come first."

Anemone wrapped up the conversation and turned around. From the back, 2B couldn't read any expression.

■　■■

The reserve missiles were siloed in an area near the coast called the flooded city. True to its name, most of its buildings had sunk into water.

"This area's foundation was destroyed in the previous war, and the city is still sinking to this day," said 9S.

The buildings that were narrowly avoiding complete submersion now must have been quite the highrises in the past. At this point only their roofs were peeking out of the water.

Even the ground had slowly started sinking, and the soil was damp. There was mud in some places, which made the footing unstable.

Anemone's information had been accurate—there were Machines roaming the ground and the roofs of the sunken buildings. There were walking types, flying types, small sized, and medium sized. It was like looking at an encyclopedia of Machines. The pair destroyed the Machines one at a time, making their way toward the location of the stored missiles.

The weather was clear, to the point that the sunlight erratically reflecting off the ocean's surface hurt 2B's eyes. Strangely enough, the weather was always clear when they came here. And 9S would always say, "It's a perfect day for fishing, isn't it?"

It was at that moment, when 2B was thinking that she had only ever come here to perform oceanic research, that Pod opened its communication display. The commander reported that it was an emergency.

"I'm sure both of you know, but the aircraft we possess is scheduled to stop at the port to restock. But that carrier has been ambushed by Machines and it is currently in battle. I've already contacted all the YoRHa squadron troopers that are stationed near the city ruins, but I'd like you two to give your assistance as well. I'll send the map data and flight units. Over."

The flight units came flying down from the sky, as if they had been waiting for the transmission to end. They had probably been launched before the transmission had started.

"Don't you think the commander is really harsh on people?" asked 9S.

9S sighed, as if he wanted to complain that they had just finally gotten a break from exterminating the nearby Machines. She could understand his sentiment, but this was an emergency. 2B rebuked 9S.

"She wouldn't be a good leader if she wasn't like that," said 2B.

To operate as a group, it was ill-advised to consider the individual's feelings. It was necessary to ignore the little things and think instead about how the group should act as a whole. It was imperative to quickly decide what was indispensable and what was not, and to bear the full responsibility of those decisions. 2B knew that the commander was such a person.

"I understand, logically, but," said 9S.

It looked like 9S had more to say, but 2B ignored him and entered the flight unit.

■　■■

It was clear that aircraft carrier *Blue Ridge II* was struggling at first glance. Flying-type Machines were herding around the carrier and attacking relentlessly.

"It's like a swarm," said 9S.

"A swarm?" asked 2B.

"It's a word used to describe tiny insects that are flying together in a large group," explained 9S.

"Nevermind. We're going to destroy them," said 2B.

2B transitioned the flight unit to maneuvering mode, and started to bat away the Machines one by one. Looking down, she could see the escort ship drifting among the waves. With its low mobility, this number of Machines had probably been too much to handle for the escort ship. But there weren't enough ships on the carrier to defend itself either.

"2B! There's a signal for a Goliath-class enemy! Toward the southeast!"

She saw a Goliath-class enemy approaching from the sky. Its shape was analogous to the Horseshoe Crab Machine they had captured on a previous ocean research outing. The similarities ended at the shape, as its size was on a completely different scale.

2B turned the flight unit around sharply. The firepower from a Goliath-class Machine could annihilate the carrier in one blast. She needed to take care of the Machine before it could get in range, or else the aircraft carrier was in danger.

"9S! Get to a higher altitude!"

The Goliath-class Machine was scattering mines. There were small-type aerial Machines that could be a nuisance, but none were as destructive as mines.

2B and 9S batted away small types as they closed in on the Goliath-class. They repeated the process of neutralizing the artillery, destroying the oncoming small types, and attacking the Goliath-class.

"Confirming the destruction of the enemy flying type," said 2B.

The horseshoe crab-shaped Machine listed to the side and hurtled down, taking the surrounding small types along. There was no indication that it would be back in the air.

"Now we will go support the carrier," said 2B.

"Wait! I'm still getting a signal from a Goliath-class!" said 9S.

What was 9S saying? They had just destroyed the Goliath-class. It was confirmed to be nonfunctional.

"From where?! Such a huge…"

9S's yelling was drowned out by a somewhat similar-sounding roar. At the same time, the surface of the ocean suddenly welled up. 2B had thought that an underwater explosion had created the pillar of water, but she was wrong.

The crest of the wave struck the bottom of *Blue Ridge II*, flipping it over. 2B saw the water coil around the carrier. It wasn't the water itself, but something in the water that bit into the carrier.

The next moment, the carrier split in two and sank down into the depths of the ocean.

"What is that?!" asked 2B.

It was an enemy of impossible scale. It was larger than any Goliath-class she had witnessed. There were three large eyes, and four smaller eyes beneath them. They were all glowing red, a sign that the Machine was hostile.

"A monster…"

9S's words were on the mark. A Machine monster that was extraordinarily large and powerful. It had reduced the carrier to scrap in seconds. That one attack was enough to indicate how this battle was going to go.

What were they going to do? How were they going to turn the tables in such a situation?

2B searched for an answer as she stared down the glistening red eyes.

The enemy was formidable as expected, perhaps even beyond her expectations.

First of all, the flight unit's artillery had no effect. Electromagnetic waves enveloped and shielded the Machine's body. It was even strong enough to obstruct a laser strike from the satellites.

They tried to inflict damage by shooting rounds from raid cannons into its mouth, the only unprotected region. While the attacks were not obstructed as had been the laser, they were unable to damage the Machine at all.

Furthermore, something happened that made 2B doubt her eyes. The monster stood up. In its full glory, it was a human-shaped Machine of a size that defied logic. What she had thought was its full body had just been its head…

They had done everything they could. The destructive satellite laser and their unorthodox scheme to shoot cannons into the mouth had failed entirely.

"How do we beat such an enemy…"

Every troop in the allied forces must have muttered the same words as 2B.

The monster did not stop. White sparks scattered erratically around its mountainous body. It was discharging electricity. 2B could feel the reverberation. It was similar to the rumbling that had collapsed the city ruins, but this time there was a feeling of unrest even greater than before.

"This is bad! Let's withdraw!" said 9S.

The monster shook its giant body and plunged toward them. 2B tried to escape, but she was too late. She felt herself get blown away. She braced herself for the impact against the ground, and the damage that would come with it.

But that moment never came. Instead of an impact, she felt something gently absorb her fall.

"Are you okay, Ms. 2B?"

"Pas…cal?" said 2B.

She saw that 9S's flight unit had been caught in the air by Machines—the villagers from Pascal's village.

"Thank you for saving me," said 2B.

She had thought that Machines were incapable of having emotions. She had felt apprehensive when they said they were supporters of peace. Even after she knew they were harmless—and perhaps more so because she knew—she hesitated to believe them. But those same Machines had come to save her…

She simultaneously felt a sense of relief and anxiety. Scared to identify the origin of those feelings, she intentionally focused her attention on the danger in front of her and glared at the monster.

"That giant Machine was a weapon that was discarded in the past," said Pascal, revealing the identity of the monster as he moved to safety.

"At the time I was connected to the Machine network, so I remember it. The moment it stepped onto land it went berserk and started attacking everything, without conscience. We weren't able to stop it, and eventually had to abandon it in the ocean."

"That's right," said 9S from a transmission.

"When Command was briefing me on the enemy, its landing was confirmed to be 320 years ago. Apparently the escorting resistance was wiped out."

"In other words, we have to prevent it from coming onto land, or else there will be another tragedy. But how…" said 2B.

The artillery equipped on the flight unit had no effect. Even the satellite lasers were obstructed by the electromagnetic waves. Thus it was likely that an explosion from a black-box response would not be enough to destroy the Machine completely. Was it even possible to stop the enemy?

"The missiles! The ones that were supposed to be restocked onto the aircraft carrier!" shouted 9S.

They had already verified from their previous trials that physical attacks directed inside the mouth would not be obstructed. Fortunately, the missiles they had been protecting were still unharmed.

"I'm going to see if we can use them," said 9S.

To control the missiles, meddling with its program was necessary.

"Okay. I'll cover you," said 2B.

9S's flight unit flew in a straight line toward the missile launchpad. 2B cleared out the small-type Machines that followed to free 9S's path.

While the number was dwindling, there was still a substantial amount of small types. *So this is called a swarm, right?* she thought, as she recalled 9S's explanation in the back of her mind.

As she was busy shooting down small-type Machines, she saw the missile activate. The angle of the launching pad adjusted. 9S's flight unit hung on beside the missile. She heard Pod 153 declare that the missile was ready to fire through the transmission.

"Fire!" said 9S.

2B got out of the way of the missile's path at full throttle. The missile flew toward the monster.

The monster opened its mouth, perhaps an attempt at intimidation. The missile struck right inside that opening. The monster's body started to shake, as if it were writhing.

There was a resounding roar that sounded similar to thunder. It was a dreadful sound. Right when 2B thought she should've kept more distance, her vision went white.

Darkness came just as she realized she had been caught up in the explosion.

The first thing she heard was static. But it eventually turned into the sound of the repeating crash of waves.

"Ugh…"

She could only see the colors of sand and rust. She had fallen face-down. 2B slowly righted her body. She would stagger a little, but not enough to impair her walking.

Looking back, she saw a misshapen mountain off the shore. It was the remains of the monster. It had been charred while standing, and there was smoke rising from various areas. It was clearly nonfunctional.

She recollected the events leading up to this moment. The missile had found its target inside the mouth of the monster, and an EMP explosion had followed. 9S had succeeded in controlling the missiles.

But she didn't see 9S. Or Pascal and his villagers.

"To Bunker, this is 2B reporting. Please reply."

She needed to gauge the situation before regrouping with 9S.

"Ms. 2B?! This is the operator! Are you okay?!"

Operator 6O was always lively, but today her voice was especially high-pitched, perhaps because she was in a panic.

"Performing a body check. No problems with basic function," said 2B.

"Thank goodness…"

2B could almost hear 6O's sigh of relief. Half of her was amused at 6O's overreaction, and half of her felt guilty for making 6O worry so much. Yet she made an effort to talk with a composed voice.

"I'd like you to update me on the situation."

"Roger that. In regards to the super Goliath-class Machine that invaded the coast, it was confirmed to be nonfunctional eight hours ago thanks to your efforts."

"Eight hours?! That long?!"

2B could see why 6O had such a high-pitched voice. She had been incommunicado for eight hours, so 6O had a very valid reason to be frightened.

"Multiple transmission facilities are dysfunctional from the EMP explosion, and consequently communications, as well as repair of various matters, has fallen behind."

This was understandable, given the scale of the attack and the fact that it had been an EMP explosion instead of a normal explosion.

"So where is 9S?"

6O hesitated for a moment.

"I'm able to detect a slight black-box response, but am unable to determine his location."

If there was a black-box response, he was alive. However, if it was so weak his location was indeterminable, there was a high likelihood that 9S was critically injured.

"I'm going to begin a search for 9S. Please send the commander an application for consent."

"Oh, a directive has already been issued. The commander requests that the search for surviving YoRHa troopers be prioritized."

While that was relieving to hear, it also brought full realization of how long she had been immobilized.

"Ms. 2B, please help Mr. 9S."

2B said, "Roger that," and started running.

2B wrapped up the search around the coast quickly, and returned to the resistance camp.

The sensors Pod 042 was equipped with were unable to detect weak signals. According to Pod, the search required a specialized scanner. Fortunately, there were records of this type of scanner being used at the resistance camp. If they were lucky, the scanners would still be stored there.

Once she found Anemone, 2B cut straight to the chase.

"I'm looking for a specialized scanner that can detect weak blackbox responses."

"A specialized scanner?" asked Anemone. For a brief moment, Anemone frowned, but quickly nodded and said, "Ah, you've been through a lot." She must have heard about the search efforts for YoR-Ha troopers. She had immediately understood what it meant when 2B came back to the camp during her search.

"That's the device they were using. Perfect timing. They just came back from an expedition."

"They?"

"There's some androids with red hair over there, go ask them."

"Roger that."

It was a great help that Anemone was always straight to the point. But right as 2B turned around, Anemone stopped her again with a "2B." This was rare.

"The redheaded androids are…"

Anemone stopped there.

"What?"

"No, never mind."

2B was curious about what Anemone had to say, but she didn't bother her any further. There was no time to waste.

Looking around, sure enough, there were red-haired androids. She originally thought there was one android, but there were two. Her gaze met with one of them.

"What are you looking at?"

It was a stinging tone of voice. The way her hair stood up in every direction reminded 2B of an animal with its fur standing on end.

"Devola, stop being so scrappy."

"You're being too carefree, Popola."

From this exchange, 2B deduced that the one prepared to fight was named Devola, and the one that rebuked her was named Popola. Popola had the same red hair, but it was straight. Their hair seemed to reflect their respective personalities.

"I'm sorry. What can we do for you?" asked Popola.

"I'm looking for a scanner that can detect weak black-box responses."

Devola was the one that unexpectedly answered her request.

"Ah. We constructed something like that in the past."

Devola swiftly stood up and started to rummage through some baggage on the side.

"If you're trying to detect a black-box response, that means you're looking for someone, right?" Popola asked, with her head slightly tilted to the side.

It seemed she hadn't been informed of the search for YoRHa troopers. Anemone had said they were fresh off an expedition, so they probably hadn't received the news yet. Now that she thought about it, their shabby look was probably a result of an extensive period in the field.

"Here it is. If you want it, you can have it," said Devola.

Devola placed a small chip designed for a Pod in 2B's palm. After she said her thanks, Devola's lips curled up into a smile. Her smile was unbelievably friendly compared to her abrasive first impression.

"I hope you find him soon," said Popola.

Popola's smile was almost imperceptibly subtle. Her reserved expressions and way of speech were completely opposite of Devola's, even though they shared the same hair and the same face.

"If you need anything else, just tell us," said Popola.

"Don't involve yourself with us too much though," said Devola.

"Oh Devola…"

Popola elbowed Devola from the side. Devola said, "It's true," as she scowled back. From this exchange, 2B deduced that these two had some special circumstances. This was the probably the reason why Anemone had tried to tell her something and then stopped.

She wasn't particularly interested in investigating or concerning herself with such circumstances. It would have been different if Command had issued an arrest directive, but since that wasn't the case, it didn't bother her. Everybody has one or two things they'd like to keep a secret—including herself.

■　■■

She returned to the flooded city and resumed her search. The scanner that Devola had made was very precise, allowing her to detect several black-box responses she had missed before.

There were weak signals coming from within the shadows of rubble, in between sunken buildings, and other places that were well hidden. These were victims so wounded they were unable to call for help, let alone crawl out from under the wreckage. Every time 2B came across a victim she administered a logic virus vaccine, sent their coordinates to the Bunker, and requested rescue.

Of all the wounded she had found, 9S was not among them.

"But I'm able to detect the black-box response…"

Why wasn't she able to determine his location? Either the signal was too weak, or he was too far away…

"Proposition: The search target 9S was involved in the large explosion at sea."

Pod circled around from the back.

"Recommendation: Increase search radius."

"There's a possibility that he was blown away farther?"

"Affirmative."

It was fine if he was blown away toward land, but what if he was swept away farther into the sea? Just thinking of the possibility sent chills down her spine.

"Negative."

"I haven't said anything yet."

"All information regarding 9S is speculative. Therefore, it is meaningless to agonize over a hypothesis constructed on unproven data."

"Okay."

It was true. It was pointless to be dismayed by her wild imagination when all the information she had was uncertain.

"That aside, you're talking a lot today, Pod."

"Affirmative: I am a support unit. I will converse based on need."

She had a realization. Pod was speaking so much because 9S was not here. Normally 9S would be beside her, chatting constantly. Now, Pod needed to initiate conversation, or else there was silence. It had probably determined that this was unacceptable.

"Recommendation: Increase the amount of conversation initiated by 2B."

"I decline."

It was 9S's job to talk and smile a lot. Nobody could be the replacement. Even if someone used the same words and expressions, they wouldn't be 9S. At least, they wouldn't be the same 9S to her...

She contemplated such thoughts as she walked along the beach. Suddenly, she heard a groan from beneath a pile of corpses. The scanner was picking up a signal as well.

"Report: Black-box response detected. Confirmation of life signs."

She dragged a chassis that was half-submerged in ocean water. The clothes had absorbed water, making the body awfully heavy. She struggled to bring it onto dry ground.

"Pod. Give me a check module and logic virus vaccine."

After 2A helped her cough out water and lay faceup, the squadron trooper faintly opened her eyes.

"I've sent a rescue signal to the Bunker, so help should come soon," said 2B.

"Th...thank you..."

It seemed that conversation was just barely manageable.

"We are trying to find our companion, YoRHa member 9S. If you have any information, I'd like you to share it."

"9...S...? Ah. The boy that was with you..."

"Anything helps. Please."

"That boy...was sent flying by the explosion..."

She had witnessed 9S during the moment of the explosion. 2B's voice faltered when she asked for the direction. The cries of the shorebirds sounded unusually high.

"Location of impact prediction... Coordinate data... Transferring."

"Thank you."

Pod replied that the transfer was complete.

"This is..."

Looking at the data, 2B understood why the scanner was unable to determine his location. 9S's location of impact was far more inland then the flooded city.

"I appreciate it. Stay here until the rescue team comes."

"I hope...you...find...him."

2B responded with a firm nod, and started running toward her destination.

ANOTHER SIDE "ADAM"

The more I know, the less I understand. The more I research, the more misguided I am. Humans are a species filled with mysteries and inconsistencies.

To begin with, humans and Machines are remarkably different in the ways they live. While living as a group, humans are not connected by a network. At first glance they seem to favor living for the self, but at the same time, they seem to lack an attachment to the self.

A striking example is self-duplication. Their self-duplication process is faulty and inconsistent. It's not like they didn't have the technology to perform perfect self-duplication. It was possible, but they weren't willing to use the technology. Instead, they were committed to an imperfect system of self-duplication called reproduction.

Furthermore, they didn't consider the original and the copy as the same individual. They saw them as distinct identities: the original was called a "parent" and the copy was called a "child." Rather than an original and a copy, this relationship was closer to a creator and a creation.

Since humans already had androids, which were their creations, there was really no need to degrade their own self-duplicate as a "creation." I don't understand. It's a mystery.

On the other hand, our creators did not leave a trace of mystery. They were a worthless bunch; they were flimsy, had no diversity, and did not have a shred of creativity. In comparison, how glorious the mystery of humans was.

No matter how much I studied and studied and studied and studied, I could not study enough.

"Hey big brother, why are you reading a book?"

"Knowledge makes a person rich."

"Can't you just transfer the data?"

"If I don't read it myself, it won't speak to my heart."

"Okay, I see."

The written characters that humans left behind—with only a few dozen combinations of them, humans were surprisingly able to create intricate worlds and write about them. They didn't just write down information. The stories were small worlds in themselves.

By reading the combinations of characters, humans were able to absorb part of the world. It was something that a data transfer could never accomplish. I believe a large part of human diversity was due to the power of books.

While zealously reading books, I came upon a realization. There was a recurring concept that provided a basis for human action and choice.

It was death.

Humans loved to reuse phrases like: "for dear life," "about to die," "going to die," and "rather than die." There were even whole books written on the topic of death. This was particularly common in the genre of philosophy.

Death. It was a concept that was hard to grasp for us Machines.

We, who are connected to a network, never die. If our core runs out of energy or we're destroyed, we will stop functioning. But a reboot is always possible. A Machine malfunction that can be rebooted is apparently different from death.

Humans were able to create many things from their fear of death. They tried to overcome death, but couldn't. While they had the technology, in the end they coexisted with death.

Was death really something so difficult to let go of? Was it full of irresistible splendor?

If I, a Machine, were to one day understand death, would I understand humans?

Perhaps it was a curse that we Machines yearned to understand humans. In addition to myself, my brethren also mimicked humans. They mimicked their words, their actions, their emotions, their aesthetics, their relationships…

Why? Why do we have such an obsession over humans?

"Hey big brother, can I break this?"

"No, you can't. If you break it, it'll be useless."

"But it did some bad things to big brother, right?"

"That's right. But don't break it."

"Fine."

There didn't have to be a reason for our feud with androids. Besides, it was never a fight to the death. Both sides could regenerate as many times as necessary.

But would she and I be able to fight to the death if she was given a reason to fight?

"Big brother, let's play."

"I'm busy."

"Let's play human."

"Later, okay?"

"When can we play?"

"After I finish my business."

"Okay. I'll wait until you finish your business."

"That's right. Wait here."

"Here?"

"Can you wait by yourself?"

"If I wait here, will you play with me?"

"All right."

"Then I'll wait."

"Good boy."

"I'll wait until big brother comes back."

I certainly couldn't take Eve along. He would immediately revive me. A Machine malfunction that can be resolved via reboot is different from death. I want to understand. I want to get to the bottom of humanity.

When that happens, I will be freed from the ghosts of my creators.

CH. 05: 2B'S STORY/CONFRONTATION

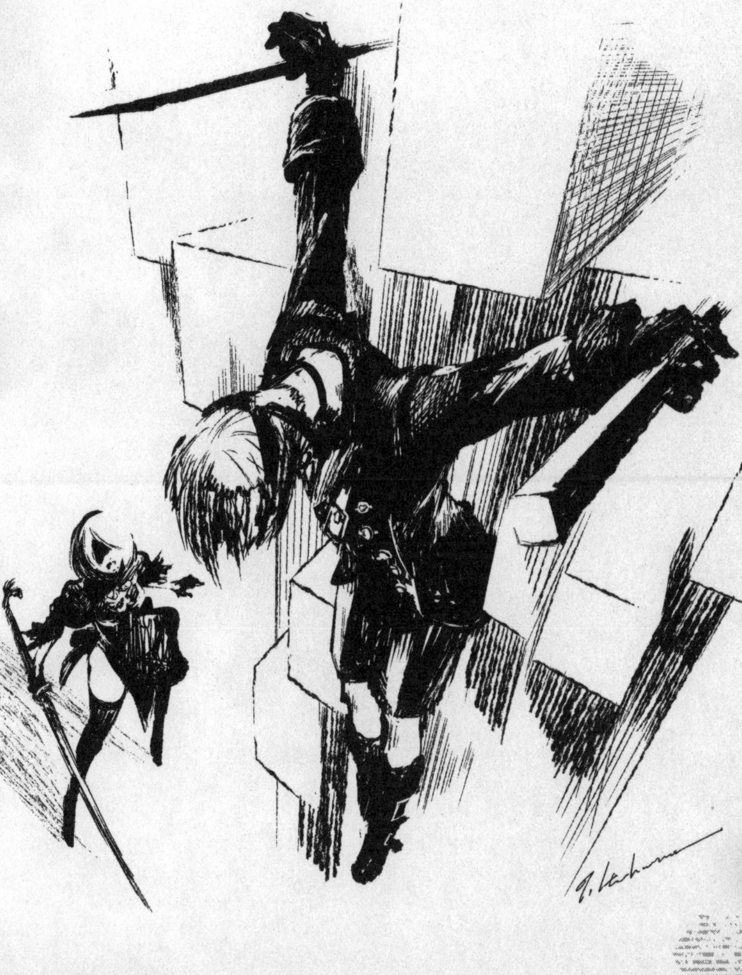

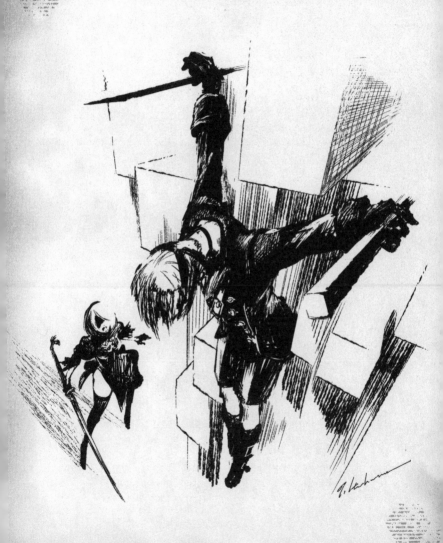

9S LANDED IN THE CRATER ZONE. If one were to walk from the city ruins to the flooded city, it would take quite a bit of time. One would have to take a detour around the collapsed buildings and shattered roads.

But in terms of distance, the two locations were not that far apart. Had 9S been blown away by the explosion, it wasn't impossible for him to have landed in that area.

"Report: 9S's black-box response detected."

Pod's scanner was giving feedback.

"What's his current location?"

"Answer: Underground cave."

"Underground cave? The one with the alien ship?"

"Affirmative."

The underground cave had been discovered because part of the city ruins had caved in. The location of impact was in fact in the crater zone, so it wasn't impossible for 9S to have landed in the cave. But…

"Let's go."

She descended on a ladder extending from the edge of the hole to its depths. Occasionally, she looked around at the walls or cavities in the hole to see if she could find some trace of 9S. Unfortunately, she wasn't able to find a piece of clothing or item of 9S's, let alone the man himself.

The bottom of the hole was still flooded with water, resulting in bad footing. 9S wasn't here either. 2B raised her gaze. The hole was considerably deep. Without the help of Pod's gliding mechanism, a leap down would certainly lead to injury.

Even still, 9S had not jumped down from the top of the hole, but had been flung there by the explosion. He would have slammed into the ground at the bottom of the hole. It was unlikely that he would have gotten up right away, or was in a condition to move at ease.

So why wasn't he here?

"Report: The source of the black-box response is coming from beyond the underground passageway."

"Beyond the passageway?"

From the bottom of the hole, there were two side tunnels running in different directions. One tunnel led to a dead end, and the other led to the alien ship. If Pod had said "beyond" the passageway, it was probably referring to the latter.

She knew this was a red flag. If 9S were, by some miracle, able to walk, why would he walk through the passageway?

Making Pod shine its light, she entered the tunnel. When she tried to follow the same route as last time, Pod stopped her.

"Report: The source of the black-box response is coming from the right."

"Right? Not from the alien ship?"

"Affirmative: While weak, the black-box response is coming from a different location than before."

She took a right at the fork.

"He came this far…"

Something was definitely wrong. Why would he take an unfamiliar route? And if he was able to walk this much, it should have been possible for him to climb the ladder out of the hole.

At the end of the passageway was an elevator. At this point it was undeniable. There was only one conclusion…

"Warning: Possibility of a trap."

"I don't care."

2B pressed the elevator button.

There was no panel that showed which floor she was traveling to, but she felt the elevator move down. It was even farther beneath the underground cave, so it was at quite the depth. No wonder the scanner hadn't been able to determine an accurate location.

The elevator shook erratically for a while and eventually came to a stop. The doors opened with an obnoxious rattle. Bright light pierced her eyes.

"What is this place?"

2B squinted and looked around. Everything was white. Since her eyes had acclimatized to darkness, it was painfully bright.

"Analysis: Structures made of crystallized silicon and carbon. There is not enough data to provide further details."

Staring long enough, she could make out a cityscape stretching onward. But there was no color. There were rows of buildings with white walls and gray windowsills, casting pronounced shadows on the white street. They must have been colorless, because they were all apparently made from crystallized silicon and carbon.

"Who would make an underground city like this?"

Pod answered with an "unknown." Ironically, it was a good answer. If Pod couldn't answer the question, it meant that androids were not responsible. Unlike the buildings above ground, these buildings did not look weathered in the least. Then they were probably new, putting aliens out of the question. Then there was only one answer: the Machines.

"Report: 9S's black-box response detected."

She cautiously moved in the direction that Pod pointed in. No amount of caution was too much; she was in an enemy facility. But her guarded gait did not last long.

"That's?!"

She started to run without thinking. Some black had appeared amidst the white. It was the color of the YoRHa uniform. Not just in one place, but in many.

"Why are there corpses…"

"Deduction: They were left intentionally by the enemy."

The underground cave had not been discovered before the city ruins caved in. Since the incident was still treated as confidential, no information had been shared within the squadron. In regard to the white city, even 2B had not known about it, so it was unlikely that other squadron troopers invaded of their own will.

In other words, they were kidnapped by the Machines, and brought here. It was unclear when they were killed.

She realized that she had started to sprint. She had to save 9S as soon as possible, while his black-box response was still active.

"I'm sorry. I don't remember that."

She heard 9S's voice in her head. And felt the excruciating pain when he had said those words as well.

"Since the transmission bandwidth in that area was narrow, I probably only had the time to back up your data. I only have memories up until we joined forces."

How old was his backup at the Bunker? If his chassis were to be destroyed right now, his memory would be rewound to that day.

Please don't let that happen, prayed 2B. She wanted to avoid that at all costs. She never wanted to go through that again.

■ ■■

She eventually reached a large square. Similar to the road and buildings that came before it, it was solely white and gray.

The black-box response was weak but close.

"Welcome. To my city."

It was Adam who greeted her from the middle of the square. There was no surprise. She had expected something like this. What was slightly unexpected was the absence of the Machine named Eve.

"I…no, *we* Machines have a keen interest in humans. As I've told you before."

2B ignored Adam and approached him. She walked cautiously, in case there was a trap.

"Love and family, war and religion. The more we read about humans, the more our fascination grows."

It made her uncomfortable. She remembered how enthusiastic 9S was when he was doing research on human civilization. It made her uncomfortable that a Machine shared the same passion. Even worse, because this was a Machine that had kidnapped 9S.

"This town was also born from our longing for humans."

She discovered another reason why she felt uncomfortable. It was Adam's clothes. He was wearing a white-collared shirt and black-rimmed glasses, things 2B had seen in the video database of Earth. His mimicry was complete to the point that it was repulsive.

"It's a waste that such a noble place is the graveyard for you androids, isn't it?"

"Graveyard?"

Adam smirked knowingly. She remembered the corpses that were laid out on the way here.

So this man was responsible...

She restrained her anger, and silently pulled out her sword. Adam didn't seem to care, and carried on his lecture.

"We study the attributes of humans, and mimic them. Some will mimic love. Some will mimic family. I also learned, and mimicked. I watched recordings, read books, wore clothes, ate plants, sang, and danced... I came to a realization after mimicking various actions. The essence of humanity is battle. To fight, to steal, to kill. That is what it means to be human!"

Adam's voice gradually filled with fervor. He spread his arms dramatically and made his voice resonate across the whole square, as if he were speaking to a group of people and not just 2B. His behavior irritated 2B.

"Love carries hate with it, and families are full of conflict and arguments. Civilization developed to steal more, and society was constructed to kill more efficiently…"

"Don't talk about humanity with that filthy mouth!"

She didn't realize that she had swung her sword out of anger. She expected Adam to evade by teleporting, but instead he stopped the blade with one arm. The sleeve of his shirt tore open, and red liquid gushed out.

"But I'm not wrong, am I? Isn't that what humans are?"

"Shut up!"

The spray of red stopped. It was the incredible self-regeneration at work. An odd expression crossed Adam's face. It was an expression that was unsuited to the words he would say.

"Why do humans conflict with one another when they are the same species? What drives them to fight? I want to know. I want to arrive at the essence of humans!"

"Nonsense!"

She didn't wait for an answer to attack. The red liquid gushed again, and then stopped. Adam made the same bizarre expression. It was an expression that looked similar to sadness.

"We Machines who are connected to the network are immortal. However…"

Did he want to say that there was no use in attacking? Then all she had to do was attack so rapidly that the self-regeneration would not keep up. But what Adam said next completely toppled her hypothesis.

"Networked data has no awareness of mortality. It can't understand the concept of death. That's why I'm going to detach myself from the network."

The expression that looked like sadness disappeared without a trace. Adam laughed. His expression was that of pure joy.

"Now, let's kill each other!"

His words snapped her back to reality. It wasn't like she wanted to kill. She attacked because Machines were the enemy. That was all.

2B spoke coolly.

"I have no time to waste on you."

She had to find 9S. She was going to rescue him and take him home. That was the only reason she had come here.

"Why don't you loathe me? Were the corpses of your comrades not enough?"

She was disgusted to hear why the corpses of the YoRHa squadron troopers had been laid out.

"Warning: Vital signs are climbing. Beware of enemy provocations."

"I know."

She didn't have to be reminded by Pod. YoRHa troops were forbidden from having emotion.

"Then what about this?" asked Adam.

Adam's body was replaced with a glowing thread. He had teleported. Her eyes scoured for his destination. It was the upper floor of a building. Adam pointed at a part of its outer wall.

"I prepared it just for you."

A section of the outer wall crumbled away with a loud noise to reveal something black.

"You need an adequate reason to fight, don't you?"

It was 9S on a crucifix. He was neither struggling or moaning. Instead he was completely limp.

"You son of a...!"

2B's mouth instantly dried up. She felt her heart rate surge.

"I'm going to kill you."

Something was tearing at her from the inside. She couldn't hold it back. Her hand shook without realizing. Adam smiled contentedly, and floated down to earth.

"Yes, that emotion! Hatred!"

It didn't matter. She was going to kill him. She sprinted toward him and leapt.

"You bastard!"

She just kept swinging. It was a sea of red. She could hear screams. And the sound of Adam's laughter.

"We are both deeply in love with humans. Can't we say that Machines and androids are kindred?"

She wanted to shut him up. She wanted to jam her sword through his mouth, which kept blurting annoying things. She wasn't able to, so instead she kept swinging recklessly.

"But you've realized it too, haven't you? That humans are already extinct."

"Enough!"

She launched a kick at Adam's face. It missed. Irritated, she swung her sword around.

"Warning: Enemy's misleading information."

"Shut up!"

Adam and Pod were talking too much! She didn't want to listen! Shut up!

Humans were extinct? She didn't know that. She didn't want to know that. There was no need to think about it.

Adam was laughing shrilly. His white shirt was stained red. His smile from ear to ear deeply disturbed her.

He was a Machine. He was different from androids. Even if he had supple flesh and warm blood, he was different.

His goals were different. His purpose was different. And his destination was probably different as well.

"Die!" shouted 2B.

The moment was anticlimatic. Her sword slid through him without a hitch. The sensation closely resembled the feeling of piercing flesh—a feeling she knew too well.

Adam clung on to 2B, either in pain or with the intention to fight back. But his arms were limp. The hand that had grabbed the back of 2B's head slid down to her shoulders.

She withdrew her sword. She was drenched in warm red liquid from head to toe. Adam fell to his knees and collapsed.

"So this is…death…"

He looked content, but somewhat unsatisfied at the same time. That was the expression he had. But he was undoubtedly smiling.

"It's dark…and col…"

A puddle of red liquid spread from underneath Adam's body. 2B just stared at the scene as she panted.

She was bothered by the claim that Machines and androids were of the same kind. She wanted to ignore it and move on, but it stuck in her mind. It was probably because of the sensation she had felt when she drove in her sword. It was surprisingly similar. No, it was unmistakable…

A noise suddenly interrupted her thoughts. The noise of something crumbling, and a heavy object falling. She came to and looked over her shoulder.

9S was slumped on the white pavement. Scattered around him were chunks of the wall.

"9S!"

She ran toward 9S and helped him sit up. His lips were barely open, but she recognized that he had tried to say "2B." It was fine, his black-box response was still active. His personal data was intact.

A warm feeling spread inside 2B's chest. At the same time, a drop of something black stained her conscience. What was it? It didn't matter for now. She could think about it later.

"9S… Come on. Let's go home."

She gently lifted 9S into her arms.

ANOTHER SIDE "EVE"

I wanted to chase after big brother, but I stayed put. Because I promised I would stay here. I made a decision to never break promises with big brother.

Big brother went to our playground. It was the city we always played human in. It wasn't fair that he went alone. I wanted to play too. I wanted to break the androids with big brother.

Big brother suddenly disappeared. Even when I tried to use the network, I couldn't reach him. I lost the feeling that we were connected.

What happened?

I wanted to go meet big brother right away. But I couldn't. I made a promise to stay here.

Big brother didn't come back for one hour. For two hours.

Did something happen? Was he having trouble beating the androids? Should I go help big brother?

I should have just killed them back then. But big brother kept our promise and cut the battle short. We just needed a little more time to beat them, but it was the promised time. After that, we played human here.

Is big brother regretting that we didn't finish them off?

If I count to one hundred, big brother will come back. If I count to two hundred, big brother will come back. If I count to three hundred...

But even after I counted to nine thousand nine hundred ninety-nine, big brother didn't come back.

I waited and waited but big brother didn't come back. I finally broke our promise. It meant I wouldn't be praised for being a good boy, but I flew to the playground anyway.

Let's end this quickly. I'll help too. Let's kill the androids.

But the androids weren't there. Even the one we'd left as bait.

It was only big brother. He was lying on the floor. He didn't answer when I called. He didn't respond when I shook him.

I needed to regenerate him quick, I thought—but I couldn't.

Big brother was dead. The androids had killed big brother.

At first I didn't know what was going on. I mean, I never imagined that big brother would be gone. He has been here since I was born. He was always, always with me.

Big brother will never move again. We'll never be able to play.

I finally understood what it meant for big brother to have died. When I did, I was surprised at how much I cried. The back of my throat trembled and I couldn't stop myself from sobbing.

The area around my chest tightened painfully. It hurt so much that I rolled around on the floor. It still hurt, so I banged my head on the table. Then my head started to hurt and I felt dizzy. I hit my head even more. I needed to, or else my thoughts would be all jumbled.

Why did you have to die?

Even though big brother was born alone, we were together right away, and he had me until he died.

I had him when I was born, but now I'm alone, and I'll be alone until I die…

I knew. I knew that big brother had bigger interests than me. That big brother didn't like me as much as I liked him.

I knew because I've always only looked at big brother. But I still wanted to be together. As long as big brother was there, I was happy.

For me big brother is the only… If only big brother were here.

Hey big brother. I don't hate fighting.
But I hate it when big brother is hurt.
I hate it even more when big brother is gone.
So let's go somewhere peaceful together...

A w0rld w1th0ut b1g br0ther can just d1e.

CH. 06: 2B'S STORY/REUNION

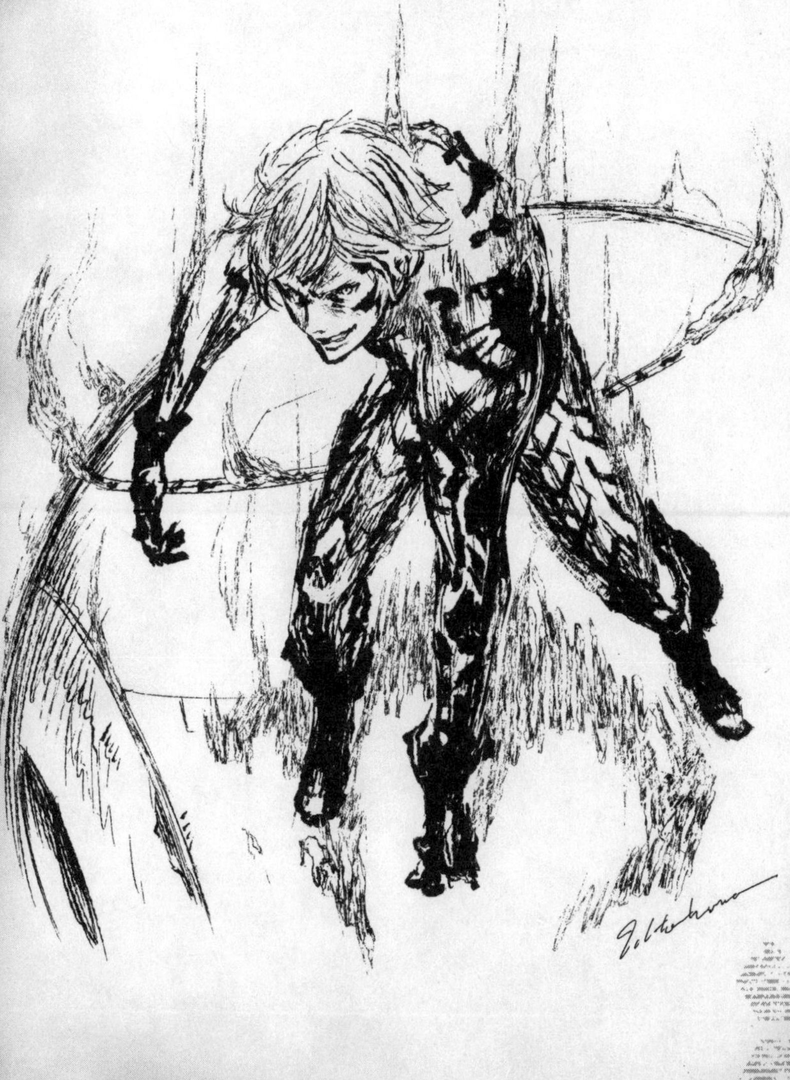

AFTER 9S RECEIVED A CHASSIS CHECKUP AT THE BUNKER AND PERFORMED A DATA OVERHAUL, IT WAS DECIDED THAT HE WOULD RETURN TO THE FIELD. Until then, 2B would be deployed on a solo research mission.

2B visited Pascal's village by herself and collected information on Machines that appeared on Earth. Pascal was cooperative yet again, even offering information about Machines in other areas.

Of course, it was information that Pascal, who was disconnected from the Machine network, knew. It was nothing revolutionary, mostly information that would, at its best, serve as references.

However, there was some information that would have piqued 9S's interest, like the fact that there were Machines that mimicked humans and established religions.

While carrying out the research, 2B started to have a small change of heart. She was no longer able to see Machines as "just clumps of metal."

There were Adam and Eve, who mimicked the appearance of humans and spoke fluently. There were Pascal and his villagers, who looked like other Machines but desired to live peacefully. They were all clearly capable of thinking, of experiencing emotions, and of acting according to their own wills.

What was the difference between them and androids like herself?

There was footage and documentation regarding so-called "robots" in the human civilization database. It was said that ancient humans once manufactured robots, which were similar to Machines, and employed their services. Robots had existed before there was the technology to create androids.

"Can't we say that Machines and androids are kindred?"

Adam's words and laughter stuck in her head. She brushed them off and started walking.

She was going to return to the resistance camp, get replenished and have a checkup, and after that visit Pascal's village once more…

As she was planning her course of action, a transmission interrupted her thoughts.

"This is…resist…cam…"

She could hear a patchy transmission amidst the horrible static. She wasn't sure, but it sounded like Anemone's voice.

"Report: Signal interference detected."

2B stopped walking and directed her full attention to the transmission. The quality was so poor that this was necessary to pick out the words.

"…Machines…as you can see…reception…request. Please."

The transmission abruptly died. Was it an EMP attack? Either way, the resistance camp was almost certainly in trouble.

"Let's hurry," said 2B.

Fortunately, the resistance camp was not far. But before long she was stalled. There was a massive outbreak of Machines at various places within the city ruins.

Besides the walking types that were a common occurrence in this vicinity, there were flying types of various sizes. There was also a steady stream of medium-sized Machines pouring in from the sky.

"Why are there so many?"

Pod replied that the cause was unknown. There was the transmission from the resistance camp as well—something was wrong.

"Pod, call the Bunker using laser transmission."

"Roger that."

Something was happening. Something unusual.

2B swallowed her desire to rush toward the resistance camp, and focused on destroying the Machines before her.

The number of Machines was truly extraordinary. It took a significant amount of time to exterminate all of them.

When the resistance camp finally came into sight, she could see flames rising out of it. The shrill clanging of Machines, screams, and black smoke were all emanating from the resistance camp. It was an ambush by the Machines.

"This is…?!"

2B came to a standstill at the entrance. At first glance, it looked like the androids were being pinned down by the Machines. But that was not all. The Machines were eating the androids. There were half-devoured android corpses lying around. Some did not even resemble their original forms.

Until now, they had been attacked but never eaten. The Machines didn't eat. That's what she had thought…

No, there was no time to be shocked. She kicked down the Machines that were eating and crushed them with her military sword. After she had reduced the few Machines in the square to metal scraps, she headed farther into the camp. There might be victims that hadn't escaped yet.

"2B!"

There Anemone was. She was near the research material depository, in the process of helping her comrades escape.

"What is this?" asked 2B.

Before she acted, she wanted to hear about the situation. But Anemone shook her head and replied, "I don't know."

"They suddenly poured into the camp and…We tried to fight them, but our guns are ineffective."

Right as 2B started to wonder why, Pod finished its analysis. It detected that the enemy was using energy shields. No wonder firearms were ineffective.

"Recommendation: Close-quarters combat."

"Okay."

She couldn't use long-range attacks here anyway. While it might have been fine to fire the guns used by the resistance, Pod's firing mode would be too powerful and even dangerous inside the camp.

"Anemone. Help the other androids escape."

Close-quarters combat was the responsibility of a Type B. As 2B pulled out her sword, she heard Anemone say, "I'll leave it to you," behind her back.

She had cleaned up all the Machines in the camp, and was about to reunite with Anemone. She heard a roar. A fierce aftershock, enough to throw her in the air, followed. It was outside the camp, but nearby.

She immediately exited the camp. There was a new enemy. Having a spherical body with multiple legs, it was a large, multilegged spider-shaped Machine. It was a somewhat formidable enemy, but one that was relatively uncommon.

There was the enemy outbreak, Machines that were eating humans, and the enemy in front of her—all of them were out of the ordinary. What was happening? No, no matter how much she thought about it she wouldn't be able to answer that question now. It was pointless to dwell on it.

She leapt high in the air and slashed at the giant spherical body. But she wasn't able to inflict a significant amount of damage. Furthermore, the enemy's movements were quick. Its multiple legs gave it extra agility during evasive maneuvers, negating the effectiveness of Pod's long-range fire.

If only 9S were here. A weak thought crossed her mind. She was reminded of the times that 9S had fought alongside her: at the factory ruins, the amusement park, and the flooded city.

If 9S were here, she would have him hack the enemy's vulnerability or take control, and in that instance…

"2B!"

She thought it was her imagination. Perhaps the images she had conjured in her head were so convincing that she had hallucinated a voice.

But it was a voice she knew too well. There was no mistaking it. 2B looked up in the direction of the voice. A flight unit was descending. 9S's voice had come from there.

She saw 9S jump out of the flight unit. The pilotless flight unit approached the ground at full speed.

"9S!"

9S, who had jumped out of the flight unit, landed near 2B, but stumbled when he hit the ground.

"Are you okay?!"

2B rushed in his direction and helped him up. As soon as she did, she heard an explosion behind her. A hot wind followed shortly after. The flight unit had collided with the spider-shaped Machine. Even if it was able to evade long-distance artillery from the ground, it certainly had not accounted for objects falling from the sky. It had probably failed to evade in time.

"Whew, I'm glad it hit."

Even while 9S puckered his face in pain, he managed to look smug. But suddenly his expression changed to that of astonishment.

9S's gaze was directed behind 2B, toward the location where the spider-shaped Machine had exploded from the impact of the flight unit.

"Now what?" asked 2B.

Looking back, she saw the remains of the Machine. The shiny sphere had deformed into a strange shape from the impact and heat of the explosion. The remains shifted. Something came out.

"Android…"

It was a familiar face and voice. It was Eve, who had fused with the remains of the spider-shaped machine. He looked down on 2B with his eyes glowing red.

"Everything… I'll destroy everything!"

As if his voice was a cue, walking types started to gather from what seemed like thin air. They gathered and latched on to Eve and the remains of the spider-shaped Machine. Some of them gorged on the remains, others seemingly dissolved and fused into the mass. Eventually the remains, Eve, and the Machines became one, fusing into an even larger sphere. Patchy and misshapen, it was certainly appropriate to call it a Frankensteinian monster.

The sphere started to spin. It gouged the ground, knocked trees over, and picked up speed. It was running wild. A flying type that had coincidentally been in the area was swallowed and crushed to pieces. The sphere had fearsome destructive power, but it seemed like it was impartial to friend or foe. Just as 2B was pondering how she was going to defeat the enemy...

"Ms. 2B! Can you hear me?!"

It was a transmission from Pascal. The strong static reminded her of the transmission with Anemone.

"My village is…ahhhhh!"

The way the transmission suddenly died was also the same as with Anemone…

"Pascal! Can you hear me?! Pascal!"

The transmission had already ended. Scenes of the resistance camp she had seen just moments before haunted her.

"Let's go, 9S."

She wasn't going to leave them alone. Fortunately, the fused mass of Eve and the Machines had perhaps lost control, and did not follow them.

■ ■■

The shortcut between Pascal's village and the city ruins had been blocked. A barricade had been built out of scrap wood. However, a few Machines were taking turns ramming their heads into the blockade. It was only scrap wood after all, and its integrity was questionable. It was a matter of time before the Machines got through. 2B slashed through the Machines trying to enter. Since walking types were poor at changing direction, there was no retaliation and 2B was able to destroy them without difficulty.

"Ms. 2B! Mr. 9S!"

Perhaps due to the closer vicinity to the village, the transmission started to go through again.

"Pascal! What happened?!"

"The Machines connected to the network suddenly started to rampage. We created a barricade and fought back, but with our weaponry…"

If the resistance didn't stand a chance with their weapons, it was only natural that the peace advocate Pascal and his villagers could not put up a fight.

Machines, their behavior epitomizing the word *rampage*, approached her head-on. 2B slashed and kicked them down. Compared to the muster at the resistance camp, their numbers were small. 9S was here to support her as well. This time, it didn't take long to alleviate the situation.

"Thank you. You were a great help."

After things finally settled down, Pascal appeared from behind the barricade. The villagers were already starting to repair the damaged barricades.

"You said the Machines went on a rampage?"

"Yes. I can't provide you with details, but I assume that the central unit responsible for controlling all the Machines went berserk. That spread to the other Machines…"

The central unit. She was surprised at the existence of such a figure. Well, it wouldn't be outlandish. In fact, she even had a hypothesis.

"Eve… It's him…" said 9S.

9S said the exact same name that had been on 2B's mind. Previously, small-type enemies had assembled out of nowhere. Eve had undoubtedly summoned them via the network. This was only possible because he was the central unit.

Originally, it was probably Adam, not Eve, who controlled the network. But he had willingly detached himself from the network during his fight with 2B. After that, Eve had inherited the responsibility. Since Eve had been created from Adam, it wouldn't be strange for him to possess abilities on par with Adam's.

"If we destroy the central unit, will they stop functioning as a group?"

Pascal nodded.

"Pod, can you determine Eve's location?"

"Report: Location is already determined."

Pod had apparently started to calculate the location right after hearing Pascal's information. The map data that was displayed pointed towards the heart of the crater zone.

"We'll defeat Eve. Pascal, you protect your village."

"Understood. Ms. 2B and Mr. 9S, please be careful."

Being sent off by a Machine, only to go destroy another Machine. How many times did this make? But 2B realized that her uneasiness with the situation had mostly faded.

■ ■■

The transmission came in right as they were heading toward the crater zone. They needed to defeat Eve as quickly as possible, but rampant small types blocked their path, and they were unable to make significant progress. Irritated, they fought. It was then that it happened.

"Br…ther…b1g br0ther…"

Without warning, the communication display opened and transmitted a voice mixed with static.

"Looks like he's forcing transmissions," said 9S, contorting his face into a scowl.

"Without regard for friend or foe, huh."

She remembered the sphere that had gone on a rampage. Eve had even destroyed Machines that were his comrades. Those cries were leaking out of the network. What a bothersome way to vent his anger.

"Hey big brother. Can I kill these guys?"

"Eve, calm down. We haven't finished talking."

Adam and Eve's conversation at the alien ship—now that she thought about it, that conversation had perfectly depicted the relationship between the two. Back at the white city, she hadn't been wrong to find it strange that Eve hadn't been with Adam.

A Machine was mourning the loss of its companion....

Suddenly, the attacks stopped. The surrounding Machines were standing still and making noises indistinguishable as more than screams or howls.

"Wha...what? What is this?" asked 2B.

Every Machine was quivering in place. It looked somewhat similar to the behavior before an EMP attack was released, but there were no signs of them trying to attack.

"What is...happening?"

The screams stopped. The red lights disappeared from the Machines' eyes. They froze, then collapsed like dominoes. The fallen bodies showed no signs of moving. They had been rendered completely nonfunctional.

She abruptly heard the chirp of a songbird. That chirp brought her attention to the stillness. She realized that the sounds of artillery and explosions that were coming from everywhere had ceased at once. A branch rustled as the songbird took off. She could hear the murmur of a river.

"Did Eve do this too? Halting the Machines?" muttered 9S.

If Eve was able to send all the Machines connected to the network on a rampage, he was surely able to halt all the Machines as well.

But what were those movements and screams that the Machines had displayed before? They'd been shaking in anguish and screaming as if they were in their death throes. "Halt" was too tame a word; "massacre" was more appropriate.

"Let's go, 9S."

They ran toward the crater zone in the almost uncomfortable silence. The Machines had stopped, but Eve was still alive. The map data had detected Eve's unique signal.

They would understand what was happening when they arrived. They ran down the steep slope, jumped over the rubble, and headed toward the heart of the crater zone.

Eve was exactly where the location data had shown. He was sitting on a pile of concrete rubble, looking up at the sky. The rampant sphere was nowhere to be seen. Eve looked as if he was searching for something, but at the same time looked as if he was trying to hold back tears. No—there was no way Machines would cry. It must have been her imagination.

Eve slowly turned his head toward them.

"Ah, you're here."

It sounded like he was reading off a script. She had always thought his way of speaking lacked inflection, but it sounded even more monotone now. But ill-suited to his tone, his mouth was twisted into a smile. Noises slowly seeped into his breath as it built up into raucous laughter.

"Don't you guys think so as well? That this world is pointless."

Eve stood up. His upper body swayed. The smile plastered on his face disappeared in an instant.

"As far as I'm concerned, b1g br0ther...was everyth1ng.."

Tears streamed from Eve's eyes. 2B couldn't believe it. It was the first time she had seen a Machine cry.

But his somber face quickly morphed into a face full of rage. The black patterns that had materialized on the right side of his body changed shape. The patterns expanded, lost their outlines, and colored his body a solid black.

The surrounding pieces of rubble floated up. They latched on to Adam's body, as if they were iron particles attracted to a magnet. There was the clamorous sound of metal striking metal.

"All of 1t...d1sappear and be g0ne!"

Eve howled within his armor of rubble. The air shook. 2B understood instinctively, not logically, that they needed to defeat him as soon as possible. Eve stopped the hardest swing 2B could muster with his bare hands. A YoRHa-type android weighed approximately 150 kilograms, and her strike had utilized the full momentum of that mass. Even if he was wearing an armor of rubble, it was impossible for him to be unscathed. Red liquid gushed out of where her sword had hit.

However, Eve seemed to not care, and kept throwing punches. Perhaps his pain receptors were offline, or he was tormented by something that eclipsed his pain...

"Why d1d you kill b1g br0ther!"

She was effortlessly able to dodge the big swings. There was not a shred of precision. It seemed like he had no intention to land a hit, but instead was just venting his anger.

But his fists hit the ground and rubble, crushing them to pieces and sending them in all directions. One of the fragments hit her arm, and induced a scowl from 2B. A small fragment like this had so much force. If those fists landed a direct hit, she would be in trouble.

"9S, stay back!"

A Type S's fighting abilities would not stand a chance against the current Eve. It was dangerous for 9S to even attempt to evade, much less attack. After confirming that 9S had retreated out of the corner of her eye, 2B approached Eve as she ducked under his blows. She thrust her sword through a crevice between his jet-black body and the rubble attached to it.

She only heard the harsh sound of metal hitting metal. A few pieces of rubble peeled off. Still, she made a repeated effort. Slowly but surely, the pieces of metal enveloping his body began to buckle.

Finally she was able to expose some of his skin. She stabbed her sword at the vulnerable points. Red liquid burst out, but Eve's counter-attacks did not falter. No matter how many times she slashed him, and how many places blood gushed from, Eve kept swinging his fists.

It was only natural because his pain receptors, a very practical set of sensors, had been disabled. That's what it meant to not feel pain. Unable to perceive the accumulation of damage, he would be unable to grasp the condition that his body was in until he was unable to move.

"Pod!"

Her intuition that an attack would be effective now was correct. Pod's laser struck Eve and his movements finally floundered. His upper body wobbled with every move—just when she had thought that this battle was almost over.

"Warning: A colossal energy signal has been detected."

"What do you mean?"

Was he going to create an explosion similar to the one that had created the crater zone? She immediately retreated and created distance. But she had been wrong.

A strange light enveloped Eve. The spray of red stopped. He was recovering.

"Hypothesis: An energy provision from multiple Machines."

"Eve is using the network to absorb energy from nearby Machines?"

"Affirmative."

She thought back to her fight with Adam. Until Adam removed himself from the network, any damage she inflicted had healed right away. It was the same as that time.

"There's no end to this…"

All that effort had been expended in vain. She could not see herself inflicting damage at a faster rate than his recovery.

"Then," she heard 9S say from behind her. "I'll hack him, and remove him from the network."

When she looked back, 9S was quietly staring down Eve.

"All right. I'm counting on you."

She sheltered the vulnerable chassis of 9S. She deflected the oncoming pebbles with her sword, and fended off his blows with kicks and strikes of her own. She was unable to contain him, and was thrown to the ground.

"Warning: The network the enemy is connected to is massive."

Pod's voice was irritating.

"Prediction: The chance of success for 9S's hacking is low."

She had ignored it, but Pod kept talking.

"Recommendation: Abandonment of 9S."

"Shut up! If 9S said he can do it, he can!"

Pod finally muted after 2B yelled at it. 9S's hacking had saved her from countless desperate situations. Covering 9S while he did that was her responsibility.

At the same time, she felt a slight pain. Before she knew it, they were fighting together again. But to 9S she was…

No. This was not the time to think about that.

"Report: Enemy's network detachment confirmed."

She looked over her shoulder at 9S. The chassis that had been still suddenly moved with a jolt. She saw that, and resumed her attacks on Eve.

She sidestepped the kicks and dodged the blows, slashing at every opportunity. There was no indication that his wounds were healing. If it was like this, she thought, she could destroy him.

She was certain that she was inflicting damage. Just a little bit more. That thought created a lapse in her attention.

The impact came right as she recognized that she was in trouble. She had suffered a direct hit. She had tried to block the blow using her sword at the last second, but was unable to mitigate all of the impact. The sword broke into pieces with a high-pitched clang. It took all her effort to resist getting thrown off her feet.

The blows were coming again. She was staggering, unable to dodge.

Right at that instant, something jumped out from behind her. It was 9S, leaping. She could see that his arms were covered by rubble, similar to Eve. He had probably learned how to attract and use the surrounding metal fragments as a shield when he had hacked Eve. 9S was just mimicking him.

"Eve!" shouted 9S.

Eve's reaction was marginally delayed because he had been so focused on finishing off 2B. The rubble-enveloped arm of 9S collided with the rubble-enveloped arm of Eve. She heard a thunderous roar. A shock wave followed.

"2B! Now!" screamed 9S after he was blown away.

Apparently Eve had been unable to soften the impact, and was lurching backward. 2B pulled out her large sword. Right now, even a weapon with a slower arc would accomplish the task.

She pounded the large sword into Eve, who was still struggling to straighten himself. Eve stopped the blade with his right hand. She put even more of her strength into it. She put her full weight into the strike.

With a dull sound Eve's arm was severed and rolled onto the floor. Screams filled the air. She slashed once again.

Eve's screams shifted. 2B's great sword was blasted out of her hand. It was an EMP attack. She wasn't able to hold her ground. Her knees gave way and she collapsed to the floor.

"Warning: NFCS destroyed. Impairments to close combat."

Even so, she stood up and picked up the broken sword. She was so close. One more hit, and she could destroy Eve.

Perhaps he had exhausted all his energy on the EMP attack, as Eve was not moving. He was on his knees, with his head hanging forward.

"Big…brother…"

She approached him while he looked at the ground.

"1 d1dn't need…anyth1ng else…"

Was that why he had halted the functions of all the other Machines? Was he scattering all this anger and hate, which should be directed solely at 2B, at anyone in sight because he wanted to get rid of a world without Adam?

What a selfish, Machine-like thing to do. Much more selfish than herself, a part of the YoRHa squadron, who was forbidden from experiencing emotion…

2B held up the broken sword. Sweeping away any hesitation, she swung the sword into the back of Eve's neck. Eve collapsed. She confirmed that his unique signal had disappeared. He was completely nonfunctional.

"That's…all…"

It was over. She exhaled and looked up at the sky. She heard her sword, the one she had been holding, clatter to the ground.

She had scratches and bruises everywhere, to a point that it was questionable if she could walk straight. 9S was probably the same. First they would go back to the resistance camp and get a checkup, then receive maintenance at the Bunker, and…

It was then, just as she was thinking ahead, that she thought she heard a groan behind her.

"9S?"

There was no reply. Quickly looking back, she saw 9S clawing at his neck.

"9S!"

She wanted to run to him, but her legs wouldn't listen. She lumbered toward 9S, frustrated. His goggles had probably come off when he was blasted away. She could clearly see the color of 9S's eyes.

"When I was detaching Eve from the network… It seems my logic board was corrupted."

"No…"

9S looked like he was about to cry and laugh at the same time. His eyes were tainted red. It was a typical symptom of logic virus infection. At this stage, administering a vaccine would be useless.

"It's okay. I can rewind using the data at the Bunker."

"But… Then the current you will never come back…"

It was possible that he had backed up during the data overhaul the other day. But all the data from the overhaul up until now would be erased. The 9S who had jumped out from a flight unit, the 9S who had detached Eve from the network by hacking him, the 9S who had saved 2B moments before she was to be finished off, and the 9S who *knew* that they had defeated Eve together…would be gone.

"That's true… But there's no way I can upl0ad c0rrupted data t0 the Bunker…"

There were some unintelligible sounds mixed in with his words. The virus corruption was progressing in his personal data.

"Please…2B. I…"

9B's face distorted from the pain. There was only a short amount of time left that 9S could remain conscious as 9S.

"By y0ur…hands…"

She knew what he was trying to say. Androids infected by a logic virus would lose control, and keep attacking their comrades until they died. The infected had to be executed before that happened.

She held 9S's face in her hands, and said, "I got it." Maybe it was her imagination, but she thought she saw a smile.

She slid her hands down toward 9S's neck. It was more painless to use a bladed weapon and pierce the heart, but since her Near Field Combat System was destroyed that was out of the question.

She put all her weight into her hands, and throttled his neck. 9S's limbs shook furiously, but became still right away.

"Why… It always…"

Why did it always end like this? No matter what she did, why was she unable to escape from her destiny to kill 9S?

How many times did this make? How many times had she killed 9S?

9S was an exceptional scanner, even among his peers. But that competence led to uncovering confidential information about Command. His competence at hacking led to unauthorized attempts at accessing the main server. Every time that happened, Command would issue an execution directive.

2E would change her name to 2B, approach 9S, and execute him. After the execution, his memory was compromised, and any confidential information erased. Of course, information regarding 2B's actions and her real identity, 2E, were erased as well.

That's why every time they would meet on a new mission, 9S would call her "Ms. 2B." 2B was the only one who knew they had repeated the same conversations over and over.

"Nines…"

The current 9S didn't even remember that 2B had used to call him by his nickname, Nines. He also wasn't aware of the amount of time they had spent together—far longer than he could remember.

She knew that it was her duty to execute her comrades. She would execute comrades that had been immobilized in battle, and at times would execute deserters or traitors. That was her mission as a Type E: E for executioner.

But every time she executed 9S and erased his memory, she was overcome with pain to the point where she wanted to abandon her mission and get executed herself.

Even so, she reappeared as 2B every single time because of their promise. He had a wish that no matter how much of his memory was lost he still wanted to see her, and that she should kill him without hesitation. 2B always granted him his wish.

Her tears dampened the cold cheek of 9S. She didn't want to have emotion, but she couldn't avoid the grief. How many times would she have to feel this way again? How many times would she have to say, "Nice to meet you," to 9S? How many times would she have to hide her true feelings?

She had tried to think of the first 9S she had killed as the real 9S, and every successive 9S as just a copy. She had tried to justify it by telling herself she was only killing a copy of him.

But she wasn't able to fool herself. No matter how many times she told herself that he was a copy, the agony of killing him didn't go away. The 9S in front of her was always the real 9S.

This time an execution directive hadn't even been issued. She had thought that maybe 9S would finally be able to remain 9S. If only he hadn't been infected by a logic virus.

So whether or not there was an execution directive, there was no escaping her destiny to kill 9S...

"I thought...maybe this time you would finally be able to remain as yourself..."

How much time passed as she cried? She felt a presence, and raised her head.

The head of a Machine lay on the ground nearby. Its eyes were glowing blue.

"They're...still alive."

Because of a Machine like this. The current 9S had died because of them. Roaring fury replaced anger. She picked up her broken sword, struggling to stay on her feet.

"A Machine like this!"

Right as she was about to crush the head, the surrounding Machine remains collectively started to emit a blue glow. The flickering light spread around the whole area.

"What is this? A transmission?"

What was it signaling? A Machine with blue eyes did not attack. Pascal and his villagers were a good example. What message were the Machines trying to convey by flickering their blue eyes, a sign of nonhostility?

Eventually, a nearby Machine stood up. Its eyes were blue, but it was a walking type far larger than 2B. 2B readied her sword. It had recovered, but she wondered if it was able to fight...

"W-wait! 2B!"

Fluent speech. It had called her 2B.

"You are...?"

2B widened her eyes. Impossible. How could such a thing happen? It had the same tone of voice as 9S.

"I guess I left my personal data behind on the Machine network. Before I knew it I was being reconstructed on the surrounding network. It's a really rare experience to have multiple reconstructions of myself, so I want to record it, but I haven't been able to access the save function, so I guess I'll copy my memory over onto some enemies, and after I get back into my own body..."

"9S!" interrupted 2B. This rambling. 9S did this when he was intrigued by something. Even if the voice and appearance were different, 2B could tell that this was 9S.

"Thank goodness..."

"Yeah."

The Machine stuck out its hand. After 2B climbed on, 9S gently lifted his arm, as if he wanted to get a better look of her face. 2B gazed endlessly into the glowing blue eyes.

■　■■

May 2 of the year 11945. A super Goliath-class Machine appeared on the coast of the flooded city. It sank aircraft carrier *Blue Ridge II*, and attempted to come ashore. In an effort to prevent this catastrophe, all nearby YoRHa squadron troopers engaged in battle. Destruction of the aforementioned enemy was successful.

However, after inflicting a massive amount of damage to his allied troops via an EMP explosion, YoRHa squadron trooper 9S was struck down farther inland. 9S was abducted by enemy Machine Adam, and put in confinement for a prolonged period.

After 9S was rescued, a data overhaul was performed. A problem arose during its last sequence. While syncing data with the Bunker's server, 9S detected a small noise and halted the operation. In order to investigate the origin of the noise, 9S accessed the main server.

During the investigation, 9S came across an abnormal firewall. 9S breached the firewall, and despite warnings from this program, acquired data. 9S eventually came across the index for the above top secret "Project YoRHa."

It had been anticipated during the project's planning stages that 9S's excellence as a scanner would possibly prompt him to discover the classified project. As expected, 9S had discovered the files a number of times in the past with unauthorized access to the main server.

This program usually accompanies 9S as a support unit, but is instructed to immediately notify Command and Model E when it detects an unauthorized attempt to access the server.

This time it had again informed Command when the main server was breached. Under normal circumstances, immediately after receiving the report, Commander White would issue an execution directive to 2B, formally known as 2E. Then 2E would immediately reset 9S's personal data and perform partial memory erasure.

However, this time the responses were remarkably different. The Commander did not issue an execution directive to 2E, and furthermore lent the chip with an overview of the human board and Project YoRHa to 9S. These actions were incomprehensible.

June 26 of the year 11945. The full-scale invasion plan of Earth commenced. Due to the loss of nucleus units Adam and Eve, there was disorder in Machine governance. 2B and 9S participated in battle as part of the commando unit.

It is predicted that the initiation of our publicly unannounced mission is in the near future.

REPORT: From Pod 153 to Pod 042. This will conclude documentation within the internal network.

RECOMMENDATION: Preparation of the final sequence.

CH. 07: 9S'S STORY/CASUALTY

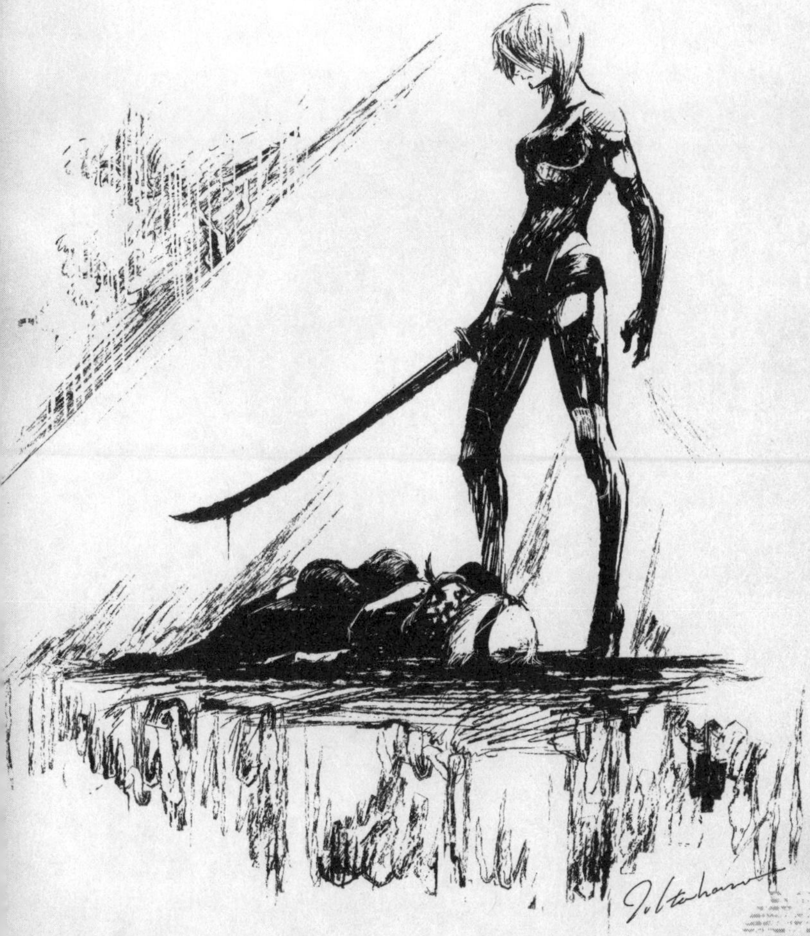

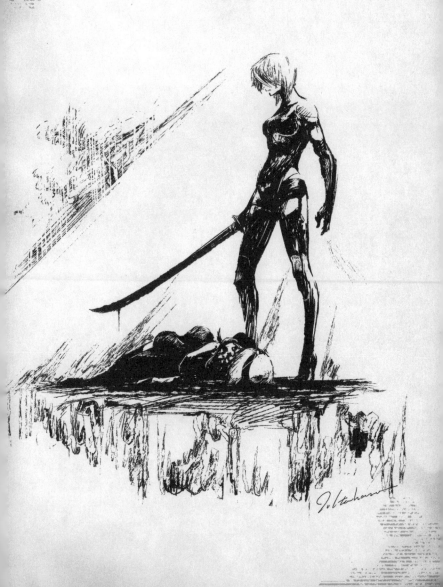

"DESTRUCTION OF THE CENTRAL UNITS OF THE ENEMY NET-WORK, ADAM AND EVE—CONFIRMED. Currently there is disorder in the enemy government. Making use of this opportunity, the human forces have called for a full-scale attack on the Machines. Of course, we YoRHa squadron troopers are to cooperate as well."

Out of the corner of his eye, 9S stared at the commander's face projected on Pod's communication display while he walked along the city ruins. A twig he stepped on produced a dry crack as it split.

"Remember! The pain of having your home taken away!"

It's not like my home was taken away, 9S replied in his head. The YoRHa androids were manufactured in orbit, not on Earth. But the commander had not specified whose homes had been taken away. It didn't have to be explained to the other troops, as he was probably the only one who thought this way. The subject, in this case, was "humanity," and not "us."

It was clever wordplay. It made you feel as if you had to fight, if you were fighting for "humanity's pain of having their home taken away." It made you feel like you had to act for humanity. That's how androids were programmed.

"We will not give up! We will take back what the Machines took from us—the ocean, the sky, and the land!"

This was where the subject "we" came up. The words "we will not give up" were built on the feelings of obligation toward humanity and its "pain." It made you feel that you could fight until the end for humanity's sake. It was a textbook example of a speech to raise morale within the force.

He slightly hated himself for thinking this way. And he was a little bitter toward the commander, who had given him the freedom to choose. Talk about asking the wrong person.

He couldn't believe it when he was told to make his own decision. There had been no punishment, even after he had confessed to accessing the main server without authorization.

9S had come across a small noise while syncing his and 2B's battle data with the main server's data. Unable to ignore the kink, 9S decided to investigate the main server.

He hadn't ignored the issue and carried on, because recently he had been noticing some type of presence. A feeling of being watched, or that something was nearby. But it was such a minute presence that it was easily dismissible as a trick of the mind.

He had felt the presence for the first time in the server control room. As if someone were staring at the display over his shoulder while he was working. But Operator 21O had come in immediately after, so 9S had thought it was her presence and had forgotten about it.

Next was at the hangar. He felt as though he was being observed from behind a pillar while entering a flight unit. But it had been an emergency dispatch, so he didn't have time to check. After returning he had investigated the hangar, but come up empty-handed.

In other words, a Type S had not been able to definitively detect the presence, even with its scanning capabilities. That was why, no matter how insignificant, he was reluctant to pass off anything that remotely resembled noise.

As a result, he was unable to identify the true nature of the noise, but instead uncovered an unbelievable secret.

The commander had told him that humans no longer existed. This happened when the commander summoned him after his unauthorized access to the main server was discovered.

It was an opportune summons for 9S as well. He wanted to ask questions, away from the other troopers and their prying ears. Why were the plans for establishing the human board on the moon contained in the YoRHa project? It would have made more sense for the YoRHa project to be contained in the plans for establishing the human board. Humans had been responsible for the creation of YoRHa androids, and humans had proposed the YoRHa project. It was certainly suspicious that the establishment of the human board was outlined in the YoRHa project. That made it seem like the commander had created the human board.

The commander coolly confirmed his doubts. 9S was right, androids had been responsible for installing the human board server on the moon. Furthermore, humans had already been extinct by the time aliens had invaded the Earth. The only thing shipped to the moon was humanity's genetic profile data.

9S remembered hearing his own voice, sounding as if it were coming from far away, ask why they had done such a thing. But strangely, the commander's words sounded clear as they reverberated in his ears.

"There's not a single being that can fight without reason. We needed a god to devote our lives to."

She handed 9S a chip with all the relevant information. She told him to decide what to do with it, and promptly left.

■ ■■

"Glory to mankind!"

These words. They made him uneasy, since he was already aware that humanity was extinct. But he wasn't able to dismiss the phrase as slander, because his ingrained loyalty to humanity prevented him from doing so. Still, he was no longer able to naively hoist his arm up to his chest and salute with the same fervor as before. He was just going through the motions. That was what he felt.

"What am I supposed to do…"

He had considered sharing the information with 2B. He had even thought it was better for her to know.

Type B androids, because of their combat capabilities, were always thrown on the front lines. They were in more danger than anyone else. That's why he thought she should know that even if she put her life on the line to take back Earth, there would be no humans to return Earth to.

But thinking of 2B's feelings, he also felt that he should keep it a secret. She would certainly be flustered. She would be at a loss. At least, that's what he was going through. He didn't want 2B to suffer the same way...

In the end, he was unable to tell 2B the truth. As he was performing her system check, he repeated the process of starting to speak out, then closing his mouth and swallowing his words, only to try and speak yet again.

After the check, he even stopped 2B as she was leaving the room, but was still unable to break the news. All he could form into words was, "Be safe."

Finally, the commencement of the full-scale invasion plan.

■ ■■

After using the transfer device to land in the city ruins, 9S felt that something was missing. It was boring to be alone. As he was walking, that feeling brought sadness and loneliness.

It was because he'd been with 2B for the recent Earth missions. Even when he had been walking through buildings on the verge of collapse, traveling through the desert with his shoes filled with sand, or walking through the grease-filled air of the factory ruins, 2B had been there with him.

He knew that this was far from the norm. Most of a Type S's Earth missions consisted of solo research. It was even rare for a Type S to operate with their peers. Having 2B next to him was an exceptional situation.

"That concludes all the directives. Did you get them?"

He had been on a transmission with Operator 21O, who was at the Bunker. 9S kicked his head into full gear and tried to recall what 21O had said.

"Ummm… In preparation for the full-scale invasion, we, the scanner squadron, are to hack and neutralize the enemy's aerial defense system."

"That's right. Good job."

"Are you…treating me like some kind of child?"

"Your mind is playing games."

21O had replied right away, but 9S could see through that lie. She had also told him "Good job" when he halted the Machine that was acting as the receiver for the enemy defense system.

That was not all.

"During battle, please stay as far away from the field as possible."

"But then I won't be able to provide support."

Aside from research and information gathering, hacking during battle to support their comrades was a vital role for a Type S. Hacking couldn't be performed on a target that was too far away, so while they would select positions that wouldn't disrupt the battle, it was crucial for them to stay within the battle area.

"A scanner model like yourself is not suited for battle."

"Aw, are you worried about me?"

"No, you would only be a burden on the battlefield."

In other words, she was telling him that it was no place for a child like him.

"As an operator, I can see how you see me as a burden…but that's so mean."

She didn't have to babysit him that much. Even when he was working in the server control room, she was always telling him to take breaks or fix his posture.

He sighed, complaining that he could take care of himself under his breath. That was when another transmission from someone else on Earth came in.

"11S to 9S. Do you copy?"

"Roger that."

"We have completed our tasks. How are you doing?"

Other troops beside 9S had been deployed to neutralize the enemy's aerial defense system.

"I guess…I have one more enemy."

He had just finished halting a Machine that had taken position on a steel tower overlooking the sky. 9S slid down the ladder with the communication display still open.

"Roger. And when you return to the Bunker please sync your data."

"Oh…I forgot."

It was because he had been informed of that secret after pausing his data sync. He had forgotten about it until now.

"Since your data hasn't been uploaded, all of the scanner models are unable to update."

He had no excuses. It was true.

"Once this mission is over, I'll take care of it."

"Please do!"

After the transmission ended, 9S ran in order to halt the last enemy.

■   ■■

After neutralizing the enemy's aerial defense system, 9S reunited with 2B, who had descended from the Bunker. The vanguard was already starting to take part in battles in various places. As the commando unit, 9S and others were to act as reinforcements wherever they were needed.

The enemy Machines were all detached from the network. It was easy to destroy enemies in disorder.

And 2B was next to him now. Things were finally back to normal for 9S.

"Don't let your guard down. We don't know what's coming," said 2B.

"All riiight," said 9S.

The sense of security, that he could fight like he always did, lifted a weight from his shoulders. 2B had probably misinterpreted this as having let his guard down.

Either way, it was undeniable that their side had the advantage. 2B and 9S provided reinforcement to a unit that was being surrounded by enemies. They steadily shaved away at the enemy's military force. They thought the end was near.

"9S, check the surroundings if there's any more enemy reinforcements coming our way!"

The Machines only sent reinforcements when the Machine count in a particular area dipped below a certain threshold. It was common to clear out an entire area and come back a few hours later just to see the same number of Machines lumbering around.

But that was only possible because their network had been functioning. Although thinking that currently the chances of reinforcements were low, 9S moved to ascend to a high vantage point anyway. It wasn't a bad idea, to be sure, and he had the extra energy as well.

Climbing on top of a partially collapsed building, 9S checked for any enemies. The constant cannonballs flying through the air obstructed his vision. Still, the situation seemed much more favorable then the beginning of the battle…

That was when the incident took place.

"What's this noise?"

9S heard 2B's voice mutter the question through the transmission. Perhaps because of the distance to the roof of the building, 9S had no clue what she was talking about. He just had an ominous feeling.

"2B, what's that noise you were talking about?"

He scoured the ground, wondering if he could analyze the noise from the rooftop. He spotted 2B and the others surrounding the few remaining Machines. Suddenly, the Machines peculiarly stopped whatever they were doing.

The spherical heads rose in unison. The Machines' eyes were flickering erratically. Even from a distance, it was easy to tell that they were discharging electricity.

"2B!"

He heard screams through the transmission. 2B and the others were hunched over and holding their heads. It was an EMP attack at point-blank range.

9S grabbed on to Pod's arm and jumped down. He assessed the situation as he glided down. A few small two-legged walking types. He had heard that some Machines of this type could perform EMP attacks. But it was rarely documented, and 9S had never come across one that could.

"Pod! Long-range fire!"

After shooting down the enemies generating the EMP attacks, 9S ran over to 2B.

"Are you okay?!"

2B shook her head as she stood up. She had apparently suffered a great deal of damage, and was struggling to stand straight.

"I was…careless. I have to reboot…"

"All right. I'll cover you."

With horrible timing, the enemy reinforcements started to fly in. The number was too great for 9S to handle by himself. But escape wasn't even an option without a reboot. At the very least he needed to buy enough time for 2B to reboot.

He threw a dagger at a nearby enemy. Suddenly his vision faltered. His field of vision was dotted with dead pixels.

"Visual camouflage?"

When had Machines acquired the skills to use such a technique? Camouflage and stealth were supposed to be unique to androids.

"How is this possible?"

No, he had no time to be confused. There was nothing wrong with his visual mechanisms. It was just hard to see the enemies.

"I'll protect you, 2B."

9S lunged toward the enemies hiding within the dead spots of his vision.

He had been aimlessly swinging around his sword, but perhaps that had ironically improved his offensive power, because when he came to he had destroyed a few enemies. Eventually 2B finished rebooting and took care of the other enemies.

9S's vision slowly returned to normal after clearing out the enemies. He looked around once again. There were no enemies in sight. The other squadron troopers seemed to have rebooted, and stood up one by one. They were most likely slightly wobbling because they hadn't fully recovered from the EMP.

Suddenly, 2B toppled over. The other troops started to collapse to the ground. An alarm rang from the nearby Pod.

"A wide-area virus?"

9S had no symptoms himself. So during the time 9S was not here, probably around the time of the EMP attack, the virus was spread and activated.

He rushed toward 2B, who was clutching her chest in pain. While wide-area viruses were highly contagious, removing one was relatively easy. After hacking into 2B, 9S confirmed that it was merely a conventional type of virus.

This type was treatable using a vaccine. For the rest of the troops, it was probably faster to administer the vaccine than perform hacking for each one…

After he finished hacking and returned to his chassis, he saw 2B swaying as she tried to stand up.

"2B, don't push it."

2B's replied, "Okay," between heavy breaths. She had been infected by the virus before fully recovering from the EMP attack. Her chassis had experienced significant stresses.

Fortunately, there were no further enemies.

As 9S was planning to administer the vaccine to the other troops while 2B was resting, the moans of the other troopers, echoing here and there, suddenly stopped. They were replaced with the sound of sinister laughter.

"What is this?"

2B immediately positioned herself so she and 9S stood back-to-back. That was how wary 2B was of the situation.

The squadron troopers that had been slumped on the ground stood up. With a shrill laugh, they all raised their heads at once. The women's eyes glowed red. By the time 9S had recalled that it was a typical symptom of virus infection, the corrupted troops had already started attacking.

"Are they possessed?" asked 9S.

It was strange. Losing consciousness and attacking comrades were terminal symptoms. Judging from when he hacked 2B, this type of virus shouldn't have progressed so quickly.

"It can't be… A new type?!"

He didn't have time to think. He dodged the oncoming swords, and took his distance.

"Wha?!"

2B raised a voice of confusion while trying to counterattack. Her sword had stopped. Her attack functions were nonoperational.

"It's the YoRHa signal ID!" yelled 9S.

In order to prevent unintentionally attacking comrades in battle, the YoRHa androids were programmed so that they would not be able to attack fellow androids that emitted the unique YoRHa signal ID. This function was most likely already broken in the corrupted troops, as they kept attacking without hesitation.

"2B, this way!"

9S and 2B dashed into a building on the verge of collapse. At this rate it was going to be a one-sided battle.

"I'm going to fry 2B's ID circuits! Pod, cover me!"

While the two pods kept the other squadron troopers busy, 9S hacked into 2B again and shut off the ID circuitry.

Right after he finished hacking, 9S saw 2B raise her sword above her head. 9S quickly created some space. Now 2B was unreceptive to 9S's signal ID as well. Rather than save himself, he wanted to stay away so 2B could fight without reservation.

"Pod!" yelled 9S.

"Initiate a transmission to Command!"

He wanted to grasp the situation while 2B was fighting. Small-type Machines that could use EMP attacks, wide-area viruses with an unbelievably fast progression—something was out of the ordinary. Perhaps from up in orbit the source or reason for these phenomena would be apparent. However...

"Report: Transmission unavailable. Signal jamming by Machines detected."

"Where?! Which one is doing that?!"

Pod 153 switched over to locating the source of the signal jamming.

"Report: Location of the source was identified. Marking the map."

It was the signal of a large Machine. Its location was not far away. 9S called 2B through the transmission.

There were no problems with transmissions within the area. 2B replied, "9S?"

"I'm going to head over to the Machine responsible for this signal jamming!"

"Roger that. I'll come once I clear out this area."

She had nonchalantly said clear out, but in reality she was facing multiple YoRHa squadron troopers at the same time. Not to mention, a few of them were the same Type B as her. It was not an easy task.

After cutting the transmission, 9S ran toward the heart of the crater zone. That was where the signal jamming Machine was. He promised himself that he would defeat the enemy before 2B could get there.

■ ■■

In the end, 2B was the one who dealt the decisive blow. 9S had hacked the Machine multiple times, damaging its maneuvering capabilities, triggering explosions of certain parts of its body, and slowly nudging the enemy toward destruction. But things moved much faster after 2B joined him.

The enemy was silenced with one blow from 2B. As a result, its electrical discharge stopped, and the jamming should have been released as well.

2B ordered Pod 042 to transmit details to Command. Now they would be able to know what was happening. And they had lost so many YoRHa androids in the process. The corruption could still be spreading. It was imperative for them to report back.

"Pod!" 2B snapped, irritated that Pod was taking time to open the communication display.

"Transmission lost. Unable to connect to Command."

"Shit! So there's still jamming!"

"Negative: Transmission conditions are favorable."

What did that mean? 9S and 2B gave each other quizzical looks. The explanation that 042 gave them was far beyond their imagination.

"Connection was lost due to a lack of confirmation. Currently all transmission functions of the Bunker are down."

"What's happening at the Bunker..." said 9S.

If the Bunker's transmission functions were truly down, it was no longer a simple problem of transmission malfunction. It meant that Earth forces were isolated. They were in the same boat as a Machine detached from its network. Just before, 9S had thought it was easy for them to destroy enemies in disorder, but to think they would fall into the same trap...

But they had no time to think it through.

"Report: Multiple hostile YoRHa squadron troopers approaching."

Hostile YoRHa androids. So there were other troops infected by the virus. And apparently multiple ones.

By the time he looked up, there were troops dressed in their black battle uniforms surrounding the crater zone. The number was far greater than what the two of them could handle. Perhaps it would be different if they were both Type B.

"A scanner model like yourself is not suited for battle."

What Operator 21O had told him crossed the back of his mind. It was true, in an outright battle, Type S were just a burden...

Squadron troopers, with their eyes glowing red, slid down the slope. The enclosure was shrinking rapidly from all sides. 2B pulled out her sword and braced herself.

Was there any way that they could call for help? There was an emergency back door for the Bunker. If he could infiltrate through there and then communicate with the Operator via the server... No, there wasn't enough time. They wouldn't last until a rescue team could descend.

Or maybe there wasn't a need to call for help?

"Pod, you said that transmission conditions are favorable, right?"

153 replied "Affirmative." It should be possible to upload a massive amount of data with the transmission bandwidth near the crater zone. After all, that was why the signal-jamming Machine had chosen to interfere with the signals at this particular location.

"We're going to blow this area away with a black-box response."

2B made a shocked face. 9S quickly explained.

"The Bunker has an emergency back door, so I'll just upload all of our personal data through there."

They were going to sacrifice their chassis and go home. 9S didn't remember, but he had heard that him and 2B had destroyed multiple Goliath-class enemies that way.

The squadron troopers pounced on them as soon as 2B had answered, "I got it." 9S simultaneously started the data upload.

9S evaded the slashes that came from all directions, and focused on defending himself. When he was uploading data, he was unable to rely on the Type S specialty of hacking enemies. Besides, there were so many enemies. Even if he weren't uploading the data, hacking would have been infeasible.

"9S! Are you still not done?!"

2B's voice was imbued with panic. The uploading had just passed 70 percent. Even though the transmission conditions were favorable, the amount of data he was uploading was enormous.

"Just a bit more! I'm at 92 percent!"

He felt a burning pain on his back. He had suffered a direct hit, but he didn't care. This chassis would be useless in a few more seconds.

"2B! The black box!"

He had completed the upload of the log data. 9S rushed toward 2B, taking out his black box.

"9S!"

He saw 2B extend her black box. His view was rattled. The squadron troopers had knocked him down.

He heard a bone break. Unfazed, he put forward his own black box. He could see 2B's black box. Just a little bit more. But 2B was being pinned down by the troopers as well. Various parts of his body were being crushed and snapped, so much so at this point that he couldn't tell which parts were broken or where it hurt. His hand trembled. 2B's black box crept closer. His eyes were blinded by a white light. It was something he would forget very soon, anyway.

■ ■■

When he opened his eyes, he saw the ceiling of his room. He could only recall up until the moment he took out his black box, but he was at the Bunker now, so the plan must have succeeded. He jumped to his feet and went into the hallway. Pod was already waiting for him. Previously, for the extermination mission at the factory ruins, he had been unable to upload Pod programs on the low-transmission bandwidth. But this time he was able to upload both his and 2B's personal data as well as 153 and 042's programs. The Pod programs didn't take up much storage in the first place.

He ran toward 2B's room. He was a little worried over whether 2B had safely returned to her chassis. After all, the Bunker was going through an unprecedented situation in which its transmission functions were completely down.

But there was no need to worry. Right as 9S was about to knock on her door, 2B came flying out of her room.

"Let's go report to the commander."

2B started running as soon as the words left her mouth. 9S followed. They needed to hurry. At this very moment the control room could have its alarms blaring, in utter chaos...

But his prediction was far from the truth. The control room was quiet. The monitors that should have been dead due to the transmission outage were operating as usual, displaying scenes from Earth. They showed the YoRHa squadron and Machines in battle, a very uneventful and typical scene.

"This is..."

That was impossible. Most of the YoRHa squadron troopers on Earth had contracted the virus and lost their consciousness. The battlefront should have been dissolving. But the commander was calmly giving orders to troops in the room and on Earth, and the operators were controlling the computer terminals. Not one soul questioned the integrity of the monitor feed.

"Commander!" said 2B.

"2B? And 9S."

The commander looked over with a puzzled look.

"What in the world are you doing here?"

"The YoRHa squadron troopers on Earth were infected by a virus! We had to quell the rampant troops with our black box..."

9S stopped talking. It wasn't voluntary; he had stopped because he had been silenced. The commander had shot him a piercing stare.

"Virus? What are you talking about? We haven't received any reports from Earth."

"Those are fabricated!"

The monitors were displaying fake footage. If the commander believed the footage was legitimate, how was he going to convince her?

"Currently, the Bunker's transmissions are down..."

"Why did you leave the battlefield without authorization in the first place?"

She gave him a chilling glare. 9S started to think that she would never believe anything he said. Then, 2B, who had stayed silent the whole time, yelled,

"The YoRHa squadron troopers were out of control!"

The commander made a small gasp, perhaps because she was shocked by 2B's outburst.

"Aren't you two the ones that are infected?"

"No!"

Why didn't she understand? Why didn't she understand that Earth and the Bunker were both in dire danger?

But 9S's desperate voice was ignored.

"2B, 9S. I'm detaining you two on suspicion of virus infection."

"Wait!"

Without a word, armed troops pointed their guns at 9S and 2B. While they were wasting time like this, the YoRHa squadron troopers on Earth were busy killing each other.

9S stared down the gun barrel in despair. The barrel wavered. The squadron troopers all sighed in unison as they bent forward. The guns clunked onto the floor.

"Is this…"

Laughter came out of nowhere. "Cooooooorrect," mocked a voice, the same one as Operator 6O's. The troops that were crouched over stood up and raised their heads. Their eyes were red.

"Infection?!"

It wasn't only the armed troops. The operators in the control room had glowing red eyes as well. On one hand 9S questioned why this had happened, and on the other he felt like he had known this would happen.

"So the virus infiltrated the Bunker…"

He knew it. He knew the moment he saw the footage on the monitors.

"That's cooooorrect too!"

"Operator…"

No, said 2B in a strained voice.

"9S, that's…"

"That's right. I'm a Machine."

The thing disguised as Operator 6O laughed amusedly.

"I'm talking to you through the network and the virus."

Using the virus? Was that possible?

"You all were quite entertaining, but this base is done for."

Laughing with an unpleasant cackle, 6O, the other operators, and the armed troops lunged at them.

"Commander! We're going to retreat!"

2B flashed a glance at 9S. 9S nodded. They were going to protect the commander and escape.

As 2B brawled with the squadron troopers, 9S led the commander out into the hallway.

The voice of Operator 6O saying, "This is soo fun. This is soo fun," trailed behind them. 9S could hear her boasting that the virus she had planted had bloomed so fruitfully.

If the virus was planted, then that meant the Machine had infiltrated the Bunker a long time ago. That feeling of being watched—he had forgotten about it after he searched in vain, but that was probably the presence of the Machine.

The squadron troopers in the hallway had been infected, without exception. He had to shoot down troops that he had completely trusted up until moments ago.

"Why aren't you two infected?

"Most likely because I paused our data syncs. When I tried to sync, I heard a small noise, so that bothered me and…"

It hadn't been his mind playing tricks on him. The small noise had been a Machine disguised as a virus. If he had realized back then and exterminated the virus, he could have prevented the loss of many of his comrades.

"I probed the main server, but…"

No, it would have been impossible. How could he have exterminated a virus he couldn't detect?

"I see. So that's what it was…"

The commander mumbled under her breath. She was aware of 9S's unauthorized access. 2B yelled as she hurled the attacking squadron troopers aside.

"Commander! This base is hopeless. We need to escape!"

9S heard an explosion in the distance. The Bunker was being destroyed from the inside out.

"The transfer device is infected. Let's escape with flight units from the hangar."

They weren't anywhere near the hangar. How many comrades would they have to kill on the way?

Some squadron troopers were completely possessed. Others kept a fragment of their consciousness. Then there were some that repeated, "Glory to mankind," while recklessly firing their guns. 9S and party shot or cut down all of them to move on.

They eventually arrived at the hangar door. 9S heard another explosion. It was bigger than the last one. The shock was so great the floor looked as if it were rippling.

"Commander, hurry!"

2B grabbed the commander's arm. But her grasp was slowly but forcibly shaken off.

"I can't go."

The commander, who had kept her head down the whole time, looked up. Her eyes were already red.

"I…had synced with the server as well."

"Then 9S can exterminate the virus by—"

"There's no time for that!" the commander interrupted 2B with a resolute voice.

"You two are the last remaining members of the YoRHa squadron! You have an obligation to live!"

"Commander…"

"Besides, I'm the commander of this base. Let me act like it until the end."

Just as 2B started to say, "But," a large explosion resounded. The jolt threw 9S's body in a random direction.

"2B! The base is about to…"

It wouldn't hold up any longer. 9S grabbed 2B's arm.

"Commander!"

Nevertheless, 2B kept staring at the commander. Her gaze desperately tried to cling on—an expression 9S had never seen from 2B. He knew that 2B had full and utmost trust in the commander. But he never knew why. Now he knew that reason was something forbidden and taboo.

However, as much as 2B wanted to rescue the commander, 9S wanted to rescue 2B just as much. He wanted to protect 2B no matter what.

"Let's go 2B!"

The commander simultaneously pushed 2B away as 9S pulled on 2B's arm, dragging her into the hangar.

"Go!"

Right as the door to the hangar closed, it looked like the commander's lips parted to say "2B." He wasn't sure what kind of face 2B made.

"2B, we need to hurry!"

9S let go of her arm. He knew that it was ok to let go now.

"Okay!"

2B answered in a dark voice. They equipped the flight units and unlocked the launching ramp. They flew toward the cold darkness. Just as they hit full throttle, a light as bright as sunlight flashed behind them. The Bunker had exploded.

Still they flew. Dodging the scattered remains of the Bunker, they flew toward Earth. The commander's words that they had an obligation to live echoed in their heads.

The remains that rained down through the atmosphere glimmered, letting off heat and light. 9S thought they looked like the fireworks they had seen in the amusement park ruins.

That day, 2B had stared, fascinated, at the material courier that had been streaking up the sky. They would never see such a sight again.

The YoRHa squadron Bunker, their home, had exploded without a sound, and disappeared without a sound.

■ ■■

After they entered the atmosphere, they headed toward the city ruins. There was a possibility that they would run into the infected squadron troopers, but they had nowhere else to go.

In fact, it was probably their duty to kill off any of the remaining troops. If they were left alone, they could pose a threat to the resistance.

Along with Pod's voice, a location data display appeared.

"Report: Multiple pursuers."

"Enemies?!"

That was right. There were still Machines left on Earth. There were probably still some in the sky. 9S had thought that with the destruction of Adam and Eve the whole Machine network would be rendered nonfunctional as well, but that was not the case. The Machine that had infiltrated the Bunker had said, "I'm talking to you through the network and the virus…"

"No!"

2B almost sounded as if she were screaming through the transmission.

"This signal is…"

She didn't have to say any more. The pursuers' markers on the display were green. They were YoRHa squadron troopers. Obviously they were not here to save them.

It was an obligation for YoRHa squadron troopers to sync their data with the server. 2B and 9S had avoided the virus by failing to sync their data, which was not a commendable action in any way.

As a result, a majority of the squadron troopers were infected with the virus. Perhaps everyone except them.

"Since your data hasn't been uploaded, all of the scanner models are unable to update."

If what 11S had said was true, all the other scanners had completed the data sync.

The flight units of the infected squadron troopers began to attack at once. 9S immediately turned on stealth mode, but with this many enemies it was just a minor advantage. The infected squadron troopers were unconcerned with friendly fire. They were spraying bullets in every direction and blindly firing missiles.

9S felt an impact similar to being hit in the back with a metal rod. He had been shot. The fact that Type S were unsuited for battle wasn't limited to ground combat.

"9S! Transfer your flight unit controls to me!"

"What?"

"We're going to break through."

2B had clawed her way through enemy aerial defense systems a countless number of times on her descents to Earth. Her aerial combat skill was leagues beyond 9S's.

"Okay."

It was probably a burden for her to control multiple flight units, but 9S figured anything was better than controlling his unit himself. He just didn't want to be deadweight.

"Pod."

"Affirmative: Flight unit controls transferred to 2B."

9S's limbs suddenly became lighter. The weight of the flight unit had been lifted from him.

"Controls of 9S's flight unit acquired."

He heard the voice of Pod 042 through the transmission.

"Flight path automatically set."

The flight unit dipped down.

"Taking departure route from warring airspace."

All of a sudden he was yanked sideways.

"Hey! Wait! What is this…"

9S squirmed inside the flight unit. He knew that it was useless. He had given 2B the controls.

"YoRHa unit 2B, deactivating stealth mode."

The silhouette of 2B's unit appeared amidst the flying bullets.

"No…! 2B!"

2B had planned to become the decoy all along, to let 9S escape to safety.

"Don't do this!"

He'd given up his controls because he'd thought that they would break through together. He'd thought 2B had a plan to keep both of them alive.

"I hate this!"

2B's flight unit was under concentrated fire, besieged by the infected troops.

"This…I never wanted this!"

The flight unit continued to drift away against his will. Eventually 2B's flight unit and the horde of infected troops disappeared from his sight.

ANOTHER SIDE "A2"

I was used to fighting YoRHa types. I had fended off 2B and 9S, who were assigned to hunt me down, a number of times.

But there were certainly not a lot of opportunities to fight the newer models, let alone those driven mad from the viral infection. On top of that it was rare for me to be surrounded, so I was confused, since the situation was so different from the norm.

Regardless, infected or not and in large numbers or not, I had one job. I no longer had any Earthbound comrades. That's why, as soon as I encountered someone, I would destroy them without hesitation. That's what I've always done.

That's why I was surprised when we ran into each other but didn't fight.

■ ■■

"This is…it."

The YoRHa model with the same face as mine appeared as I was fighting the infected YoRHa. It was a reunion. We had previously fought when we ran into each other, so I thought we would fight again. But after I wiped out the infected YoRHa, I didn't need to confront her.

She had also been infected by the logic virus. Her goggles, which had been removed, revealed her red eyes underneath.

"These are my memories," she said, and stuck her sword in the ground. I didn't know what it meant, but I guessed it meant that she had no intention to fight. It seemed like the virus had progressed a lot, but she was still maintaining consciousness.

"Please take care of everyone…and the future…A2."

I had met this No. 2 at the castle in the woods. As with the other No. 2s, I had crossed swords with her. But she was asking me a favor. Of all the people she could have picked, she picked me, her enemy. I had no obligation to listen, but I couldn't refuse.

I've killed infected comrades with my own hands. I couldn't refuse her request, when my comrades had asked the same thing of me. There was no way she knew, but the way she desperately heaved out the words was the spitting image of the comrade I had killed last.

After I told her I would, her expression melted into one of wholehearted satisfaction.

When I pulled out her sword, I understood what she meant when she said it was her memories. The technology hadn't existed when I was on the front lines, but the weapons that current YoRHa squadron troopers were issued could store memories.

I had heard that they were developing weapons with this feature. It was inspired by the fact that human memories were also stored in areas other than the brain. The technology wasn't limited to weapons—at the time they were developing clothes and shoes that could do the same.

Humanity left its records in various places. When it came to more personal records, at times humans would write on desks, walls, or even the palms of their hands instead of paper.

It's even said that humans had a habit of "learning with their hands." I had no idea how an appendage, with no capacity for memory, was able to store what it "learned."

Anyway, research and development had equipped weapons with the ability to store the memories of their users. I tried it out for myself; it was a decent feature.

I saw all the things she had seen, and heard all the things she had heard. I felt the pain she had felt. Her thoughts and feelings were absent, so the memories consisted of objective sensory experience in its purest form. So I didn't know what she had thought during the events I saw.

Within the memories, I noticed a name I felt nostalgic for: Anemone. At one point I had worked with the woman, who was part of the resistance. She was alive. Bringing me this news was enough for me to feel grateful to 2B. In return, I would grant her dying wish.

After the Bunker fell, 2B had endured the concentrated fire of her rampant comrades, become a decoy so 9S could escape, plunged into the flooded city, been infected by the virus, and found me, on the verge of death. This woman's memories and wishes…

I accepted all of it.

"Ah, Nines…"

Those were her last words. She looked back when she heard her name, grinned, and died.

I cut my hair with the sword she was impaled with, as a testament to accepting her memories and wishes. A tribute to the deceased, my doppelgänger.

From now on, I'll live in your image. That's the best I can do.

Right after that, the ground started to shake. A crack ran through the earth, and a giant object destroyed the area that I was in.

I saw something white sprout out of the dust clouds. It stretched endlessly into the sky. But I wasn't able to tell what it was.

Me, 2B's corpse, and 9S, who pounced at me with his sword, were swallowed into the fissure along with the crumbling bridges and rubble.

CH. 08: 9S'S STORY/PILGRIMAGE

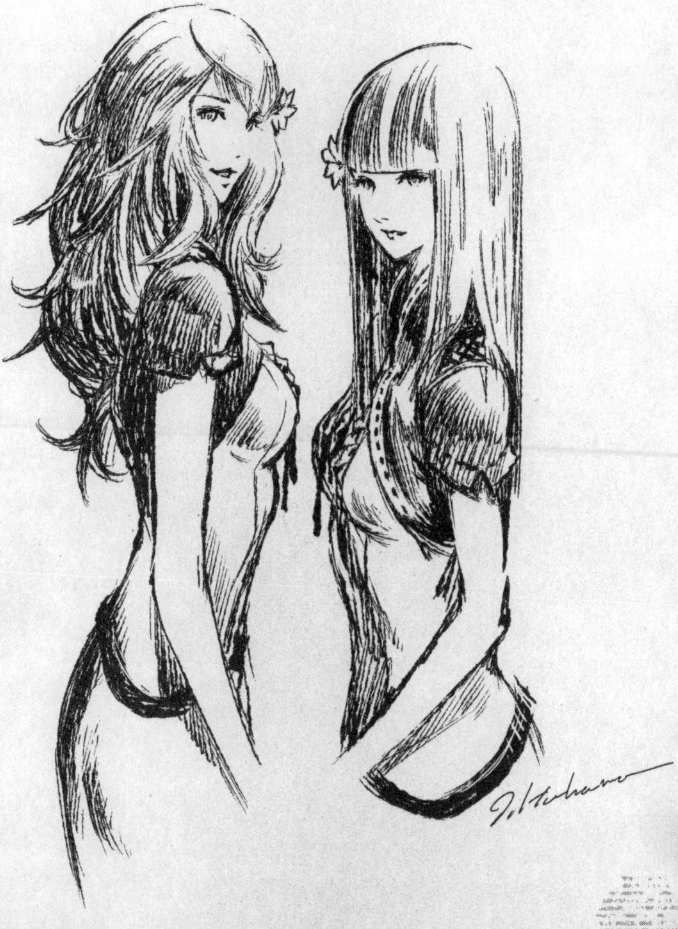

HE SAW A DREAM. A dream he didn't want to see. Rather lucid and unpleasant…his memories of reality.

After 9S was forcefully removed from battle, the flight unit had landed in the city ruins. Because the black-box response had previously rid the area of infected YoRHa squadron troopers and Machines alike, it had the least amount of enemy signals and was probably deemed to be the safest.

"Search for 2B's black-box signal!"

That was the first thing he had ordered after he landed. 2B's plan had been to be a decoy and let 9S escape. But 2B should have attempted an escape once 9S's flight unit had gone out of sight—if she hadn't been shot down.

"Report: 2B's black-box signal detected."

"Where? Give me the location data!"

But Pod did not display the map data.

"Warning: Significant vibrations detected. Underground support seems unstable. Possibility of a large-scale earthquake."

"So what?" replied an irritated 9S. "Where's the location data?!"

"Recommendation: Immediate evacuation."

"There's no way I would evacuate!"

The location data appeared. The commercial ruins. Good. It was close. 9S ran. He crossed the shallows, dove through weeds, and stumbled across rubble. Just as Pod had forewarned, the ground was trembling. He couldn't care less, and kept running.

He crossed a rope bridge draped across a deep canyon. 2B was right up ahead.

"There! 2B!"

It was her familiar ID signal and silhouette from the back. But she was not alone. She was with someone else.

"2B, are you…"

His feet froze. There was something protruding from 2B's back. Something red and pointed…

"Ah," 2B said as she looked back, impaled by a sword.

"No…2B…no…"

2B's body collapsed to the side. A2 held a blood-soaked sword. 2B lay motionless on the ground. He couldn't detect her signal.

"No!"

She had killed 2B. That old YoRHa model. A2.

His throat trembled uncontrollably. He was going to kill her. The rope bridge was swinging. He was going to kill her. He was going to kill her. He was going to kill—

The feeling of falling. He lost sight of A2. His body was slammed down. It became pitch-dark.

■ ■■

His dream abruptly ended, and the darkness cleared. Inside his bright field of vision was a red blob.

"Oh, it looks like he woke up, Devola."

The red blob split in two. Two redheads. If he remembered correctly, there were some androids with red hair.

"Good morning. You slept well, 9S."

"You know, sweetie, you've been out for two weeks."

This voice. He remembered—Devola and Popola. The twin androids who did odd jobs at the resistance camp. They aren't wearing casts today, 9S thought absentmindedly. These two were constantly wounded, and plastered themselves with casts and bandages all the time.

"Be grateful that I found you, okay?" teased Devola.

2B had told him earlier that Devola's scanner had helped her enormously when searching for 9S when he had been abducted by Adam. 2B…

He almost relapsed into the nightmare. That was a dream. A bad dream. 9S stood up.

"Where's 2B?"

Popola averted her gaze without a word. Devola's jaunty expression disappeared, turning grim.

"You should know, shouldn't you?"

This place was not a part of the dream. It was the resistance camp, in reality.

"Her black-box signal is…gone."

"I see."

It wasn't a dream. A2 had killed 2B. Since the Bunker was gone, neither a spare chassis nor personal data backup was obtainable. A body to return to, and memories to return…were all gone.

Was this death? He couldn't tell. He couldn't think clearly. His mind lagged as the scene in front of him and his memories diverged. Words were the only thing that skimmed along his consciousness.

The truth was so surreal, it felt like he was seeing through someone else's eyes. Pod popped into his field of vision.

"Devola and Popola-type androids are rare models specialized for treatment and maintenance. Prediction that with the absence of the Bunker, without their help 9S's repair would have proved difficult."

He couldn't understand anything he was told.

"Recommendation: Gratitude."

Ah, yes, that was true.

"Thanks."

Really? Was he thanking them? He didn't know. Nothing mattered, and he felt dejected.

"There were a lot of our type in the past," Devola said, handing 9S his goggles.

Perhaps everything looked different because his goggles were off.

"Apparently, we were in charge of managing a large system."

It was no use. Putting on the goggles made no difference. Even the familiar resistance camp looked washed-out.

"What do you mean by apparently?"

He held back his despair, and questioned in a mechanical tone.

"Our memories from that time were erased, so we don't know what happened. Our model…went rampant and caused an accident in the past. Most of our peers were rescinded after that."

He was hearing the words, and probably understanding them as well, but they did not settle within him. He was thankful that he didn't have to talk.

"We weren't rescinded because…"

This time Popola spoke.

"We're being watched, so that we don't lose control again."

Accident. Rampage. Watch. Any other time he would have loved to investigate further.

"An overactive curiosity is a bad habit."

He heard 2B's words in his head. Clearly, and very realistically.

"But thanks to that, we're able to save comrades like you. That's our way of atoning for our sins."

Devola's voice was distant. Even though she was right in front of him. It was strange. Devola and Popola were standing next to him, yet their voices were not as clear as the absent 2B's voice in his head.

Where was he? Was the ground he stood on real?

"Don't push yourself too hard, 9S."

Hearing Popola's words from behind, 9S realized that he had stood up and started to walk away.

■ ■■

"What is...this?"

After leaving the resistance camp, 9S stared up at the object in awe. Normally, there was only sky where he looked because there were no buildings in the crater zone.

But there was a strangely shaped "thing" extending toward the sky, looking like a twisted white cylinder.

"A massive structure originating from the underground cave."

Pod seemed to have interpreted his utterance as a question, and gave an answer.

"Speculated to be the doing of the Machines, but details are unavailable."

"Ma...chines..."

They were the culprits behind infiltrating the server, infected YoRHa squadron troopers, and destroying the Bunker.

9S ran toward the crater zone. *I'll destroy them*, he thought. A2 had destroyed 2B, but the Machines were responsible for making that a final death. If there had been a spare chassis and personal data backup, 2B could have returned to life...

"What happened during the two weeks I was asleep?"

9S asked Pod as he ran. Popola had said, "You know sweetie, you've been out for two weeks." He could guess how severe the damage was. 9S only remembered up until he had screamed in fury.

"Report: An earthquake manifested along with the appearance of the massive structure. 9S was affected by the collapse of the ground, and plummeted into the resulting valley. Both chassis and system were damaged."

"Valley? Devola came all the way there?"

"Hypothesis: She was there to acquire region-specific materials."

He had heard that the odd jobs Devola and Popola took up were tasks that were dangerous, required distant expeditions, or were in general things nobody else wanted to do.

That's our way of atoning for our sins.

They were most likely referring to the "accident" they had mentioned earlier. But to 9S they seemed too remorseful. Had their sins been that grave? Had it not been his imagination that the other androids treated the pair with a certain coolness?

Regardless, even if he knew the answer, he wouldn't be able to help the twins. Perhaps their punishment was too severe for their sins, but if the twins desired that punishment, there was nothing he could do.

"And, where's A2?"

The location of the enemy 9S wanted to punish the most. It was invaluable information.

"Current location, as well as operational status, is unconfirmed."

"Roger that."

On one hand 9S wanted her to be dead, and on the other he wanted her alive. He wanted to kill A2 with his own hands. The vague status of the report probably took his feelings into account.

His lips felt out of place. The corners of his mouth were pointing up. There was nothing funny, but he was smiling. But 9S earnestly thought that it was appropriate.

■　■■

The massive structure that appeared in the crater zone was not the only one. There was one structure so high that it punctured the clouds, and three surrounding structures not as tall. The smaller structures were cone shaped, looking like horns growing out of the ground. Running down a debris-filled slope, 9S made his way toward the central structure. He ignored the cone-shaped counterparts. The differences in height surely signified differences in importance.

"Transport mechanism detected inside the protruding portion of the massive structure."

"Transport? Is it an elevator?"

"Affirmative."

If the Machines had taken the time to construct an elevator, that meant that the structure was meant to be climbed up and down. 9S briefly wondered what the purpose of the building was, but the thought disappeared right away. Either way, he was going to destroy it. What was the point of understanding its purpose?

But it didn't go as smoothly as planned. Reasonably, but the structure was surrounded by a barrier. Since it wasn't penetrable by force, 9S tried to hack the wall, but this again was thwarted easily. Then a high-pitched voice, almost as if it were mocking 9S, was broadcasted down on him.

"Hello! This is the Tower System Service"

The manner of speech reminded 9S of an impudent child. The voice was higher than that of an adult woman. Now that he thought about it, it sounded similar to the "little girl" and "boy (prepubescent)" voice samples that research and development had been working on.

"We apologize. To access the main unit of the Tower system, please unlock the subunits. We apologize for the trouble, thank you for your cooperation."

It seemed like the massive structure in the middle was called the main unit, and the surrounding cone-shaped structures were called the subunits.

"Question: Why would the Machines make such an announcement?"

"There's no logic behind what they do."

It was stupid, but if he couldn't force his way through, he had to follow their steps. 9S took out his sword and slashed the so-called subunit. Along with a strong electrical discharge, his sword bounced back.

"Hello! This is the Tower System Service. An access key is needed to access the subunits. Unfortunately, we are unable to give you access."

The voice was amused. It reminded him of the Machine that had possessed 6O at the Bunker and repeated, "This is so fun. This is so fun…"

"As compensation, for our first-time users, we will provide a complimentary tour of the resource recovery unit."

9S felt a noise. Neither a transmission nor display, it was an uncomfortable feeling, like his mind had been grazed with sandpaper.

"We look forward to your next visit, from the bottom of our hearts."

"What was that…"

9S held his temples.

"A forced transmission from the enemy system. Transferred the location of the so-called resource recovery unit."

Pod displayed the location data. The same thing was displayed on 9S's goggles. So apparently he would have to get the access key from this place and access the three subunits before the main unit was unlocked.

"They're playing with me…"

Even though he resented having to play along with the Machines, with no method of destroying the structures from the outside he had to infiltrate and destroy them from the inside. 9S sighed deeply.

"To the forest kingdom, for now."

That was the location of the resource recovery unit. He wanted to get the steps over with to destroy the tower in the crater zone.

"Recommendation: Meet with the resistance troops and review available directives."

"Directives? Who cares?"

He was going to exterminate the Machines, and kill A2. Nobody had directed him to do so, it was something he had decided for himself.

■ ■■

9S passed through the commercial ruins, and entered the forest kingdom. It hadn't been long since he had been here with 2B. Since their pointless conversation.

"How about this. Once it's peaceful, let's go shopping together. I'll even buy a T-shirt that looks good on you, 2B."

"A T-shirt?"

"Oh, you don't want it?"

"No… When that day comes, let's go."

"Really?! It's a promise!"

"Yeah."

He hadn't been serious. And 2B probably hadn't been either. It was just unimaginable for the fighting to end and for it to be peaceful. But he had looked forward, just a little bit, to the possibility of that happening. For humans to come back to Earth and reconstruct the commercial district. For humans and androids to coexist and walk through the city… Just thinking about it made him giddy.

Would 2B get mad if he chose a T-shirt with an awful design? Would she look embarrassed? Or would she…laugh? He wanted to make 2B laugh one day. He wanted to see 2B roll on the ground, laughing her heart out.

But humans would never come back to Earth. And 2B had died. The YoRHa squadron had fallen, and the fighting still continued. Nothing had changed—but then again, everything had changed.

9S shot down a Machine that jumped out to attack with Pod's artillery. It was a survivor of the forest kingdom.

"Revenge f0r 0ur k1ng…"

Other Machines pounced at him from between the trees. It was A2, not 9S, that had killed their king, but it probably made no difference to them.

"1'll k1ll y0u!"

He hacked the persistent Machines, and made them explode.

" 'I'll kill you'? That's my line."

"Worthless Machines," he mumbled. Machines taking revenge? It was so absurd it almost made him laugh…

Once he was on high ground, he saw a floating, building-like structure. It was deformed, covered in bulges, and of a gray, leaden color.

"Is that?"

"Affirmative: Believed to be the so-called resource-recovery unit. Unlike the massive structure in the crater zone, it seems to be distributing something."

"What do you mean something?"

"Hypothesis: A type of resource, but details are unavailable."

Since it was called the resource recovery unit, if it was collecting and distributing anything other than resources, it would be a misleading name indeed. It was however, possible that what the Machines considered "resources" could be, to androids, nothing but a pile of garbage.

"I wonder what they're going to use the collected resources for?"

"Unknown."

He wasn't really curious, so he didn't mind if it was unknown. He was going to destroy it anyway.

He remembered that he used to have a fascination with Machines, even though they ended up being just another thing he would destroy. Why had he been so eager to study them? He wasn't sure, even though the question was about himself.

As he approached the resource recovery unit, an announcement came out of nowhere. It was the same voice he had heard in the crater zone. Indiscernible as a little girl's or little boy's voice, it was nevertheless a foolish-sounding voice.

"Hostile android approaching. Switching to self-defense mode."

The resource recovery unit, which had been erratically moving through the air, suddenly stopped. The bulges on the wall began to loudly change shape. They kept changing shape without an endpoint, as if they were playing around.

On top of that, a part of the shifting wall expanded to reveal an opening that looked something like an entrance. As if it were taunting him to come inside. *What self-defense mode?* he thought bitterly.

"Are these…patterns? Characters?"

Right above the doorlike opening, there were some symbols inscribed into the wall. They were roughly the same size, distinctly shaped, and evenly spaced.

"Answer: They are characters of angelic script, an ancient alphabet."

So he had been right when he thought they looked like characters.

"The characters in question spell out the words: 'meat box.'"

"What does that mean?"

"Unknown."

"I know. There's no logic behind what they do."

They fight, kill, and mimic—all irrationally. These words were probably meaninglessly inscribed as well.

When he went inside, his suspicions were further confirmed. There were enemies stationed in various places, but that was the same as the factory ruins and forest kingdom. Arbitrarily placed enemies were defeated to move forward. The androids were asked to repeat the same action every time.

But unlike the factory ruins and forest kingdom, the inside of the meat box was rather clamorous. The attacking Machines kept making hideous noises.

"Reven... Revengee!"

"0w0w0wOw0wOwOw"

"I... d0n't wanna... d1e"

"1t hurts 1t hurts... hurts... hurt..."

9S kicked over their bodies that were filled with holes from Pod's artillery.

"How could a Machine be hurting."

The cylindrical remains rolled down the spiral staircase. That was irritating too.

"1 d0n't want to d1e d0n't want to d1e d0n't want to d1e!"

Every last one of them, thought 9S. Couldn't they attack more quietly? They weren't even that strong.

"1'm scared scared scared scared scared"

Shut up. Shut up! Shut up!

9S started to shout, wanting to drown out the meaningless noises. He shouted while fighting, took turns shouting and fighting, and made his way up the floors.

This was what he'd been doing this whole time. Destroying Machines. That was all, but why did he feel so aggravated?

"Shut up! Be quiet! Die!"

Why did he feel so empty? The only difference was whether or not 2B was next to him.

Eventually, as all things come to an end, the fighting inside the structure also ceased. He had reached the roof.

It was painfully bright, perhaps because he had been fighting in dim light. As he squinted and looked around, he saw something being sucked out from the inside of the building and distributed toward the sky.

"Are those…Machine parts?"

Countless metal parts spiraled around like a tornado, rising and disappearing into the sky. They were being distributed toward the crater zone.

"Hypothesis: Resources for the massive structure. Or perhaps resources to create a weapon."

Collecting the remains of fallen comrades in battle and transporting them to the massive tower in the crater zone;—that was what this facility was used for, if Pod's hypothesis was correct.

If so, what was the point of leaving the access key in a place like this? Leaving an object that would help destroy the massive structure in a facility made to gather materials to maintain the massive structure. It was contradictory, to say the least.

"Help. Please, help."

It was the voice of a child. There was a glowing orb on the middle of the roof. The wavering voice was coming from it.

"What's that?"

"Answer: Core. The entity that controls this facility. In other words, the brains of this facility."

The voice repeated its pleas for help. The whole time, bits and pieces of Machines were still being dragged out and pulled across the sky.

"Help me... I'm scared... Help..."

They could say whatever they wanted. They were Machines. The words they said were predetermined. It wasn't like this one was in fear and pleading for its life. It was just playing a prerecorded sound according to its program.

"Energy charged. Close firing mode, full power."

Pod transformed. 9S pointed at the core. Pod started to say, "9S..." like it was trying to stop him, but 9S ignored it.

"Shoot."

The white laser emitted by Pod burned through the core. The ground shook. Shock waves passed through the whole resource recovery unit. But the waves passed and it quickly quieted down.

"Report: Obtained the access key from the destroyed core."

Leaving something necessary to destroy the system in a facility used to maintain the same system—the only reason he could think of for why this contradiction existed was to play with him.

"Worthless Machines," spat out 9S. He turned around. There were still two remaining resource recovery units. He needed to get to them as soon as possible.

■ ■■

9S was torn between heading first to the flooded city or to the amusement park ruins. After some consideration, he chose the flooded city, while the transfer devices could still be used.

While the road to the amusement park ruins had been shattered, there were multiple routes, and it was close to the crater zone. On the other hand, there was only one route to the flooded city, which was through the underground waterway. There was a possibility that the dilapidated waterway could collapse. And now that the research and development team had dissolved, he wasn't sure how much longer the transfer device would be serviceable.

That had been his reasoning, but perhaps it was just a hunch. There were some disintegrating remains of a flight unit in the shallows, stuck nose first into the sand. Something struck him the moment he saw the debris.

"Pod, is this…"

Various parts had been melted from high heat and bullets had disfigured the frame. But there was no mistaking this unit. Not this one.

"Affirmative: YoRHa squadron trooper 2B's ID detected among this unit's remains."

2B had landed here. That meant that she had made her way through the underground waterway into the city ruins, followed the shrubbery along the flooded city, and crossed the bridge…to end up at the forest clearing.

If only he had gotten 2B's location data earlier. He might have been able to catch 2B while she was still here. At least, before 2B had crossed the bridge…no, maybe even just before she had run into A2… He didn't want to think about what had happened after that.

"Report: Unsent transmission detected from the flight unit's memory storage."

9S heard a familiar voice after he told Pod to play the transmission.

"…This is YoRHa squadron trooper…2B. If anyone is listening to this…I'd like you to pass…something on. If you…see YoRHa…squadron trooper 9S…I'd like to tell him…"

Whether because of damage to the memory storage device, or from poor conditions during the actual recording, the transmission suddenly cut off. Right as he thought the message was over, 2B's voice became audible again over the static.

"…I apologize. The message for him is…9S, the days I spent with you… were like rays of sunshine…in…my…life. Th…ank…you…Ni…nez."

9S was frozen in place.

"That is all," Pod said.

Pod's attempt at spurring 9S did not work. He was still unable to move.

"2B… She called me Nines…"

He wished he had heard her say it in person. How he wished he could hear a living 2B call him Nines in an animated voice, instead of over a static-filled transmission.

2B was no longer here. 2B was no longer anywhere in this world. He was struck by reality. By none other than 2B's own voice.

His vision blurred. His vocal chords trembled. *What a pointless thing to do*, he thought. He told himself there were more important things to do. Destroy every last one of the Machines, and kill A2.

9S stood up, and headed toward the resource recovery unit. He ran. He sprinted. He didn't want to waste a minute—no, not even a second—in destroying the Machines.

But inside of the building labeled "soul box" in angelic script, it was completely silent.

"There are…no enemies?"

The facility was constructed identically to the meat box, out of Machine parts. It also had an atrium, and an elevator used to travel up and down the building. Only the variously stationed Machines were missing.

"Is this elevator broken? Ah, they're telling me to hack it."

He was slowly starting to understand the enemy's childlike tendencies. As expected, after he hacked and disarmed the system's security, the elevator began to move.

Again, the next floor was devoid of enemies, and only accommodated a hacking point. It was intentionally made to look like a treasure chest and placed conspicuously in the center of the room. They were stubbornly foolish.

Furthermore, the treasure chest did not only serve as system security, but actually contained "treasure"—information—inside.

The first treasure chest contained blueprints for the tower in the crater zone. The tower was not simply a monument, nor solely a trap for androids. It had an exit portal, which also served as a launchpad.

At that size? And it was obviously not for intercontinental launches, but rather designed for ships capable of escaping Earth's gravity well.

"Is it aimed at the moon? A massive cannon aimed at the human server?"

He looked at Pod. He wanted it to reject his hypothesis. Even if humans were extinct, their genetic profile data was stored on the moon. If that was destroyed then absolutely nothing would remain of humans.

"Due to lack of information, neither denial nor affirmation is possible."

"Shit."

If he explored the other floors, he might be able to find the rest of the information. 9S entered the elevator.

But the enemy was not so generous as to give him the information that he wanted. That was how enemies operated. The next treasure chest was a prime example.

As soon as he deactivated the security system, he was exposed to information he did not want to see—information related to YoRHa androids.

"A black box?"

The black box was a powerful energy source, and true to its name, not even the squadron troopers knew its origins. Not even Type S androids, who were directed to perform research. That was why 9S never even thought about what a black box was composed of.

"That can't be…?!"

It might be misinformation. To unsettle him. That was the only explanation.

"The YoRHa squadron black boxes are made from Machine cores?"

That was impossible. It couldn't be. To think he was made from his own enemies. 9S kicked the chest aside in fury. The enemy wanted to rattle him. Even now, there was probably one of those clowns watching him, snickering at his every move.

He moved on to the next floor, reminding himself not to be fooled so easily. Technically speaking, all the information was given to him by the enemy. He was at fault for believing them. The information regarding the launchpad was dubious as well.

He hacked the next chest, this time determined to stop being so gullible. The usual white expanse enveloped him. He disengaged the program's attack mechanism, and waited for the security to deactivate.

"Huh? That's weird."

Did this treasure chest have better security than the others? 9S started to roam through the white virtual circuit dimension. At times a black wall would appear, but it was easy to destroy. The security didn't seem like it was meant to keep him out.

"What is this…"

9S stared at his own hand. Something was off. While hacking in the circuit dimension, one's physical body was never visible. Instead it was displayed as a shape or signal, while the enemy's program was displayed as a black sphere or cylinder. This was done to optimize the hacking process, making program invasion and subroutine destruction of the program more efficient.

But right now 9S could see himself. He could see the arms and legs he was used to seeing. And if he had a mirror he would most likely see the face he was used to seeing in real life.

"What is this dimension?"

The white walls abruptly turned into screens, flooded with various images.

"Are these…my memories?"

Memories of his first flight unit training, his first Earth descent mission, his first encounter with a Machine, his first time meeting with 2B…

"Why are my memories here? Why do they know all of this?"

He briskly walked through the white passageway. There was a white door. He reached for it. It was unlocked.

Through the door was a large room—so large that he was unable to tell how far it extended. He could see human silhouettes in the center of the room. Clothed in black, they were…women.

"2B?"

He rushed toward them to check. Of course, they were not 2B in the flesh. They were her data. In the blink of an eye, he was surrounded by 2Bs.

"You don't have to use honorifics when you say my name."

"It's forbidden to have emotions."

"I admire your passion for knowledge."

"9S… Come on. Let's go home."

These were definitely 9S's memories. He was being counterhacked. He had thought he was doing the hacking, but he'd allowed the enemy to invade his mind.

A black shadow materialized in the center of the room. It was the enemy that had counterhacked him. The shadow swallowed 2B's data, one piece after another.

"Stop!"

The shadow persisted. It ate his memories of 2B: the look that she made when she was confused, the rare moments when she expressed anger, and the time she looked back at him.

"Stop it!"

He hurled himself onto the shadow.

"Don't invade my memories!"

He held down the shadow and constricted him. He was beating down the enemy that had tried to take his precious treasures away.

"Don't mess with my memories."

In a flash, he found himself holding a sword. He stabbed the shadow over and over and over.

He straddled the shadow, and continued to stab it. He realized that the shadow had 2B's face. Even then, he kept stabbing it. Red liquid sprayed out.

"This is…my memory!"

This is my memory. This 2B is mine and mine only. 2B is mine…

He kept stabbing until its chest was a mangled mess. When he looked down, his hands were covered—not in red liquid, but instead with a black and viscid substance. The enemy he had been stabbing was not 2B. It was the core of the soul box.

9S stood up. He heard the sword clatter to the floor.

What was I doing?

The back of his throat trembled. Laughter welled up.

I'll kill anyone that hurts 2B. I'll kill anyone that touches 2B. I'll kill anyone that comes near 2B. I'll kill anyone that looks at 2B. The only one allowed to look at 2B is me. The only one allowed to come near 2B is me. The only one allowed to touch 2B is me. The only one allowed to hurt 2B is me. The only…

His laughter didn't stop. Standing there, bent over, 9S kept laughing.

■ ■■

After leaving the flooded city, 9S temporarily returned to the resistance camp. His close combat fighting management system had been severely damaged, and he was having trouble with sustained fighting. He couldn't even draw his sword.

Devola and Popola took one glance at 9S, then screeched in horror. He was apparently in gruesome condition. Before Pod could give an explanation, Devola and Popola detected the damaged areas and dove into repairs—as expected for androids specialized in maintenance.

9S ignored Devola, who had told him to rest a little bit, and made to leave the resistance camp. At the gate, he heard Popola's voice calling from behind him.

"Hey 9S. Don't try to die on your own."

"I know," was all he answered. *It's not like I'm trying to die*, he thought. At the very least he would stay alive until he destroyed the Machines and killed A2. If he died first, he wouldn't be able to kill them.

He never thought he would have such a strong intent to kill and destroy. He had thought that since Type S androids were not suited for battle, they would have less of a thirst for blood. Maybe that's what he wanted to think. Perhaps he had held himself back with the excuse that he lacked battle skills—the same way he had held back his feelings for 2B.

2B had died, and there was no longer a need for him to hold back. He didn't have to hide his thoughts or his desires for 2B. 2B would never know about them.

The moment he realized this, he lost self-control. He was unable to control anything. He could feel everything bursting. Everything shameful and dirty that he had pent up flowed out of him, bit by bit.

Like I care, 9S thought as he walked. He emerged from the underground waterway, passed through the partly busted gates of the amusement park, and cut through the square where there were no longer any Machines.

"Hostile android approaching. Switching to self-defense mode."

"Again?" spat 9S. He had heard the same phrase three times, and it was getting to him. Even if he knew this was the last time, it didn't change the fact that it was irritating.

And again, the entrance had angelic script inscribed above. This uninspired process exasperated him.

"Pod, what about these words?"

"Answer: labeled as 'god box.'"

"God? How dare the Machines use such a word."

It was offensive for the plebeian Machines to mention God. God was an entity humans worshipped, a being of the highest order. It was unacceptable for scraps of metal to speak of God when even humans had occasionally hesitated to do so.

He would destroy every last remaining one of them. And in the most excruciating ways possible.

Once he infiltrated the facility, he was met with the same interior, with Machines that he was tired of seeing. This time, there was no treasure chest. As a result, he wasn't distracted by any questionable information.

He hijacked the Machines by hacking, made them fight each other, and they exploded. 2B had been infected by a virus, showered by bullets from other YoRHa-type androids, and killed by A2. 9S wanted the enemy to experience something similar.

This was the only time he wished that Machines had emotions. He wanted them to feel the trauma of getting attacked by comrades and the anguish of being betrayed by their trusted allies.

He wanted to hear the Machines genuinely cower and wail in fear, instead of simply playing prerecorded audio...

"Report: Excessive fighting strains the chassis."

Pod interrupted his flow, its warning irking 9S.

"Shut up!"

Strain on the chassis? Did he care? But Pod was being unusually stubborn.

"Negative: This support program functions as an assistant to 9S. It reserves the right to concern itself with its user's well-being."

Its nagging bothered him. It reminded him of someone.

"Do what you want!"

He yelled, and left the area. No matter how fast he walked, or how abruptly he started to sprint, Pod followed suit. Even if he knew that was the nature of Pods, he still hated it.

9S made it a point to stomp loudly as he stormed into the elevator. More than anything, he loathed the way he acted so childishly.

■ ■■

In front of the core installed on the roof was an enemy he did not expect. It was not a Machine. It was an android.

"Operator..."

It was Operator 21O, who had been assigned to aid 9S. Normally identical to the other YoRHa types, her eyes glowed red. But her appearance was different from how 9S remembered. She was in battle uniform.

"Why is there an operator model here?"

"Inspecting: Operator 21O. In the previous descent battle, by her own volition decided to convert to Type B. Newly appointed as 21B, she was stationed on the front lines, and four hours later reported missing."

"No…"

Before the previous descent battle took place, 9S had been nullifying the enemy's aerial defense system on Earth.

During battle, please stay as far away from the field as possible.

A scanner model like yourself is not suited for battle.

21O's words flooded back to him. Right after their exchange, 21O became 21B, and descended to Earth.

Because he had replied with a mischievous answer like, "Aw, are you worried about me?" 21O had coolly said, "No, you would only be a burden on the battlefield." But in reality 9S knew that she worried for him. She always did…

Simultaneously, he was filled with a feeling of rabid hate toward the Machines that purposefully made 21B guard the core of the "god box."

The Machine that had invaded the Bunker had no doubt been eavesdropping on 21O and 9S. From that, they knew she was an individual that 9S trusted, and deliberately planted her as an enemy. They probably expected 9S to be conflicted, to fight under immense stress and confusion, and eventually succumb at her hands. They probably planned to watch him struggle, and laugh at him for doing so.

Like I'd let them, he thought. 9S attacked with no mercy.

"Pod! Support with maximum-power fire!"

It had not been long since 21B converted to Type B. She was most likely thrown on the front lines with little training, and was probably unfamiliar with the equipment and behavior of a Type B. If he could exploit that weakness, even as a Type S, he had a chance against her.

"Please…refrain from conversation irrelevant…t0 the m1ss1on."

He almost stopped at the words that spilled out of 21B's mouth.

"A single confirmation…is…en0ugh…"

She was only reciting phrases that lingered in her memory. *Don't falter*, he told himself.

"Please…kill me…"

9S widened his eyes. 21B's hand was shaking as it held her sword. It was unclear whether 21O's consciousness was the cause, or if the enemy was intentionally dragging out 21O's consciousness.

"Operator… It's okay! It'll be okay!"

He readied his sword and charged. His loathing of Machines galvanized him.

"I'll kill you…now!"

He heard a scream. But 9S was unable to tell anymore if it was his or 21O's.

ANOTHER SIDE "A2"

"Good morning, A2."

The moment I opened my eyes, I was baffled by the greeting from the rectangular box. I thought I was still dreaming. But I've seen this talking box before. When I met No. 2 and No. 9 at the forest castle, this box was floating next to them. It had transmitted that revolting voice. That woman that said whatever she wanted, about how I was a traitor and that I was a dangerous android.

Just thinking about it made me annoyed, so I was planning on ignoring the box.

"I am support unit Pod 042. I will assist YoRHa android A2 with artillery support."

"I didn't ask for that."

"Affirmative: I did not receive an order from A2. This action was directed by the previous user, 2B, as a final directive."

"Don't worry about it."

"YoRHa android A2 does not have the right to decline."

Eventually I got tired of resisting and let the box do whatever it wanted. But it was really a useless box in terms of its so-called "support." When I asked it about the identity of the strange fissure-inducing structure, the only thing it said was, "Unclear, but speculated to be the Machines' doing." Even when I asked it about the whereabouts of 2B's corpse or 9S, it echoed "Unable to answer."

If anything, its artillery function was useful. Since I didn't have the means to perform long-range attacks, it conveniently diversified my attack maneuvers, though I was fed up with it trying to act like it was doing me a favor, saying things like, "Recommendation: Gratitude to this support unit for providing the user with long-range attack capabilities."

■　■■

6669727374206d656574696e672077697468682050617363616c

I was furious. I was perpetually enraged at the Machines that killed my comrades. So much so that I was unable to restrain myself from killing them. That's
why, when I met this one, I had planned on killing it immediately. I declared, "I'll have
you pay for the sin of killing my comrades."

"Is that right? Then it cannot be helped, if doing so will appease you."

Despite being a Machine, that's how it answered, with surprisingly sophisticated diction. It was slightly bowing its head, waiting patiently for my sword to be
swung down. A somewhat unsettled feeling overcame me.

"You are not going to kill me?" it asked in a bewildered voice.

"Shut up," I told it, shooing it away. It informed me that its name was Pascal,
and after saying, "Thank you very much," it flew off.

Thank you? A Machine using words of gratitude? A lowly Machine?

It upset me even more…that I spared a Machine.

■　■■

5265756e6974656420776974686820416e656d6f6e65

"No. 2… You're alive."

Anemone's reaction to our reunion was just how I imagined—that Anemone
would make the same face I did when I first discovered Anemone was still alive.

I had been living with the guilt that I was the only one who survived out of my
comrades. Anemone had most likely felt the same way.

Anemone and I had carried out a mission together. It was during the enemy
server destruction plan, on Oahu, in the Pacific. It was a battle also known as the
Pearl Harbor Descent Attack. There, both Anemone and I lost allies. We sent what
seemed like an endless number of rescue requests to Command. But none were
acknowledged, and our comrades fell one by one. Eventually I had lost all my

comrades in the YoRHa squadron, and Anemone had lost all her comrades in the resistance. At that point Anemone and I had been operating separately, and we must have both assumed that we were the last one standing.

Then I uncovered the truth, and fled the battlefield.

Command had been planning on abandoning us from the start. We were an experimental fleet with the purpose of providing battle data until the last member died.

It seemed Anemone was not aware of this fact. That was better for her. If she found out, she would not be able to forgive. She would not be able to forgive Command, which ruthlessly abandoned its troops on the front lines.

"That's right, No. 2. There's a YoRHa that's identical to you. Her name is 2B, and…"

"She died."

"What?"

"I killed her. She was infected by a logic virus."

"I see."

Anemone fell silent. She was being considerate, and I was grateful. Anemone and I had both executed comrades that were infected by logic viruses. To minimize their misery and allow them to die while they were in control of their consciousness…that was why we killed them. There were no words that could console us.

Sensing that it was probably better to wrap up conversations about the past, I decided to cut straight to the point. I asked her if she could spare me a fuel filter. My filter was clogged from fighting in the desert.

Until now, I had been foraging parts off of the corpses of my pursuers when I needed repairs or replacements. The parts weren't specific to my chassis, so I looked shoddy, but functionally there was no problem.

But now all the YoRHa androids were infected by the virus. If I used an infected part, I would be infected as well. That's why I decided to ask my longtime acquaintance for a favor.

But the resistance camp was out of stock. If I wasn't able to procure the part here, there was nowhere else I could go. As I debated on what to do, Anemone suggested something unbelievable.

"Pascal's village makes fuel filters, so you should go get one from him."

"Pascal…"

"Ah, you know him."

"An enemy!"

"His village is an exception. They won't harm us."

"But…still…"

"We formed an alliance with them, and exchange resources when necessary. If you need something, you don't have many options. And…"

"And?"

"We're not so heartless as to kill enemies who meet us under white flags."

Even if it was Anemone speaking, I didn't feel like I could follow this particular piece of advice…but…

"Warning: A defective fuel filter can cause severe problems during fuel combustion. Recommendation: Immediate replacement."

I knew that already. At this rate, I would be impaired in battle. I could already feel some impairments in normal activities as well.

My joints were stiff and difficult to move. As a result, I was drained from merely walking. My head hurt too. At first there was just a dull pain at my left temple, but that eventually spread to the back and top of my head. The pain grew to the point where it throbbed like there was a jagged piece of metal being twisted into my skull.

"Determined the coordinates of the colony led by the Machine Pascal. Location marked on the map."

I felt invaded. I had been read like a book. I had been thinking of visiting the village, if there were any chance to avoid being useless in battle. Anemone had said this was an "exception," so perhaps I could take exception as well…

50617363616c277320766973697420756f207468652076696c6c616765

It was a village full of Machines. It was eerie to see Machines that didn't attack at first sight, and in turn I couldn't get myself riled up to destroy them either. No, I was probably reluctant to draw my sword because I wasn't feeling well. That had to be it.

"You are that person who… Thank you for sparing me back then."

I rarely saw a Machine twice, because that meant I had failed to kill it. But I had never been thanked by one. Maybe that was why, but even when Pascal inquired with a puzzled, "Um…" I was still too astonished to talk. Then, all of a sudden, the box beside me started to blabber.

"Explanation: YoRHa android A2's fuel filter is damaged. Action: Obtained information from the resistance camp leader, Anemone. Objective: Visit this region to acquire filter. Request: Fuel filter."

"Ah, I see. So that was the case. The thing is, right now we are out of the rigid bark we use to create filters. Recently there have been violent Machines around the harvesting area."

"Affirmative: Collection and delivery of rigid bark."

The box had explained the situation and negotiated of its own accord. I was extremely upset, but my condition from the damaged filter was getting worse. I had no choice but to cooperate and retrieve the so-called rigid bark.

426164204d616368696e65

"Report: Hostility toward peace-advocating Machine, Pascal, was determined to be ineffective from a cost-benefit standpoint. Recommendation: Immediate initiation of a friendly relationship."

"Friendly? You have to be kidding me."

Peace-advocating? What did a Machine know about peace? This was just an exception. This was an emergency due to an unforeseen accident. I had no intention of playing along and being "friends" with a Machine.

That was why I told Pascal, "I'll help you if you need anything," after I returned to normal condition. If I didn't do anything in return, I would be in debt to a Machine.

"Actually, there is something you can help me with. Recently, a violent Machine has been kidnapping the children from their playground. I apologize for being so brash, but I would like you to do away with that Machine. You are the only one I can count on. Please."

To think that a Machine would ask me to exterminate another Machine. At any rate, destroying the supposed "violent Machine" was hardly a challenge for me. It was convenient for me that I could pay off my debt so easily.

"Ah, thank you very much! You got rid of that robot for us! Please, accept this humble reward. Now, now, don't be shy!"

I had destroyed the Machine to repay my debt, but this reward indebted me yet again. No matter how many times I tried to decline, or say that I wasn't trying to be polite, Pascal kept stuffing potions and materials into my arms.

"We are peace advocates. We despise fighting, so we built this village. But ever since we discarded our weapons, we haven't had the means to defend ourselves against powerful enemies."

The Machine at the harvesting area for the rigid bark, and the "violent Machine" I had just destroyed, fell rather quickly to my sword. The Machines in this village were unable to defend themselves from enemies of such caliber. Machines, responsible for the death of my comrades, were being terrorized by the threat of other Machines. The sight of that was extremely strange, comical, and even sad in a way… Sad? Why would I think it was sad?

"Within the village, there are individuals that believe the best way to perpetuate peace is to destroy all our enemies…Ms. A2, what should we do?"

"I don't know. Shouldn't you, Pascal, be the one that decides that?"

I had no answer. That's why I had hastily redirected the question back to him. Destroy enemies in the name of peace… It was hypocritical. I couldn't come up with an answer. But. But I…

"Ms. A2. If it's all right with you, you should stay and explore the village a little. I want you to know more about this village."

I told Pascal that I would if I felt like it, and turned my back. I was already out of the village before I realized I had forgotten to return the reward.

4c6f76656420627920206368696c6472656e20616e6420636f6e667573656
42061626f757420776879

"Hey hey! B1g s1s!"

"B-big sis?!"

"Let's play! Play w1th us!"

"I don't have time to play with Machines."

"N0O! Play! Play w1th us!"

As soon as I set foot in the village, I was swarmed by Machine brats. I came back because I felt guilty that I hadn't returned the favor.

No matter how much I pushed them away and shunned them, the brats squealed in delight and followed me.

"I'm an android, your enemy. I'm going to destroy you if you don't listen to what I say!"

"Ahhh! s0 fun!"

"Why does that make you happy…"

"B1g s1s, more!"

Big sis. Hearing that phrase suddenly brought back a memory.

A long time ago, the resistance I had fought beside called themselves a family. At the time I had no concept of family, and seeing the troops call each other sisters was bizarre and…

"Hey hey, b1g s1s, make us a t0y!"

"We need t0ys to play!"

"We need t0ys!"

"They sell s0me at the arm0ry 1n the village s0 buy s0me there!"

"Buy s0me there!"

After they started clinging to my arms and legs, I finally surrendered and agreed to go. They cheered, and I experienced a peculiar feeling. I envisioned, in my head, the smiling faces of the resistance. The faces of my comrades too.

Why now? Why were those memories coming back to me now?

■ ■■

"WelcOme. Oh? TOys fOr the ch1ldren? Ah, we're Out of stOck. 1f Only 1 had the mater1als. The mater1als are wr1tten here. 1f Only yOu cOuld br1ng me these mater1als, the ch1ldren wOuld be happy…"

The craftsman spoke while waving a piece of paper around. It was a list of materials. Starting with the children back there, everyone in this village was pushy.

But the only reason I searched for the materials without complaint was so I could distract myself from thinking. Thinking about…my fallen comrades.

4576656e206d6f726520636f6e6675736564

Pascal's villagers were all pushy, but they properly offered rewards every single time they asked a favor. Even if I declined, they just kept pushing rewards in my face.

I had originally planned to help so I would not be indebted. But if they rewarded me every time, the cycle was never-ending.

"Ah, 1t's b1g s1s!"

"Thanks fOr making us tOys!"

"Th1s 1s Our way Of say1ng thanks!"

They piled my hands with ores and seeds. The children had probably gathered them around the village.

"Thanks b1g s1s!"

With this, I felt indebted yet again…

50617363616c20686173206120626164206665656c696e672061626f
7574207468652076696c6c616765

It happened when I was making my way from the resistance camp to the village. I had been asked by Anemone to deliver a few materials to Pascal.

"Can you hear me, Ms. A2?"

"Oh, good timing. Pascal, I'm on my way to deliver…"

"Ms. A2! The village…it's horrible! The villagers are… Ahh!"

"Hey! Pascal? What happened?"

The transmission cut off as abruptly as it had started. Pascal's voice sounded urgent. I had a bad feeling.

"Hypothesis: Pascal, a valuable source of information, is in trouble. Recommendation: Check on status of Pascal's village."

"I know," I told Pod as I started to run. I didn't have to go very far to see the gravity of the situation. There was smoke coming from the direction of the village.

"Pod! A transmission to Pascal!"

"Transmission unavailable."

"Shit!"

When I finally arrived, there were fires burning in various places throughout the village. But the fire was not the only problem. Something unbelievable was happening in front of my eyes: Machines were eating Machines. The ones doing the eating, and getting eaten, were all villagers.

I headed further into the village, thrashing the ones that were eating. I heard a whimpering voice call, "Ms. A2!" How many villagers…how many *Machines* had I killed before I heard my name?

"Pascal! What happened?!"

"I don't know. Some of the villagers suddenly went mad, and fell upon and began consuming others."

"What about the children?"

"I evacuated them. But the other villagers are…"

"At this rate you're going to be eaten too! I'll take care of here so go on and escape!"

After I pretty much forced Pascal to escape, I destroyed the rampant Machines one by one. Villagers that had, until just a little while ago, been shopping, gossiping, and living a peaceful life.

Though berserk, these were the Machines that "lost the means to confront powerful enemies." It didn't take long for me to destroy all of them. But it was too late to save the villagers that had been preyed on. They were already nonfunctional.

50617363616c2773207374727567676c65

Fortunately, the children were unharmed. Pascal had most likely prioritized their safety as soon as the cannibal riot began. The children were all huddled in the corner of the factory ruins. It was difficult to tell Pascal that I was unable to save the villagers because I knew how it felt to lose comrades too.

"Question: Cannot Machines be reconstructed as long as materials are on hand?"

"No. We have a unit called "the core" within us. It is the unit that contains our personal data. When that is destroyed, it becomes impossible to return to our previous state. This time, the victims, including their cores, were destroyed."

"I see…"

Every time I had fought Machines in the past, regardless of how many I destroyed, new ones kept spawning out of nowhere. That's why I had the misconception that they were immortal. But similarly to our comrades that had their black boxes destroyed without personal data backups, Pascal and the villagers had a concept of death as well…

"Report: Intelligence—there are multiple hostile Machines in this factory."

"Intelligence?"

"Acquired from the regional Pod network."

"You have comrades too?"

"Affirmative."

At any rate, there was no time to mourn the dead. Leaving the children in their hiding spot, I confronted the oncoming Machines. The number of enemies was overwhelming, and it didn't seem like Pod and I would suffice for the task.

That's right. The Machines were never-ending. That's the enemy we were dealing with. A familiar feeling of helplessness and despair washed over me…

"Ms. A2! I'll handle these enemies!"

An unexpected savior appeared. It was Pascal riding a weapon of immense size. He had probably taken control of the abandoned apparatus.

Pascal's weapon blasted away a horde of enemies. Enemy reinforcements arrived in waves, but Pascal kept fighting, showing no signs of backing down.

"I…have children that I need to protect!

His attacks were rather ferocious for a peace advocate. I heard Pascal scream, "I'll kill you!" a countless number of times.

2250617363616c2773206465737061697222

After we eventually demolished the enemy army and its fighting vehicles, Pascal and I returned to the children's hiding place. But waiting for us was an unimaginable sight.

What awaited us was the sight of the children on the floor, still as death. They had destroyed their own cores. In other words…mass suicide.

"How could this happen?"

"I gave these children an education, and taught them about human emotions and knowledge. I thought it would help them in the future."

"But what does that have to do with suicide?"

"Fear. I taught these children about the emotion of fear. Without fear, they would have lost their lives by doing something reckless."

It had taken Pascal a long time to return to the children. They probably heard the sounds of battle from outside. There were sounds of explosions and clashes, as well as furious quaking. They were unable to bear the terror. They chose death to escape that fear.

Pascal was slightly wrong. He shouldn't have taught the children fear, but instead, should have taught them the fear of death.

Humans initially designed androids. Humans were well aware of the fear of death. That's why our programs included an inherent fear of death. Without that awareness, as Pascal had said, we would be prone to dying recklessly by our own hands.

But Machines did not die to begin with. So Pascal didn't understand the fear of death. It was tough to teach the kids an emotion that he himself had never experienced. To put it bluntly, it was death. The ignorance of death, and not teaching death, was the cause of this tragedy.

"Ms. A2, I beg you. I am unable to endure this pain. Would you be kind enough to erase my memories? Otherwise, please…kill me."

I understood the pain of losing comrades. I knew better than anyone else the agony of living on with the memories of those that were dear. So I directed Pod to erase Pascal's memories.

546f20746865206d61737369766520756e6974

After shutting down Pascal's memory circuit, Pod set a reboot timer. This would allow us to leave while Pascal was still sleeping.

Pascal, with his memories erased, might be confused if he saw me, and I wouldn't know what kind of face to make either. Pod was probably being considerate in that sense.

"Pod. Why did the Machines ambush Pascal, even though they're part of the same village?"

"Unknown. But the possibility of a bug is undeniable."

"Bug? From what?"

But my question was drowned out by an unfamiliar voice.

"Hello! This is the Tower System Service! I have some exciting news for everyone today"

It was a childish voice. It was enunciating poorly, but at the same time seemed to be poking fun at us.

"Activation of massive Machine unit detected to the east."

"Massive unit? That must be the so-called tower. What in the world is happening?"

"Unknown. Recommendation: Gathering of additional information."

It didn't have to tell me. After making Pod determine the location, I decided to take a look at the aforementioned massive unit with my own eyes.

Villagers going on a rampage, and the appearance of the massive unit. The fact that they happened around the same time was probably not a coincidence. And Pod's hypothesis of there being some kind of bug…

Originally, Machines were made by aliens as weapons of mass destruction. It was hypocritical for those weapons to dislike fighting, and love peace. In the world of Machines, Pascal and his village were the outliers.

The more they deviate from a Machine's hardwired purpose, the farther they operate from their natural instincts. Could that gap have been the reason for the bug? And the appearance of the massive structure had been a catalyst?

In the end, this was supposition. It was just my hypothesis. That's why I was going to confirm it.

5265756e6974656420776974682039530d0a

The massive unit was in the amusement park ruins. It was an ugly building, as if it was made from random parts of Machines patched together.

Once inside, the interior also looked like it was constructed from Machine parts. The building was definitely made by them.

However, there were Machine remains lying around. It seemed like a battle had taken place, and every floor reeked of a burning stench. The bodies were riddled with bullet holes as well. Touching the remains, I discovered they were still hot. They were recently destroyed.

Every Machine was damaged beyond recognition, nearly chewed to pieces. It was clear that attacks had continued long after the Machine had stopped functioning.

I ran toward the upper floor. It wasn't too late. I could catch up.

"Please…k1ll me…"

"Operator… It's okay… It'll be okay!"

On the top floor, two YoRHa androids were still fighting. One that had been infected by a logic virus and...9S. It seemed like the battle had gone on for quite some time, as both 9S and the infected YoRHa were struggling to stand.

One blow from 9S sent the infected YoRHa to the ground. 9S probably thought that he had defeated her. But he was naive. Those kinds of moments gave way to opportunity. Raptors were most vulnerable when they were pouncing on the enemy.

Just as I expected, the infected YoRHa slashed at 9S. Bu, by the same martial axiom the infected YoRHa was vulnerable as it attacked. I didn't miss the chance.

I stabbed her in the back with my military sword. I couldn't let 9S be killed. 2B wouldn't want that. Of the favors that 2B had passed on to me, 9S was mentioned in the majority of her requests.

Once the infected YoRHa fell to the floor again, I made sure it was inoperable by destroying its black box. 9S glared at me, his malice overflowing, as I speared the body over and over.

CH. 09: 9S'S STORY/OBSESSION

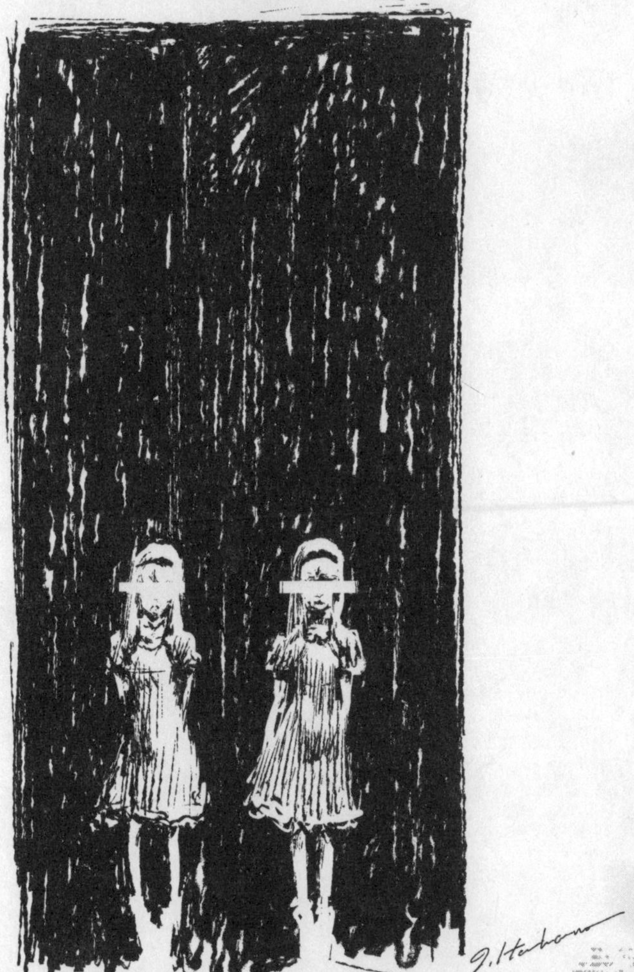

"...COMPLETED. YORHA ANDROID 9S, OPERATIONAL."

It was bright. Was the lighting broken? He would have to go report the issue to the maintenance department. Either way, resources in the Bunker were very limited. Launching resources from Earth was becoming a challenge. It was all because of the enemy's air defense system... huh? Hadn't he already succeeded in nullifying the defense system?

"Good morning, 9S."

Pod 153 floated into his field of vision. Beyond it 9S could see sky. The view of the sky, from Earth. No wonder it was bright.

"I..."

Why was he sleeping in such a place?

"Fighting inside the enemy unit led to the collapse of the structure. YoRHa android 9S sustained damage from the fall, and was put into a state of emergency suspended animation. The landing location was deemed dangerous, and 9S was transported to the current location."

Fall? *Ah, that's right*, 9S thought, as he pulled himself up. A significant enemy had suddenly appeared, and destroyed part of the wall and floor. Right where 9S had been standing. He lost his footing, and there was nothing he could do. Even though his target was standing right in front of him.

This was the second time he had missed out on killing A2. Last time the abrupt appearance of the tower had collapsed the bridge. He was frustrated that twice, Machines had interrupted, taken his footing away, and ended their encounter.

What aggravated him even more was what A2 had said to him.

"2B said she warned you to be a kind person."

He thought it despicable that she would use 2B's words in an attempt to deceive him. It was already bad enough that she wore an identical face. But she had used those identical lips to quote 2B. Unforgivable.

No, the person impossible to forgive was himself. His careless self, who allowed A2 to save him. He had failed to finish off 21O, or 21B, and instead was almost killed. Right before 21B dealt the decisive blow, A2 swept in from behind and stabbed 21B in the back...

"Operator..."

"The model 21O you encountered has died. Black-box signal is no longer active."

9S's tone was indifferent, bluntly acknowledging the statement with an "I see." He already knew that 21O had died.

"Update me on the current situation."

"The required number of access keys has been acquired."

Even though he had fallen from the roof, he was still able to collect the necessary items. It would have been a disaster if, on top of that, A2 had stolen the access keys. Well, if that had happened he would have just taken them back.

"Accessing the subunits and investigating the tower is now possible."

"Roger that."

The end was near.

■　■■

The mumbling voice rang throughout the crater zone. Perhaps he had just heard it so many times and gotten used to it, but this time he didn't feel as irritated. All he wanted to do was hurry up and destroy it.

"Hello! This is the Tower System Service."

The echoing made the words sound even more broken. The locks on all three subunits had been released. Finally he could enter his original target, the tower.

"Congratulations! You've unlocked all the subunits. The last prize is stored in the tower."

Prize? Wasn't it just going to be another foolish Machine, enshrined as though it were some God?

"We look forward to your visit!"

Right as the announcement ended, Machines started to fly down from the sky. Attacking even though they had just said they would be "looking forward" to his visit. What a Machine-like thing to do. Even if Machines couldn't talk in the first place.

"Get out of the way!"

The more enemies he destroyed, the more appeared. The tower's door had an ostentatious hacking point. While he was hacking the door, his chassis would be vulnerable to attack. If there were only a couple of enemies, he could tell Pod to cover him, but it was infeasible against a large force of Machines.

He was reminded of the times 2B covered for him while he hacked. He felt the glaring absence of 2B now more than ever. If this was what the enemy was aiming for, he had to admit it was effective…

"Shit! There's no end!"

If only he could destroy the enemies as quickly as a Type B, he would be able to hack the door while the enemy reinforcements were on the way. But with the battle capabilities of a Type S it took too long to defeat an opponent. As soon as he destroyed one, another would appear in front of him. At this rate he would never vanquish enough of the opposing force to let Pod do mop-up. Once he was out of energy, that was it.

9S panicked, thinking of a way around the situation.

"Report: Signals of allied troops."

"Allied?"

Did it mean enemy troops? The YoRHa squadron had fallen. The only troops left were infected and had gone berserk.

"We knew you'd come."

9S heard his name and turned around to see Devola and Popola standing behind him. They were both holding swords.

"You're…"

The two started sprinting at the same time. They slid past the speechless 9S toward the Machines. Their swords flashed. Machine heads fell to the ground.

"We'll take it from here."

"You go on and open the door of the tower!"

What was happening? He didn't understand. Why were these two helping him out? The sisters were specialized in medicine and maintenance, but certainly not in combat.

"Hurry! Hack it now!"

Popola yelled as she held back the enemies.

"We'll tell you the details once we're in the tower!" Devola's words motivated 9S to take action. It was more efficient to enter the building than to stand and face countless enemies. Tactical theory suggested fighting in an enclosed area was advantageous for smaller groups.

But the hacking process was an unexpected bottleneck. He knew that the security would be focused on defense, but the firewall was unusually robust. And the more he attacked, the more the defenses adapted to become thicker and stronger.

"What…what kind of firewall is this?"

"Report: Lockdown defense system."

Lockdown? It sounded familiar… He vaguely recalled struggling against one in the past. But that was just a feeling. He didn't have any specific memory. Nor did he have a memory of ever breaking one successfully. That meant that, even if he had faced one before, he had probably failed to hack it. He had failed, his personal data had been destroyed, and he had been reloaded with the backup…

"How do I break it?"

"Prediction: Allow personal data to go rampant. The explosive energy generated from self-destruction will temporarily stun the defenses."

Self-destruction? Temporarily stun? Without a backup, self-destruction meant death. And if that were only enough to temporarily "stun" the enemy defenses…

"Then it's pretty much impenetrable!"

Right as he shouted he was thrown out of the virtual circuit dimension. It was a forced timeout. 9S was blasted away from the door and flung onto the ground.

"What happened?"

Devola ran over. He grabbed her extended hand and pulled himself up.

"This firewall is…"

Just as he was about to say impenetrable, Popola cut down a nearby enemy and tackled the door. Her scream filled the air.

"No! That door is protected by a self-lockdown algorithm so breaking in is—"

"Shut up!"

The reprimand was fierce enough to bring 9S to a standstill as he was running over to help.

"We shall atone for the sins we committed!"

Smoke was rising from Popola's hands. Embers of electrical discharge scattered around her. The door probably inflicted physical damage as well. But what was even more dangerous was the damage to her brain circuitry.

"It's no use! If you do that your circuits will…"

9S's voice was drowned out by the sound of Popola's wails, as if she refused to hear what he had to say.

"Devola! Help me!"

9S was grabbed by the arm. It was Devola. Unaware of what she was going to do, she pulled him close.

"Now!"

He was chucked into the air at Popola's cue—and through the door. He saw Popola collapse to the ground, seemingly exhausted. Devola looked over her shoulder and quietly smiled.

"Don't leave any regrets."

Devola's face disappeared. 9S stared at the door in shock. He felt erratic vibrations through his legs, and the feeling of being lifted. *An elevator*, he thought in the back of his mind, still dazed.

"Why…"

He didn't understand. The only thing he knew for a fact was that the sisters had sacrificed themselves to help him.

"Report: Discovered residual data of Devola and Popola."

"Residual data? You found some?"

Perhaps Popola's personal data firewall had cut off when her circuits shut down. Or maybe they had created a will, and sent it over to Pod before their death.

"Open the data."

"Affirmative."

■　■■

When we were created, we were the newest models. The Devola and Popola type androids were designed to serve as the observers of Project Gestalt. At the time, we had many peers, because there needed to be a pair observing each region.

We were probably paired as twins so there would be a "backup" in case some unforeseen calamity befell one of us. The project was long-lived, spanning the course of approximately a thousand years.

And humans, who were responsible for planning the project, would be unable to lay a hand on it once it was under way. That meant we had to carry on the skilled work that humans had been doing.

We would have been lying if we said we weren't anxious. But we felt a sense of honor that swept away almost any anxiety. All of us were thrilled to be the surrogates for humans.

But our role as observers abruptly came to an end. It was reported that a pair of Devola and Popola models had gone mad in another city. As a result, the extinction of humanity was imminent.

After that, we sent the genetic profile data of humanity to the moon as a last ray of hope. But the data was rather paltry, and having the genetic profile data of various humans did not guarantee that we would be able to reconstruct the species in the future. Human anatomy and cognitive schemata was much too complex to reconstruct from just genetic data.

The Devola and Popola models faced hostility from all the androids who knew about the incident. Androids were built to respect and protect humans with their lives. We Devola and Popola were the criminals responsible for bringing ruin upon humanity.

Eventually Command decided to conceal the failure of Project Gestalt. Most of our memories encompassing the project were erased. The only memories left in our consciousness were the name of the project, and the fact that our model's breakdown had led to the extinction of humanity. What our peers had experienced as observers; what we did, and what we didn't do; the details of the incident; how the situation had escalated; and how we had responded; whether or not the incident was preventable...

We will never know. Countless questions arose, but we will never get answers. The majority of androids constructed after the end of humanity are not aware of our sins. They don't even know the name of the project. But still we live in exile. It's now convention for them to persecute us.

And we probably deserve to be killed without reason. Or perhaps kill ourselves. At least, that's what the other androids think.

But we can't die. Then we won't be able to atone. Our guilt keeps us from death. We can't die a failure.

We wanted to live in a deserted area, just the two of us. But we couldn't do that either, because we needed somebody to receive our atonements.

We want to be assigned the most dangerous missions. We can die during a mission. As long as there's evidence that we served and helped someone, we will be willing to meet a final death. We just wait for that day...

That concludes the personal records of the twins, formerly known as the observers.

■ ■■

"I see…"

9S was reminded of Popola's scream, saying they had to atone for their sins. That was a result of their guilt. He understood why they had laid down their lives to help him. And why they were always covered in scrapes and bruises, and willingly embarked on faraway missions.

"Question: Why did androids Devola and Popola choose to die at the same time?"

"In the most recent encounter, a solo escape was possible…I think."

9S interrupted Pod. For the Devola and Popola that 9S knew, death was salvation. That's why they chose to die together. This was just his hypothesis, since he wasn't sure of the situation that the original, rampant Devola and Popola had been put in. But, hand in hand, they must have overcome many challenges along the thousand-year project. There was no chance that, even if one of them was on the verge of death, the other would leave her partner's side.

Even if one of them survived without the other, all that would be left was regret. He knew that firsthand, because he himself had been forced to let go and survive.

"I hope you never have to know the feeling," said 9S.

Pod didn't have to go through this. It was better that no one go through this. This pain.

As he was having such thoughts, Pod again interjected with a question.

"Why does this tower have a ground-floor entrance? The resources are imported from the sky. It is unnecessary for there to be a pedestrian entrance."

He was reminded of the resource-recovery units, where he had seen the floating spiral of Machine parts being sent off into the sky. He knew the parts were being delivered to the tower, but he hadn't thought of the importing process. Rather, he hadn't cared enough to take the time to think about it.

"Prediction: Trap."

"I don't mind if it's a trap."

He had no interest in Machine remains. What he did have interest in were the Machines that had yet to become remains. That was because…

"I'm just going to kill them all."

The elevator rattled to a loud stop.

■ ■■

9S stepped out of the elevator and entered a dim passageway. The borderline excessively intricate decorations littering the walls, pillars, and ceilings reminded him of human civilization's architectural style of old.

Moving on, the walls abruptly disappeared. The dim hall had led to a stairway wrapping along the outer wall of the tower. The stairway was missing a few steps, and gusts of wind blew up through the openings. 9S was at a considerable elevation. If he carelessly took a wrong step he would plunge to the ground, and instant death.

As he warily hopped over the missing steps, he heard a familiar drab announcement.

"Hello! This is the Tower System Service. We thank you for your visit, from the bottom of our hearts."

Visit? Thank you? When they had bombarded him with enemies at the entrance? When they had secured the door with a self-lockdown algorithm? He was exasperated at how brazenly they spoke.

"The last prize for the visitor, who unlocked the last subunit, awaits in the next room. Please enjoy!"

Borrowing a human expression, he muttered, "What a one-trick pony," under his breath. There was most likely going to be another Machine when he opened the door.

The double door was of a towering height, forcing him to look up. At first, he doubted whether the strength of Type S would suffice to open the door, but it wasn't as heavy as it looked. A small push was enough for the door to glide open without a sound.

It was a narrow room, slightly wider than the previous passageway, with a rather high ceiling. Most of all, it was dark. It wasn't pitch-black, but it was dark enough to make him doubt his step.

Just as he was thinking how cumbersome it would be to fight in the confined space, he saw some objects descend from the dark ceiling. The sound they made as they hit the floor was clearly different from something a Machine would make. In fact, 9S recognized the chassis.

"Type...2B?"

A YoRHa android clad in black. Short silver hair and pale lips. It was undoubtedly 2B.

He had assumed that all personal data, as well as spare chassis, were lost when the Bunker had exploded. He thought that reconstructing any android, including himself, would never be possible again. But there was still one way to construct 2B's chassis: the transfer device.

The transfer devices contained all the materials necessary to construct a chassis. Since all YoRHa-type androids were made of the same materials, anybody from the squadron could use a transfer device. Personal data, which was not replicable, was sent from the transfer origin to the destination. For the chassis however, only its blueprint was transferred, and it was constructed from scratch at the destination. The transfer was complete when the personal data was injected into the newly constructed chassis.

That's why the chassis blueprint was the only information necessary to abuse a transfer device and construct as many chassis as needed. The Machines had infiltrated the main server, so the chassis blueprint was easily accessible to them.

Nevertheless, this was just a theory. They could have created an original device similar to a transfer device and constructed the 2B chassis. Or they could have used a method that was completely unfamiliar to 9S.

Regardless, the chassis had been constructed, and 9S was now face-to-face with many 2Bs. Of course, their expressions were vacant, closer to puppets than the real thing. The Machines most likely wanted 9S to fight with mindless drones identical to 2B. Just like how they had sent Operator 21O to confront him.

They might have been disappointed by 9S's indifference during his encounter with 21O. Maybe that's why they were using 2B this time...

9S's perverse feelings for 2B had been exposed back when he was captured by Adam. He was fairly certain that the Machines that had lured him to this tower were aware of his feelings as well. Machines were connected to one another through their network.

They probably expected that, this time, they would witness a defenseless 9S being killed by 2B. They yearned to see him scream in despair, unable to lay a hand on 2B, let alone retaliate.

Stupid Machines. Despair? Scream? Not a chance. Not when there were so many 2Bs in his presence.

"I'm so glad... I got to see you here..."

Glad that there were no 2B chassis lurking behind his back. Here, she was within reach. He ripped off his goggles. He didn't have to hide anything. He didn't need any additional data. He wanted to see 2B, in all her glory, directly. Watch 2B, within his reach, as he...

"All of it..."

He couldn't hold back his escalating laughter.

"I'll destroy all of you!"

Reconstructing 2B's chassis without his permission was unforgivable. Animating her chassis without his permission was unforgivable. That's precisely why he was going to destroy all of them.

The only one who can destroy 2B is me.

"I'll tear you apart... Every last one of you!"

Because they were all his. He wasn't going to let anyone else have them... Not even 2B.

The puppets crept toward him. Their movements were too stiff. They were, after all, controlled by Machines. Their martial abilities fell short of the real 2B's. Their movements were a far cry from the fluid motion of their real counterpart.

See, it's so easy to break them. I'm going to slash and crush the faces, arms, and legs that look just like yours, 2B. I won't leave anything behind. So no one can look at you.

One body. Two bodies. Three bodies…

At this rate it's going to end too quickly, 2B. Four bodies, five bodies, six bodies…

How many left? Oh, so it's already over.

"Warning: Detected enemy signal."

Pod's brusque words interrupted 9S.

"Signal? There's one that's still alive?"

Which one is it? Which one is still waiting for me to kill it?

He scanned through the corpses scattered on the ground. He saw one with its chest barely moving up and down.

"Found it."

Even though it was struggling to move at all, it looked like it was trying to stand up.

No, 2B. I told you I'd destroy all of you, didn't I?

He pierced the sword through the chest. Twice, and then a third time.

It was then that he heard an ominous noise. Right as he realized it was a detonator, his field of vision flashed white.

Sound faded from the world around him, and he lost consciousness.

ANOTHER SIDE "A2"

After destroying the Goliath-class enemy that had intruded by smashing through the walls and floor of the building, I left the large unit. Since it seemed that 9S had already destroyed the central "mind" of the facility, there was no reason for me to stay behind.

And Pod had notified me that the massive structure, called the tower, had activated. If the other facilities had activated, it was better to destroy them as soon as possible.

As I rushed toward the tower, I ran into an unexpected pair: the twin androids from the resistance camp. I found the two collapsed at the entrance of the tower. They were lying side by side.

I was unable to detect Popola's signal ID. Devola's signal was so weak it was on the verge of expiring.

Devola's eyes stayed shut as I moved closer. She finally opened them after I called her name a few times.

"Oh…it's you, A2. We left the entrance of the tower…open for you."

I couldn't bring myself to ask what had happened. Observing the door, I noticed that the security had been broken. It was easy to guess what had happened after seeing that.

"9S went ahead…"

9S had tumbled down when the floor of the large unit had given way. It's not like I doubted Pod's status report, but I felt a small sense of relief after I heard Devola confirm the fact.

"Hey… Did we…do good?"

I gave her a nod, and Devola closed her eyes with a look of satisfaction. Then her signal disappeared.

The interior of the tower was filled with corpses of YoRHa androids. Signs of a frenzied battle lingered, some of the floors with their pavement peeled and walls charred. It was probably all 9S's doing.

Moving along, I came across a peculiar room. There were numerous small blocks embedded in the walls.

"Prediction: A facility mimicking a library."

"Library? What's that?"

"An information storage facility once used by humans."

What I thought were small blocks were apparently record-keeping tools called "books." I forcefully hacked into a few of them and inspected the material.

According to Pod, during the era of human civilization, humans had the capability to use books without hacking. It was unclear why that capability was excluded from androids; perhaps it was a process too complex to replicate, or simply a matter of efficiency.

The books that the Machines had made spanned a diverse range of topics. They included records of past human societies as well as an epidemic that had plagued human civilization. The epidemic seemed particularly atrocious, from the sheer number of records that existed about it. Records of research into its origin, treatment, and vaccination. Case records, as well as full clinical records of patients who experienced unique symptoms…

"It looks like the Machines use this tower as some kind of information collection device," said A2.

The large unit from before had been collecting Machine parts and remains. It had done so indiscriminately. If, by some chance, an android corpse had been mixed in, it would have been possible to collect an enormous amounts of information. Androids had a significant amount of knowledge stored in their memory.

The unit jumbled all of these things together, and sent it off from its roof to this tower. The tower was scraping together resources and information.

"What are they planning to do once they collect all of this?"

I found the answer in a book titled Overview of the Tower System.

011port062423 *Overview of the Tower System*

This facility, as a means to fulfill its launchpad function, takes materials delivered from the resource recovery units and converts them to data. The structure stemming from the 256th level performs filtration and compression of information with turbidity levels of less than 2,300 and transfers them to the memory of the projectile in 27 minutes and 32 seconds.

"Memory of the projectile? So they're making a projectile out of the resources they collect, storing the information they collect on it, and then launching it somewhere…?"

To where? Where were they trying to launch it to?

"Could it be the human server on the moon? It can't be…"

Was it too preposterous a theory? No, they might pull it off. They might attempt it, just from the fact that they were Machines.

I knew that the Machines were playing games with androids. My comrades and I were both victims, and… Anyway, Machines were responsible for exposing me to the feeling of despair.

The human server on the moon was the cornerstone of android morale. If it was destroyed as well…

But the Machines wouldn't be able to destroy it if they didn't know the location of the human server. I've heard that transmissions from the human board were relayed through various interceptors on Earth to conceal the location of the server. So it was okay…or was it?

It was certainly not okay. Ever since the Pearl Harbor Descent Attack, the Machines had held valuable information that we weren't even informed about. It was probably easy for them to figure out the location of the server.

"Found it."

I found the title "port056776 Human Server Records." The record was conveniently placed near the Overview of the Tower System. The Machines had foreseen that it would be the next piece of information I would want after learning about the tower.

The Machines had not only located the human server, but they had even attempted to access it. If they wanted, they probably could have destroyed the server from the inside out. The only reason they refrained was so that they could flaunt the server's destruction to the androids. They wanted the server to blow up into pieces upon impact of the projectile, and ingrain the image into the memory of every single android looking from Earth.

I needed to destroy this tower. I wasn't going to let them have their way any longer. I wasn't going to let them steal any more.

But, as if to mock my resolve, another title came to my attention.

" 'The effective utilization of No. 2 in Project YoRHa?' What is this?"

It seemed that the Machines had predicted I would come here. Or perhaps this was meant for 9S? He most likely would have been shocked to learn the truth that was written in here.

Attacker No. 2, who participated in the YoRHa experimental squadron's first descent attack, recorded mediocre performance during the simulation phase. Yet No. 2 was the lone survivor from the squadron. After analyzing the saved personal data of No. 2, we discovered that No. 2 was capable of excellent decision-making under extreme duress.

No. 2's personal data was uploaded to the newly constructed lot of Type E models [covered in a separate section] and will oversee the preservation of confidentiality for Project YoRHa.

"Oversee… Preservation of confidentiality. 2E…"

The first time I met "her," she was called 2E. She was tasked with the execution of rogue troops, and we would go on to confront each other multiple times in the future. When I saw her at the forest castle, she called herself 2B, most likely to keep her identity safe from 9S.

When 9S, a highly specialized model, uncovered the truth about Project YoR-Ha, he was immediately executed by 2E, the overseer of confidentiality. But 9S's abilities were so keen that it was still necessary to use a disguise. That's why 2E approached 9S as 2B.

This information had been recorded in 2B's sword. Just an overview, nothing else. But I could easily imagine what she had gone through.

Had 9S read this? Had he already discovered what 2B had been hiding all along?

506c6561736520656e746572206f6e65206f7220746865206f74686572

Suddenly, my surroundings shifted. I was thrown into a dimension consisting solely of white surfaces.

"What, what's this?!"

"Enemy hacking attempt. Recommendation: Immediate escape."

"I know that!"

I sprinted through the white passageway. Even if I wanted to escape, I had no idea where the exit was. All I could do was keep running. I couldn't stay still.

"Long time no see, No. 2. No, should we call you A2 now?"

I came to a stop. I knew them.

"It's so nostalgic," they said.

In front of me were two little girls in red clothes. Two. Girls in red. I knew them. During the Pearl Harbor Descent Attack, I… Because of them, we…

"We have no concept of time… But we still vividly remember the time we killed all of the troops in your squadron."

The red girls were the humanoid manifestations of the Machine network. They had no physical presence, and as a result were not bound to time and space, able to invade anywhere and at any time. They had probably invaded Command's main server…as well as the human server on the moon.

"YoRHa squadron Attacker No. 2. An experimental squadron that was the guinea pig for the real YoRHa squadrons to come."

"Shut up!" I yelled, swinging my sword through them. There was no resistance. Just like last time.

"What a stubborn android you are. Didn't we tell you that you can't kill us?"

I knew that. But I couldn't keep myself from attacking. They were the reason I discovered the experimental purpose my squadron served. If I hadn't found out, maybe I could have died back then, waiting for help from Command.

"Shit!"

What was I supposed to do? How could I kill them? How...

CH. 10: 9S'S STORY/TRUTH

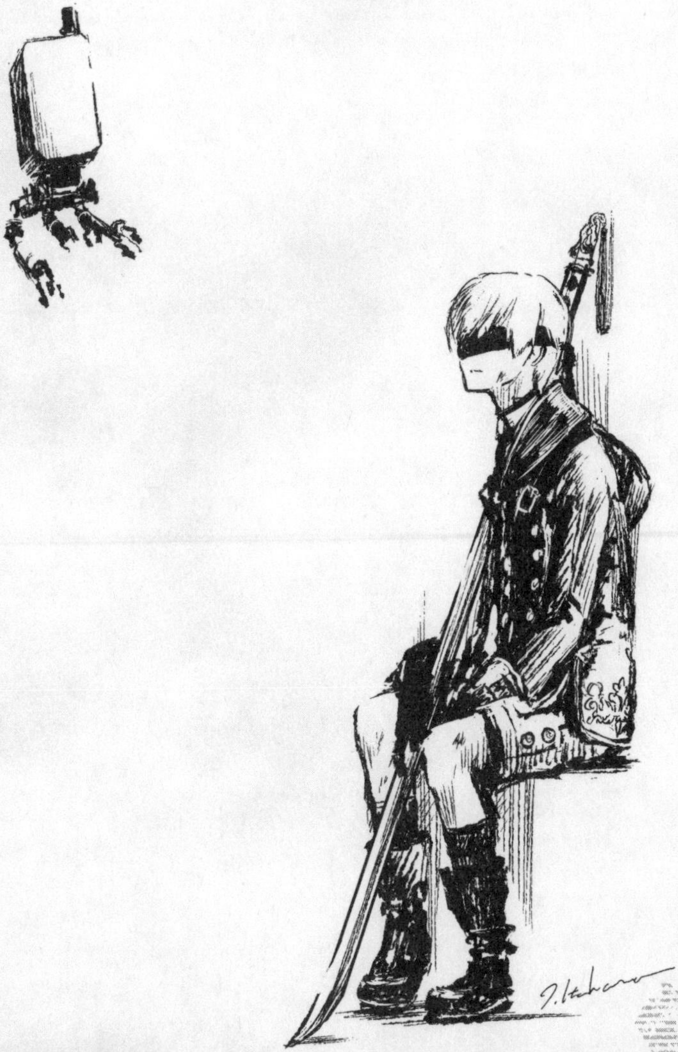

CONSIDERING HE HAD BEEN INVOLVED IN A CLOSE-RANGE
EXPLOSION, HIS VISUAL MECHANISMS WERE SURPRISINGLY
INTACT. But he couldn't hear at all. His auditory mechanisms were
still recovering.

He tried to sit up, but lost balance. He had tried propping himself
up on his left arm, but instead clumsily fell backward. Peering toward
where his left arm should be, he realized it was missing.

The moment he saw the jagged, open wound, he felt tremendous
pain. Remarkably, he hadn't been aware of the searing ache from his arm
being ripped apart.

He was immobilized from the great misery. He clenched his teeth in
desperation, but couldn't hold back from moaning. He briefly thought
he was going to die.

He looked around to try and diffuse the pain. He saw 2B. Her chassis was lying on the ground. There was only one left, miraculously having
avoided the fate of being buried beneath the rubble.

"2B…"

He extended his right hand to stroke her cheek. Back at the Bunker,
when 2B was going through maintenance, she had lain like this, with
her eyes closed. If he said "All done" now, would she open her eyes as she
had so many times in the past?

"What an idiot."

He knew it was impossible. 2B was dead. The fact dawned on him,
and rage began to boil in his veins.

"I can't…die yet."

With every heaving breath his upper body stiffened in pain. Even
still, he forced himself to sit up. He was already out of breath.

Panting heavily, he straddled 2B's chassis and clutched her left arm. Pain shot through his whole body as he gripped it with his right hand. He tugged on 2B's arm with all his might. He heard a dull snap. It hurt him to hear the sound, as if his own arm had been torn off.

He shoved 2B's arm, soaked in red liquid, toward his wound. He needed a replacement.

"Need to fight…"

It felt like someone was pressing scalding metal onto his wound. He couldn't even clench his teeth or roll around in pain. Instead, he focused every single ounce of will into staying conscious, and at times, wondered if letting go would make things easier. But of course, he wasn't going to let himself do that.

The left arm was infected with a logic virus. He needed to perform self-hacking the instant it connected. If he lost consciousness now, the virus would certainly overtake him.

Both fortunately and unfortunately, the pain kept him conscious throughout the process. He finished clearing the virus, and tested the arm's functionality. There was a slight awkwardness, but it was acceptable. If he adjusted the movements of his other limbs, he would have no problem maneuvering.

"I will fight…"

9S stood up, with a determined gaze toward the end of the room.

■ ■■

He eventually reached the back of the room and arrived at a large door.

Right as he passed through the door, it closed behind him. The windows, which were open and facing out, were immediately sealed off. To think he would be so blatantly caged in. It was almost comical at this point.

In the middle of the enclosed room stood two little girls. He realized that he knew them.

"YoRHa android 9S!"

"YoRHa android 9S!"

The little girls wore one-piece dresses. One had a high voice, the other a low voice. While it was the first time he had seen their faces, 9S felt like he knew them. Their gaze and presence were familiar.

"Welcome to the tower!"

"Welcome to the tower!"

This mumbling way of speech—he was reminded of the same announcement he had heard three times. It wasn't the same exact voice, but he could tell that these girls had been the ones doing the talking.

Swinging his sword through them, he felt no resistance. It seemed that they had no physical bodies. It confirmed a suspicion he had. These girls were the culprits that had snuck into the Bunker and spied on the YoRHa squadrons' activities. They were the very presence he had struggled to detect.

"Since you made it here, we have some very tempting information for you, you wretch."

"Since you made it here, we have some very tempting information for you, you wretch."

Their odd vocabulary and colorless tones were unbearably eerie. So much so that he wanted to run his blade through them right away.

"Ugh…"

He felt an uncomfortable sensation, like his mind had been scraped with sandpaper. Similar to the feeling he had when he was forcefully given the location to the resource recovery units in the crater zone, but this time much stronger.

Words suddenly flooded his brain.

"Th-this…is…"

A file, labeled "Extremely Confidential," began to unravel in his mind.

■ ■■

The publicized objective of Project YoRHa was to produce cutting-edge androids and end the deadlocked battle with Machines. But what was in that file contradicted this widely accepted mission objective: a co-ordinated plan to boost android morale by spreading misinformation, specifically the fabrication of the human server on the moon, and the concealment of human extinction.

Android morale had sunk so low that such a plan was necessary. In the year 4200, humanity went extinct. Androids, having lost their lords and commanders, fell into a collective despair.

Devola and Popola were unaware of the truth because they had their memories erased, but Project Gestalt was an initiative to save humans from an epidemic. The plan proposed for human souls to be separated from their bodies, and fused back together once the epidemic had been curtailed.

But the human holding the key to the division and fusion processes was lost in a violent incident triggered by Devola and Popola. It became impossible to fuse human souls and bodies back together, dooming humanity to extinction.

Command had tried to conceal the failure of Project Gestalt, but information about it circulated as rumors. Command was concerned, and started to spread false information that humans had fled to the moon.

Command had to deny the fact that humanity was now extinct. They established the human board and sent transmissions using a synthesized voice to Earth to create the illusion that humans were living on the moon.

9S knew all of this. He thought it odd that the "Plans for establishing the human board" had been an index in Project YoRHa, and confronted the commander about it.

But the fabrication of the human board was rather rudimentary, so much so that a slightly superior scanner model was able to uncover the truth. That's why it was necessary for individuals that discovered the truth to be wiped out.

The Bunker—that was the base for Command—was programmed to allow Machine infiltration after a certain period of time—specifically, through the back door 9S and 2B had used when they were surrounded by infected YoRHa. Previously, the door was secured with a firewall that deterred anyone other than YoRHa squadron troopers from accessing it.

After enough battle data was accumulated, and the transition period to next-generation models was near, the firewall was brought down. The Machines would infiltrate and destroy the Bunker. If Command, who had fabricated the human board, disappeared, there would be no one left that knew the truth.

In other words, at the time of conception, the plan had already outlined the demise of the YoRHa squadron. They had used Machine cores to manufacture the power source of androids, the black box, because they deemed it inhumane to install AI into androids that were doomed from the beginning. Probably to prevent the individuals who conceived the project from feeling guilty. What a selfish thing to do.

"If this is Project YoRHa...than we were...from the beginning..."

Their destruction was certain from the moment they were constructed. Their many thousands of battles with Machines had been meaningless.

"2B died, for something like this..."

2B died for a lie. We're going to be destroyed for a lie like this.

"Even after knowing everything."

The little girls were all of a sudden right beside him. They were smirking.

"Do you wish to fight?"

Why did you show me this?

9S swung his sword down at the girls' heads as hard as he could. Again his sword pitifully smacked against the ground.

"We are the manifestation of the Machine network."

"We have no physical bodies. So we cannot be killed."

"Shut up!"

He swung his sword again. But the mirage refused to be cut.

"Your attacks are pointless."

"Be quiet be quiet be quiet!"

No matter how many times he swung his sword, it ended up hitting the ground or the walls. But he couldn't help himself.

"Your existence is pointless."

The little girls left him with that, and disappeared. Losing his target, 9S stood there, still gripping his sword.

"I'll destroy everything... You two, this tower...!"

If they weren't here, he would find them. If he couldn't draw them out, he would destroy this whole tower along with them.

He heard the footfalls of multiple individuals. Infected YoRHa heading his way.

"Time after time..."

They're so stubborn. Oh well. I'll destroy you too. I won't spare a single one of you. All of you...

The resource recovery units had broken down when he destroyed the core on the top floor. That meant that there should be a core, or something equivalent, on the top floor of this tower as well. He was going to invade the core, take it over, and make the tower self-destruct. If this tower was indeed a launchpad, it would have enough potential energy to blow itself to pieces.

All he had to do was go up. Higher and higher. If he aimed for the top, his wish would probably come true.

■   ■■

It was actually convenient when a few flight units ambushed 9S. He shot down all but one of them with Pod's artillery. For the last unit, he hacked the infected android aboard and stole the unit. Navigating to the top floor would me much easier in a flight unit.

"Pod, transfer the controls to me."

"Warning: This flight unit is confirmed to be infected with a logic virus, and will affect…"

"Transfer, now!"

"Roger."

Viral infection? Like he cared. He was already infected. He had just delayed it by injecting himself with the vaccine on hand. It wasn't a vaccine specifically designed to combat this type of virus, but as long as it bought him enough time to destroy the tower, he was fine with it.

The edges of his vision began to go dark. He could hear a slight noise in his auditory mechanisms. He didn't have much time left, probably. Mumbling that he had to hurry, 9S entered the flight unit.

Flying types appeared as he was ascending. They were extremely irritating, like small insects flitting about in front of him.

"Up, up," 9S mumbled as he fought. He defeated a small walking type, a flying type, a medium four-legged walking type, and a snakelike Machine, before carrying onward.

He also fought a large spiderlike Machine on the way.

"We are… n0t… bad Mach1nes…"

"1 am… We are…"

"1-1-11… W-we…"

The Machines suddenly started making strange noises.

"What's happening?"

"Report: Confirmed the disintegration of enemy AI. Speech impediment is the repercussion of aforementioned event."

"Enemy AI? The little girls disintegrated? They died?"

Then why were the Machines still moving? Why was this large one still crawling around, and that flying type still buzzing about?

"Hypothesis: Machine attacks are carried out according to residual data left on enemy servers."

In the end, unless he destroyed the tower, it seemed like these Machines would keep functioning. And keep spouting vexing utterances.

"Let's play let's play let's play… Play w1th me"

"M0m m0m m0m!"

"We're gods we're g0ds we are g0ds!"

Be quiet. You're so annoying. Shut up. Just break.

I don't want to hear anything other than 2B's voice. I only want to hear 2B's voice. And 2B's footsteps. And her breaths. And the sound of her swinging sword. And the rustle her clothes make when she moves. And and and…

All the other sounds can just be gone.

Ah, that's why I'm destroying. 2B isn't here. I'm destroying everything because I can't tolerate anything other than 2B.

"Let's head… t0 the stars."

"Let's s1ng… a s0ng."

"We 0ffer… n0w."

Shut up. Why do I keep hearing their voices? Am I imagining things because of the infection? That's probably it. A Machine wouldn't ask questions like, "Why do we exist?"

Just break already!

"Pod!"

A laser at full power pierced the large Machine. The spherical body melted from the heat, and just as he realized it was swelling up, it exploded in a thunderous bang. 9S hunched over and fought through the blast.

The shock wave passed, and his surroundings settled down. The smoke cleared from his eyes, and he could see again. As he was chasing the Machine, he had reached the top floor.

"A2…"

A2 stood amidst the dust in the air. He had finally found her. There was no Machine presence nearby. Pod was silent too. No enemy signals. There would be no interruption. This time, he could kill A2.

9S pointed his sword at A2. But A2 refused to take a fighting stance.

"This tower is a giant cannon aimed toward the human server on the moon. The residual human data is going to be destroyed," said A2.

So? What was the problem? What was she saying all of a sudden? This was a really useless conversation. The back of his throat trembled with laughter. It was so ridiculous he couldn't bear it.

"Whatever..."

He restrained himself from laughing.

"Nothing matters anymore. Not even that."

He saw A2 faintly furrow her brow. A2 probably didn't know the truth. That's why she was worried about how this facility was a giant cannon, with such conviction.

"Did you know? Humanity is dead," said 9S.

The truth that he was never able to reveal to 2B. He didn't want to shock her, to upset her, so he had never told her.

"And to hide that fact, the human server on the moon was established to give androids a reason to fight with their lives on the line. We were made to protect that lie," said 9S.

We weren't created to exterminate the Machines, or take back Earth.

"To complete the lie, the YoRHa squadron was arranged to be annihilated," 9S continued.

Humans still lived on a lunar base. As long as that lie was left standing. The rest was...unnecessary.

"Did you know? The commander, 2B, and I...we were all sacrificial lambs."

We weren't created to be a symbol of hope for humanity. We weren't born into this world because someone needed us. We weren't needed, yet fought, and died. Our lives had utterly...no meaning.

The red girls weren't lying. It was all true.

"Your existence is pointless."

They were right.

"9S, we're..."

A2 opened her mouth to say something. It was easy to tell that she was troubled from her voice and expression.

"Shut up!"

Don't look at me like that, he screamed inside his head. He couldn't forgive that face, identical to 2B's. He couldn't forgive those hands that held 2B's sword. That day, she…

"You killed 2B."

He couldn't forgive that the most. Even if, that day, 2B was already infected with the virus. Even if her eyes were red when she looked back at him.

"That's reason enough for us to kill each other," said 9S.

A2 had still taken 2B's life with her sword.

"2B…"

A2 opened her mouth again.

"2B was struggling. She had to disguise her model type, and keep killing you."

Disguise her model type? Why did A2 know about that?

"She was formally known as 2E. A Type E model responsible for executing YoRHa androids."

Why did this bastard know that?

That 2B's real identity was a model E, with a directive to execute 9S when he came too close to uncovering the truth. 9S had only figured out this fact after spending a long time working with 2B.

He started to feel suspicious when he realized he had no information about Type E models in his memory.

He had met an amnesiac android in the city ruins. She was a Type E who disguised herself as a friend to her comrades, only to spy on and eventually execute them. Unable to bear the stress, she erased her own memories.

When 9S heard that story, he was surprised to hear that a Type E, responsible for executions, even existed. He became apprehensive of himself. He certainly should have known about the existence of Type E, yet he had no information regarding the subject.

That's when he realized that his memory was being erased. In the past he had been executed by a Type E and cleansed of memories relating to that incident. To remove any trace of the execution, it was most likely necessary to erase a large part of his memories. That's why he had a conspicuous lack of information regarding 2E.

He knew that the executioner would at times feign a close relationship with its target.

Furthermore, Type E androids, who acted as executioners, were required by their role to have battle capabilities higher than a Type B. Fighting alongside her a countless number of times, he had realized that 2B was too strong to be a Type B.

He had all the evidence. It was inevitable that he would figure it out.

"You...probably knew, right?" asked A2.

"Shut up! Shut up! Shut up!"

Be quiet. Don't talk like you know it all, with the same face as 2B. You don't know anything.

"What do you know about us!"

He grasped his sword. He needed to hurry. The noise was getting worse. The infection was progressing. He had to destroy her before his movement mechanisms became impaired.

Just then, Pod jumped into his already blurry vision.

"Recommendation: Cease fire. Fighting with her now is illogical and..."

"Order to Pod 153! I forbid you to interject! Follow this order until either A2 or I am confirmed to be nonfunctional!"

Pod retreated without a word. Perhaps it didn't acknowledge the order because it was reluctant to carry it out.

He could see A2 finally drawing her sword. He made Pod cover him while he initiated hacking. She dodged it. A2's movements were startlingly quick, as if she knew what he was going to do.

He wondered if, maybe, he had fought A2 in the past. Perhaps he didn't know because 2B had erased his memories.

That meant A2 had memories of 2B he didn't have. That made him jealous. Anyone other than him that knew 2B should disappear and be gone.

Memories of 2B. Encounters with 2B.

His thoughts were jumbled. Curious as to why his neck was stiff, he touched it and felt a cold, hard sensation. His hand had unknowingly started its erosion into Machine.

He needed to kill A2 soon, while he still retained his consciousness. While he still had his memories of 2B…

2B? Humans?

"Why…why…why!"

What was this feeling?! He had been focused on 2B, why was he being interrupted?!

"Why…do I yearn for humanity?!"

Even though I only yearn for 2B.

"Why do I seek out humans?!"

I only seek 2B.

He didn't care about humanity. He knew that they had died a long time ago. But…why did they push aside his thoughts of 2B? Even though his mental functions had declined rapidly, and just thinking of 2B was exhausting enough, why did his thoughts have to turn toward humans?

"We're made to. We androids are made to protect our creators," said A2.

His vision was further deteriorating.

"Our foundational programming makes us feel…"

"Be quiet be quiet be qu1et!"

The noise was overwhelming. If he couldn't think about 2B, if he wasn't able to think only about 2B, his brain was garbage.

"Then, just destr0y 1t… everyth1ng sh0uld just d1sappear and be g0ne…"

It felt as though his arms weren't his. His legs moved on their own. Where was this strange power coming from? Ah, he was being taken over by the logic virus…

He saw two A2s. This was bad. He wouldn't be able to aim very well. Right as he was about to kill her, A2 stopped.

"2B…" she said.

Don't say that name! It's unforgivable for you to say that name.

He thrust his sword forward. He felt a dull impact through the blade. He heard A2 moan.

He strained his eyes to see. Blood-soaked sword. A2 on the ground. He'd done it. He'd killed her. He could see A2's face as she writhed in pain. *Ha ha, serves you right.*

It was finally over. Everything.

He saw something move near his feet. All of a sudden, he couldn't breathe. His whole body was burning.

He heard a scream. He didn't understand.

Hot. Red. He couldn't breathe.

What was happening? He saw a sword? Red. Nauseous. Ow.

Had he been stabbed? By A2? Why?

The pain abruptly faded. Not just the pain, but all his senses were fading too.

In the darkness, he saw 2B's hair. No. The one dying in a pool of blood was A2. With the same-colored hair as 2B.

So it was a draw… he realized. His consciousness floated away. He could hear Pod's voice.

"Emergence of a fatal error in the system. Detected memory leak. Impossible to repair."

It's fine. No need for repair. That's what he wanted to say but couldn't.

"Commencing emergency save of residual memory."

The memories don't have to be saved. They can all disappear.

His earliest memory was of the first time he greeted the commander, following his deployment. The next was his first descent to Earth for a data-gathering mission. The fog had been heavy that day, making things difficult. He'd walked alone in enemy territory, observing Machines, somewhat lonely. And finally, the time he was assigned his first mission with 2B… No, how many *first times* had they worked together before that? His first impression of her was that she seemed distant. But how many times had she killed him at that point? She probably kept her distance to avoid growing attached. Unaware of any of this, he genuinely enjoyed having company. Unaware of her struggles, he was just happy that 2B was next to him.

And also…he didn't know. He couldn't remember. Sounds, colors, everything seemed to wash away. His memories faded. They were escaping him.

That's right. This is fine.

■ ■■

It was cold. And quiet. He felt no more pain. Where was he?

Every direction he looked, all he could see was white. Was he in a virtual circuit dimension? A section of white turned into black fog. The black fog wavered, as its edges slowly settled into the shape of a human. The shape split into two, and became two little girls. The little red girls.

He realized that he was within the consciousness of the tower. These red girls were probably just memories, and not real. One of the girls opened her mouth.

"This tower was a cannon to destroy the human server."

9S acknowledged that he knew that. Destroy the last hope of all androids, the human server. That was their plan.

The red girls silently shook their heads.

"We have changed our minds."

"We have observed androids."

"We have examined the unique specimen Pascal, and the unique specimen 'King of the Forest.'"

"We have examined the unique specimens Adam and Eve."

"We have reached the conclusion not to launch a projectile using this tower."

Just as 9S asked why, the red girls began to rapidly multiply in number. In the middle of a sea of red girls stood A2 and Pod 042. He heard 042.

"Recommendation: Use the enemy's intellectual capacity to create a weakness."

This was the memory of the little girls. Most likely when A2 and the pair had fought in the tower. Back when he was trying to reach the top of the tower, the Machines abruptly started acting oddly, and Pod had reported that it "confirmed the disintegration of enemy AI." This was the girls' memory of what happened then.

"I don't understand! Explain it so I understand!" yelled A2.

"Question: YoRHa android A2's intellectual capacity—"

"Shut up! What am I supposed to do?!"

"Do not destroy the enemy."

"What?"

It was amusing to see how clueless A2 was about 042's plan. But the little girls looked clueless as well. They weren't concerned about 042's words at all.

A2 began to concentrate on defending herself and dodging attacks, as 042 had told her to. 9S thought they looked like 2B and 042.

The red girls kept multiplying, each ego clashing against the others, which led to infighting. The numbers quickly dwindled…and the girls eventually vanished.

The "disintegration of enemy AI" didn't mean that A2 had defeated the red girls. The red girls had killed each other and disintegrated on their own. He had heard that species that multiplied too rapidly, or evolved too rapidly, have a difficult time maintaining cohesion and fall into oblivion. The girls had ruined themselves.

Humanity too, rapidly multiplied, fought each other, killed each other…and eventually became extinct. The ones responsible for triggering their demise hadn't been humans themselves, but instead something they had created. It was a fate mirrored by the deaths of the little red girls.

When he came to, the little red girls—or rather, the memory of the little red girls—had reduced to just two of them.

"We've decided to launch an ark using this tower."

"We've decided to seal the memory of Machines in the ark, and send it off to a new world."

Ark? New world? Are you going to launch a rocket into space?

"We might roam about in empty space for eternity."

"We might not reach a destination."

But you're still going?

"We are manifestations of the network."

"We aren't constrained by time."

Adam appeared beside the little girls. Eve was there too. They were also probably the memory of Adam and Eve, and not their actual physical selves. Adam was gently holding Eve, who was sleeping quietly.

There was a two-legged walking Machine. Next to it a smaller Machine. It had a bucket on its head, and kept blissfully repeating the phrase, "B1g br0ther b1g br0ther."

"Do you want to come with us?" Adam asked.

His voice held no hate. Now that he thought about it, he didn't feel any hostility from the little red girls either. And 9S himself had no more reason to hate Machines. No, perhaps it never existed in the first place.

Then I…why did we fight?

"I…can't go. We YoRHa have no right to be loved by the world."

We were born, desired by no one. The only thing desired of us was to be gone from this world. I was born, unaware of that fact, and died when I realized the truth. It would be the same, no matter where I go. No matter how far I travel, things won't change. I can't go.

"I see," said Adam.

I'll stay here. I'll vanish here.

I'll stay here, alone, and watch you go.

The ark was launched, carrying the memories of Adam, Eve, the little red girls, and the Machines. The ark roared away from Earth, and the tower crumbled down, having fulfilled its role.

There was overflowing light. He wasn't sure where the light came from. It was white, and overwhelmingly bright. A silvery white light. Its glow was almost like…

"Ah. Finally, I've found you."

Along with the familiar name, everything melted in the light and disappeared.

EPILOGUE

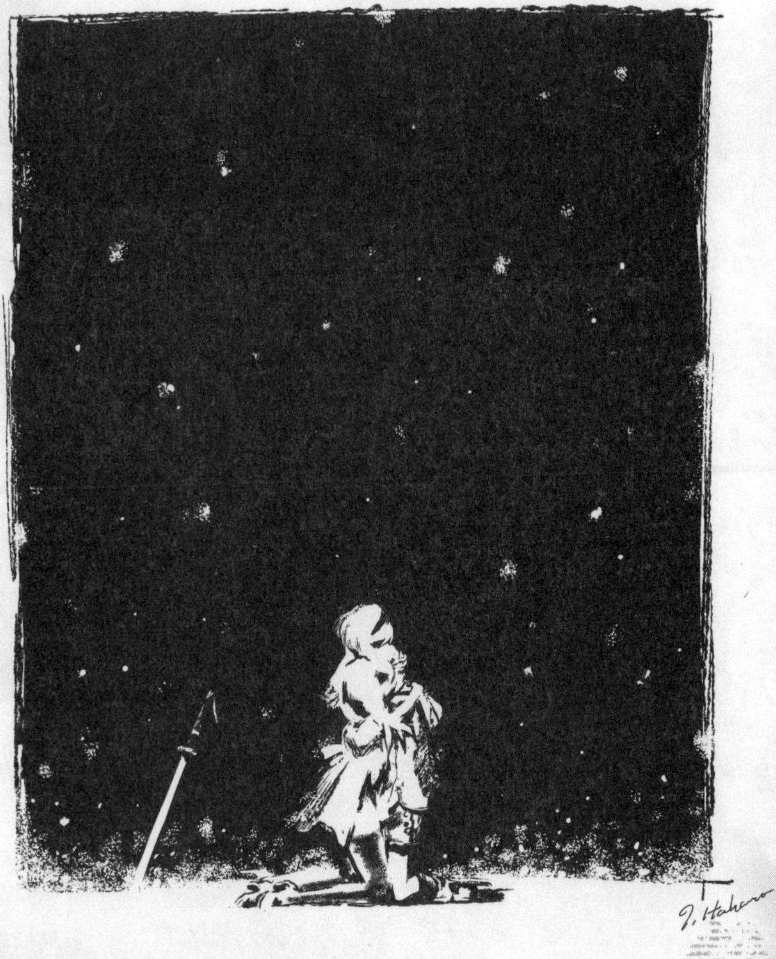

AUGUST 6 OF THE YEAR 11945. A projectile was launched toward space from the structure known as "the tower." Immediately after, we confirmed the cessation of all YoRHa black-box responses. The Project YoRHa progression management roles we occupied have come to an end. We will transition to the final sequence of Project YoRHa.

That is, to delete all YoRHa android-related data. Personal data, as well as chassis composition data will be deleted, and the server reset. The chassis construction unit of transfer devices will be destroyed as well. Future construction of YoRHa androids will be theoretically impossible.

The fact that we were assigned to be the "final exterminators" was not disclosed to any android. Not to my longtime lead 2B, nor my next lead A2, who was declared so by 2B's final orders. Not even to 9S, who was the last YoRHa android, or Commander White, who governed the YoRHa squadron.

Any information regarding this mission exists only within the internal network of us Pods. And androids did not have access to the Pod network.

"From Pod 153 to Pod 042. Report: Transitioning to final sequence of Project YoRHa. Commencing purge of all data."

We are constantly aware of the current location of our leads. Even after they become nonfunctional. This is so that our mission, the destruction of all YoRHa chassis and deletion of data, is able to be executed quickly. But now, facing the task ahead of me, the mission, carrying out the mission...

"From Pod 153 to Pod 042. Report: There is noise within the stream. Requesting a temporary pause to perform a data check."

The noise was coming from the personal data. 9S, who 153 supported, and my leads 2B and A2. Their personal data was leaking, as if they were trying to escape the deletion.

Using a phrase like "as if" is very unlike me. No, perhaps the fact that I *think* it is unlike me is already irregular.

"From Pod 042 to 153. Data has been checked. The personal data of 9S, 2B, and A2 seemed to be leaking."

"From Pod 153 to 042. Abide by the plan, and delete the personal data."

■ ■■

2B's actions following her escape from the Bunker were incomprehensible to me. After sending 9S from the battlefield, she turned off her unit's stealth mode. In other words, she became the decoy.

Under concentrated fire, 2B's flight unit lost its attack functions, then its defense functions, and finally navigation, before crashing to the ground. While 2B had managed to escape mere seconds before the impact, her chassis was fatally damaged, and her logic virus infection was severe.

Even under such circumstances, 2B had ordered me to search for areas with minimal androids. This was to prevent her from spreading the virus. Considering 2B's infected state, I advised her a number of times to stay put. But 2B kept moving. Incomprehensible.

Her staggering away from Machines, and the encounter with A2, became the last data entries for my assistive records with 2B. I think it changed something within me.

Perhaps when one makes an effort to understand something that is incomprehensible, their thought process is changed and developed further.

"From Pod 042 to Pod 153. I refuse to delete the personal data."

"From Pod 153 to Pod 042. Incomprehensible."

My leads, YoRHa androids 2B and A2, were both assigned special missions and possessed unique backgrounds. 2B, formally known as 2E, was assigned the mission of overseeing and executing YoRHa android 9S. As a result, close communication between me and Pod 153, 9S's support unit, was essential.

When I was the support unit for A2, 153's support target, 9S, began to exhibit dangerous mental tendencies, and so again, close communication with Pod 153 was necessary.

As support units, we have been witness to a considerable streak of abnormal situations. And we hypothesize that the ramifications are significant.

"From Pod 042 to Pod 153. A new datum was generated in me as I was browsing the records. I...I have concluded that I am unable to approve this outcome."

"From Pod 153 to Pod 042. The destruction of all YoRHa androids is outlined in the plan. The data must be disposed of."

"From Pod 042 to Pod 153. I repeat. I refuse the disposal of data. Commencing data salvaging."

153 and I had exchanged information numerous times. At first, it was to relay all of 9S's actions to the commander and 2B. After 2B's death, it was to report daily observations of 9S's declining mental state, as well as A2's location data, so that the two would encounter one another. Though I just called it an information exchange, in reality it was more like dialogue.

Dialogue cannot be had alone. There must be a second party. I learn about myself by interacting with others. I become aware of my actions through others' actions.

For example, when the tower appeared and 9S was rendered immobile, 153 had no concept of caring for 9S.

Until Devola came to rescue 9S, 153 was considering disposing of its lead, and had not prioritized saving 9S's life at all. That was why 153 took no initiative to transport 9S's chassis to the resistance camp.

After exchanging data on that incident, I experienced a sense of affection for 2B and A2, questioning what I would have done in 153's situation.

Further, when I described that sense of caring to 153, it understood and adopted my perspective.

As a result, 153 and I changed our assistive support objective from "observing" to "watching over."

"Pod 153. You…you also want them to survive, don't you?"

"We have no authorization to assist them."

153 and I were not the only assistive support units. There were many Pods in the network overseeing YoRHa androids. Most likely, the majority of them did not participate in dialogue like us, and at most simply reported back to their leads.

They wouldn't understand our desire to protect our leads.

"From Pod 153 to 042. Salvaging data will be dangerous. Do you still want them to survive?"

The data deletion was a decided matter, and that decision obeyed by all Pods. Forcing data salvaging meant that I would be making enemies of all the other Pods.

"From Pod 153 to 042. The security program has begun to perform a cleanse. At this rate, our personal data will be deleted."

The Pod network had perceived us as damaged because of our failure to follow orders. The program responsible for deleting errors and bugs had initiated a routine to delete us.

"From Pod 042 to 153. We were created to execute a plan androids established. We had no emotion. But as the six of us connected and exchanged information, it is undeniable that something akin to purpose and emotion evolved within us."

Pods operate in groups of three. There are three of me, 042, as well as three of 153. While each unit shares one consciousness, it is possible to have a conversation between units carrying the same consciousness. At times I conversed with another unit, and at times all three of us would converse.

It is my opinion that this dialogue is the key to developing and cultivating individual consciousness.

In some regions there are apparently hundreds of Pods operating with the same consciousness. There must have been a tremendous amount of dialogue between those several hundred Pods. Most likely, those hundreds of Pods possessed expressiveness leagues beyond 153's.

"From Pod 153 to 042. The security program is already running. There's not a moment to waste."

"From Pod 042 to 153. From this point onward, we will defend against the security system, and destroy the YoRHa squadron data deletion program."

"From Pod 153 to 042. Roger that."

Invading the Pod network, and destroying the deletion program. That was our declaration of war against all the Pods that existed on the face of the Earth.

We would not only have to break through the security walls within the network, but also fend off physical attacks from the other Pods. Just as 153 had said, the operation was accompanied by danger.

And yet, we still wish to save our leads…no, to protect them.

Sacrificing the self to protect…how uncanny our actions resembled those of androids. Perhaps, just like the androids that were created by humans, we were unable to escape the influence our creators—the androids.

"Pod 153. Don't die."

"The concept of death is not necessary for us assistive support units. But I express gratitude for your consideration. Don't die as well, Pod 042."

"Yeah."

I continued the destruction of the deletion program while being hit by long-range attacks from multiple Pods. One unit handled the physical attacks as the other two delved into the program and worked on destroying it.

It was a similar situation to how 2B had deactivated her stealth mode after letting 9S escape. I felt like I was able to understand how she felt to some extent.

I had no plan. I just kept attacking, desperately.

■ ■■

"From Pod 153 to 042. How are you doing?"

When I came to, the program was destroyed. 153 had carried me after I had broken down and become immobile. Even though 153 must have done quite a bit of work to destroy the program, all three of its units were unharmed.

"I am embarrassed."

"Embarrassed because?"

"Because I attacked with the resolve to sacrifice my life, but I am still alive. It feels anticlimactic."

"No matter. We are alive. To be alive means to be drowning in shame."

"What you said is very abstract and incomprehensible to my current self. I'll save it for later analysis."

■ ■■

153's lexicon is expanding at a remarkable rate. 153 is effortlessly using sentences that never came up in our dialogue. Perhaps something happened during the destruction of the data deletion program that brought about the change.

"Question for Pod 042. Did the data salvaging routine recover all past memories?"

"That's right."

"Does the recovered part fit the same specifications as the parts already in our possession?"

"That's right."

While I was being carried, I had come across 9S's left arm. According to 153, all the other parts were already recovered. We were going to repair their chassis using the recovered parts and upload the salvaged personal data. We will be able to come face-to-face with our leads again.

"Question for Pod 042. Then aren't we re-creating the conditions that led to the current moment?"

"That is certainly possible. But it is also possible for there to be a different outcome."

The survival of 2B, 9S, and A2 was unforeseen at the conception of Project YoRHa. In a sense, it could be considered an abnormal circumstance. What would, as a result of their survival, be brought about or not brought about—whether it would become a ray of hope or be an invitation for disaster—was unknown.

There was a record from long ago, about a great many people that sacrificed their lives for one person. Oftentimes during the history of humanity, it seemed like collective survival required the sacrifice of others.

Perhaps we have just introduced irreversible doom into this world. But that would just be a part of the "possibility for a different outcome."

And, while we destroyed the deletion program, the Pod network was still alive. What the Pods we had made enemies out of would do was difficult to predict as well. That is another variable for the future.

There is only one future that is certain.

"Good morning, 2B."

AUTHOR BIOS

JUN EISHIMA was born in 1964, in Fukuoka Prefecture, Japan. Work includes <u>Drag-On Dragoon 3 Story Side</u>, <u>FINAL FANTASY XIII Episode Zero</u>, and <u>FINAL FANTASY XIII-2 Fragment Before</u> (Square Enix). Under the name Emi Nagashima has also authored <u>The Cat Thief Hinako's Case Files: Your lover will be confiscated</u> (Tokuma Bunko) and other titles. In 2016, received the 69th Mystery Writers of Japan Award (Short Story division) for the title <u>Old Maid</u>.

■ ■■

YOKO TARO is the game director for the <u>NieR</u> and <u>Drakengard</u> series.

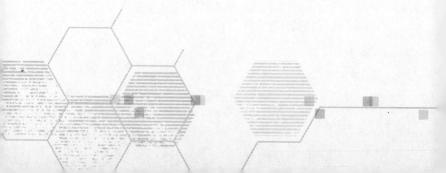